TRUSTING YOU & OTHER LIES

Also by Nicole Williams

Almost Impossible

TRUSTING YOU

& OTHER LIES

NICOLE WILLIAMS

EMBER

Text copyright © 2017 by Nicole Williams
Cover photographs copyright © 2017 by PeopleImages/Getty Images

All rights reserved. Published in the United States by Ember, an imprint of
Random House Children's Books, a division of Penguin Random House LLC,
New York. Originally published in hardcover in the United States by Crown
Books for Young Readers, an imprint of Random House Children's Books,
a division of Penguin Random House LLC, New York, in 2017.

Ember and the E colophon are registered trademarks
of Penguin Random House LLC.

Visit us on the Web! GetUnderlined.com
Educators and librarians, for a variety of teaching tools,
visit us at RHTeachersLibrarians.com

Library of Congress Cataloging-in-Publication Data is available upon request.
ISBN 978-0-553-49877-6 (trade) — ISBN 978-0-553-49879-0 (ebook) —
ISBN 978-0-553-49880-6 (pbk.)

Printed in the United States of America
10 9 8 7 6 5 4 3 2 1
First Ember Edition 2018

For anyone who's ever risen from the ashes,
even after being burned

ONE

For the one thousandth time, I shifted in the backseat, trying to get more comfortable, but I should have known better. Nothing about this summer was going to be comfortable, not even the leather seat that was supposed to be all ergonomic and crap—making road trips a dream, my dad had claimed. After doing almost six hours of hard time in the backseat, I could confidently say that my dad's definitions of *dream* and *nightmare* had gotten crossed.

The air-conditioning inside the Ainsworth family Range Rover was blasting from the front seat, where my parental units sat, but they might as well have been on opposite poles of the planet for as much as they'd acknowledged each other on this four-hundred-mile-and-some-change road trip.

I adjusted my seat-heat, dialing it up a notch when I noticed my mom crank up the air-conditioning from frosty to arctic. A faint sigh slipped past her lips as she angled the vents toward her face. Any other human being would have been sprouting icicles out their nose from the way that glacial air was blasting at her, but instead she continued to fan her face, like it was still too warm.

The leggings and tunic I'd thrown on were not holding up to the cold front, so I snagged my North Shore Track & Field hoodie from my backpack. I pulled up the hood and tied the drawstring around my face. Despite the sweatshirt, a shiver rocked me right before the seat-heat started to do its job. My mom might have been born and raised in the Northeast, but I was Californian born and bred. I didn't do below sixty degrees unless I was sporting a couple extra layers.

"We're almost there." Dad pointed at a sign on the side of the road, but I couldn't have read it if I'd wanted to. We'd been hauling ass ever since he'd pulled out of our driveway in Santa Monica.

"Still looking through that brochure?" Dad glanced back at Harrison, my ten-year-old little brother, who was sitting beside me and thumbing through the camp brochure I knew he'd memorized fifty flip-throughs ago.

Harrison, or Harry as I called him despite my mom's protests that the nickname was much too "ordinary," scooted his glasses higher on his nose.

"Fencing's that thing where they wear the weird masks and dance around each other, right?" Harry asked.

"That's right. It's kind of like medieval sword-fighting, but with blunted swords that won't totally maim or injure the opponent." Dad glanced at Harry again, which made me all kinds of uneasy given he was speeding into a sharp corner going at least fifty miles per hour.

"That sounds sick!" Harry pulled a pink highlighter from his side pocket and drew a surprisingly straight line over *Fencing* under the activities section of the brochure. Most of the few dozen others were already highlighted. Everything besides basket-weaving, papier-mâché, and cake decorating were highlighted in different colors depending on Harry's level of interest.

He had a key for it and everything. A yellow highlighter meant he was interested, a green one meant he was *very* interested, an orange one meant he'd be camped out the night before so he could be first in line, and a pink one meant he'd sacrifice a litter of puppies to do it. For a kid whose life had consisted of textbooks, music lessons, and computers, this was the adventure of a lifetime—almost as major as winning a lottery to go to the moon.

For someone like me, though? A teen girl who'd planned to spend her last official summer at the beach, playing volleyball during the day and huddling around bonfires at night before going away to college next fall—this was like serving a life sentence in a maximum security prison, the guards being my parents, my cell being some "rustic" cabin smack in the middle of nowhere.

I wanted to spend the summer before my senior year at Camp KissMyButt in Flagstaff, Arizona, about as much as I wanted to be locked in the same bedroom where I'd found my former boyfriend rounding second base with my former friend at a party a few weeks ago. Keats—former boyfriend, current buttmunch—had blamed it on his overconsumption of tequila that night. I'd blamed it on his underconsumption of self-control over his whole life.

Whoever was right, the outcome was the same. We were done. Through. Good-bye and good riddance.

That was my mantra, though my conviction lagged sometimes.

"Sick, sick, *sick*," Harry said as he continued to devour the camp brochure.

"Harrison, please stop talking like you're auditioning for a rap video." My mom's eyes were closed, like they'd been the majority of the trip, but now she was pressing her temples, which meant a headache was coming on. She'd had headaches for as long as I could remember. She blamed them on the California sun and not being used to so much sunshine, even after two decades of living beneath it. Lately, her headaches had been a lot more frequent. The sun wasn't to blame for the majority of them now, though.

"Sorry, Mom." After drawing another wide pink line through *Fencing*, Harry added a few exclamation points on either side of the word. "Fencing sounds both mentally and physically stimulating." Harry smiled up at her, but she didn't see it.

Harry was Mom's little clone, her shadow for the first five years of his life, and the child she deemed worthy of living vicariously through. I'd always been more of my dad's carbon copy and used to love knowing I'd gotten all my drive and ambition from him.

I didn't feel that way anymore.

"So? Can I do it?" Harry flipped to the last page of the brochure.

Mom twisted around in her seat just enough so that she could look at us when she opened her eyes.

Harry took after our mom in the looks department—fair skin, dark hair, slight build—but everyone said I had her eyes. That had been a point of pride, but then things changed. The person who used to be my mom seemed to have disappeared, and I wasn't so sure I wanted the same eyes as the person sitting in the front seat now.

Before Mom glanced my way, I made sure I'd angled my body as far as I could toward the door and stared out the window like the sight of pine trees and blue skies was killin' it on the first Saturday of summer break. The same day when all my friends were getting together at Laguna Beach to kick off the first beach party of the summer. I'd had my headphones on the entire trip, too, but I'd only listened to music from home to the Arizona state line. I'd kept them on the rest of the way, though, because they spared me whatever awkward talks my parents had in mind for this trip.

"Can you do what, Harrison?" Mom asked when her eyes wandered his way.

"Fencing." He shrugged.

Mom's forehead creased into several deep wrinkles as her mouth drew a hard line. "I don't know if that's a good idea. What about pottery? Or cake decorating? Don't those sound like compelling options?"

Harry looked at our mom like she'd just suggested he slip into lederhosen and take up yodeling, but she didn't see it. She'd already twisted around in her seat and squeezed her eyes shut as she massaged her temples.

Harry crossed his arms and put on the face Dad made when he wasn't happy. "I don't want to spend my whole summer learning how to bake. Or make stupid pots. We're going to one of the most adventure-filled places in the country." Harry thrust his hand against the front of the brochure, where, I guessed, he was reading one of the quotes. "I want to fence, and mountain bike, and fish, and climb a rock face—"

"Climb a rock face?" Really, if she rubbed at her temples any harder, she was going to give herself brain damage. "I don't think so, Harrison. Be reasonable."

It was really hard to keep the listening-to-music act up and stay quiet. Who told a ten-year-old boy to be reasonable? Who actually expected they were capable of it?

Beside me, Harry slumped in his seat. The brochure fell onto his lap as he stuffed the highlighter in his pocket.

"Hey, we'll see. Okay? Let's take it one day at a time. No need to leap right in." Dad reached his long arm out and patted

Harry on the knee a few times, like that was all it would take to make a kid feel better after crushing his summer vacation dreams.

I had to shift in my seat and bite the inside of my cheek to keep my mouth shut. My parents could mess each other up all they wanted if that was what they were into, but when it came to dragging Harry into their three-ring circus, I got a little touchy. Last time I'd gotten a "little touchy," I'd lost cell phone privileges for two weeks.

I distracted myself with my phone. I'd played enough games on the trip so far to qualify for gamer status, so I decided to do a quick drive-by of the social media scene. My dad had assured me there was Wi-Fi and cell reception up here at this Camp BlowsBigTime, but I wasn't going to take his word for it. Dad's word wasn't exactly golden these days. I'd caught him in so many lies I'd stopped counting.

This might be my last chance to check in with friends and make a few final words before dying to the world for the next couple of months.

I replied to a few friends' comments and posts, trying to distract myself from why I'd really logged on—to check Keats's profile picture. It was still the same—the photo of the two of us staring at that sunset like we'd figured out a way to freeze time. When I found myself relaxing into my seat, a smile starting to form, I dropped my phone in my lap and cursed under my breath.

That guy was not worth smiling over ever again.

My phone buzzed against my thigh. When I turned it over, I saw it was a text from my best friend, Emerson. **You're not thinking about him are you?**

I cursed under my breath again. The girl claimed she had psychic powers—I was a believer. *Thinking of who?*

Emerson had never been Team Keats for no other reason than believing that dating such a good-looking guy who was also fully aware of it was like handing my heart over to a rugby team to use for practice. I'd defended him, saying he couldn't help it if girls fell over themselves to brush his shoulder passing in the hallway. They could keep right on loitering at his locker and sliding into the seat beside him in class—he wasn't open for business.

Turned out, I'd been in serious denial, as I'd discovered the night I found my "closed for business" boyfriend getting it on with "her" a couple of clothing pieces away from moving on to the next stage. What sucked even more was that the girl I'd caught rubbing crotches with my boyfriend wasn't the kind of girl you'd automatically think would be the boyfriend-hunter type. She was on the track team with me, got good grades, and was well liked and respected by the male and female populations of North Shore. It would have made it easier to hate them both if she had a reputation of low standards and zero class. But she didn't. And neither did Keats.

Of course, realizing that made me do what any other teenage girl would—I spent the next week and a half analyzing what the hell had happened. Was it me? Was it her? Was it him? Was it something she had that I didn't? Was it something he felt for her that he didn't for me? Was it because I'd held out for so long that a certain part of Keats's anatomy had finally fallen off like he'd predicted it would if we waited much longer? If overthinking a situation became a high school sport, I'd be the captain of that team, too, and lead it to another state championship.

"Her" had a name, of course, but it was one I'd never speak again. Get caught kissing a good friend's boyfriend? Yeah, that landed you smack in you're-dead-to-me territory.

Good girl was Emerson's reply, immediately followed by BTW, summer sucks without you.

As a new policy I'd adopted a few months ago, I made it a point not to smile when my parents were around. I didn't want them to get the wrong idea that I was happy being in their presence, and I sure as hell didn't want them thinking I was thrilled with the sudden detour in my summer vacation plans. I occasionally set that no-smiling policy aside when Harry was close by, though. I didn't want to take it out on him when I was mad at them.

I might have let a smile slip when I read Emerson's text, though.

Summer sucks without you too, I typed, holding my breath when it took a few extra moments to send. We were winding higher and steeper up the gravel road, which only looked wide enough for one car, making me wonder if there was another way down. If there was, I'd find it. I'd use it, too. I was four months from being eighteen—an adult in the eyes of the law—and my parents were treating me like a kid in dragging me up here.

Emerson's text vibrated in my hand. How's the fam?

I scanned the inside of the car and frowned. *How do you think?*

Things have to get better soon.

I wiggled further down in my seat. *They couldn't get worse.*

Emerson's reply came about five seconds later. She made other text-savvy teens look like amateurs. Have you talked to them about you know what?

My knuckles went white from the fists I was making. I practically had to pry my fingers open to text her back. *No. Not sure how to work that into a conversation.*

How about . . . Hey Dad and Mom, about that eviction notice I found under that stack of unpaid bills.

8

I swallowed as I punched in my reply. *Ugh. I'd rather be in denial over it like they are.*

I glanced over at Harry. He'd flopped his head against the headrest and closed his eyes. When Dad glanced in the rearview mirror, I accidentally caught his gaze. I got back to admiring the ocean of trees and tried not to make a face. I was already sick of trees. And I was expected to spend ten weeks surrounded by them and not go insane? The ozone had a better chance of repairing itself with a hot glue gun and a roll of plastic wrap.

My phone vibrated with Emerson's text. *You should talk to them about it.*

My foot started bouncing. *They should talk to me about it.*

Fine. Someone should talk to someone about it.

I didn't text anything back right away. I was too busy distracting myself from throwing my fist through the window. Dad had lost his job two years ago, and I got how tough that must have been for him, but instead of picking himself up and dusting himself off, he decided to let it snowball out of control. He still hadn't found a new job, money was running out, he and Mom only communicated in glares and shouts, and now there was an eviction notice.

He'd lost his job, but you would have thought he'd lost everything else as well from the way he'd been acting. Mom too. Once upon a time he'd been like a hero to me. Now he barely played a walk-on role in my life.

The only reason we were able to afford this vacation was because the guy who owned the cabin was an old friend of my dad's. He'd given us some kind of friend discount, which I later discovered meant a total discount. As in, we were getting to stay for free. Our cabin was older and didn't get rented out anymore, but I didn't enjoy feeling like a charity case.

So, yeah. Trust issues. I had them. Big-time. Side effect of the most important people in your life lying to you.

Beside me, Harry gave the faintest of moans. Of course I was the only one who'd noticed. "Hey." I gave his knee a soft squeeze. "You okay?"

Keeping his eyes clamped closed, he nodded.

I noticed Harry shifting in his seat, like he couldn't get comfortable. His face was starting to turn a familiar shade of green as his hand went to cover his mouth. I'd seen this enough times to know what was happening.

"Dad, pull over." I leaned across Harry's lap and punched one of the half-dozen buttons on the door's armrest. Harry's window whirred down, letting in a blast of fresh air. For summer in Arizona, the air was surprisingly cool. I was expecting it to be blistering hot and the air to smell like BO. This was almost refreshing.

"Hello? Calling all parental figures." I snapped my fingers next to Dad's ear. "Puke coming. Pull over."

Of course that would get his attention. Dad loved this car. It wasn't even his, and it wouldn't be his when the lease was up because he couldn't afford to buy it or anything like it. He wouldn't even be able to scrounge up enough money or credit to buy one of those domestic four-doors in the used car lots he cringed at as he drove by.

"Need me to pull over, Harry?"

Harry shook his head, angling his nose so the fresh air was streaming straight into it. "No. Keep going. I'll be okay."

"Harry," I urged, knowing what he was up to. He was trying to be tough. He wanted our parents to stop treating him like he was a piece of ancient family china that needed to be handled with the utmost care. To him, pulling over would be a defeat. Sucking it up and keeping his breakfast down was a win in his book.

That was messed up in my book.

"Harrison?" Mom chimed in.

"Harry?" The first thing Dad's eyes went to was the light beige carpet at Harry's feet. *Yeah, that's right, Dad. Worry about the carpet in the car instead of your kid whose stomach was unleashing on him. Way to have your priorities straight.*

"I'm *fine*. Just keep going," Harry whined, curling into a ball.

Dad's gaze went back to the carpet at Harry's feet before he punched the gas, because we weren't moving fast enough at fifty.

Harry was in crisis mode. He was desperate to prove to our parents that he was strong and capable of more than just wiping his own ass and tying his shoes. This was his summer. Since this clearly wasn't going to be mine, I had all the time in the world to help him with his agenda.

"Here, this will help. . . ." Twisting around in my seat, I dug through the stuffed third-row seat for the mini cooler I'd packed with essentials like Junior Mints, Red Vines, soda, and . . . There it was. I pulled the mini ice pack from the cooler and pressed it to the back of Harry's neck.

Harry had been prone to car sickness since the day he left the hospital and yacked all over his coming-home outfit. I didn't know why I was the only one who seemed to notice that any time he was stuffed in a car for longer than an hour his stomach staged a revolt, but it would have to remain a mystery. I'd stopped asking questions like that when I realized there weren't any answers. At least no good ones.

A moment later, I reached into the cooler to pull a Sprite free. I cracked it open, and an eruption of fizz and tiny bubbles floated into my face. "Drink this. Car sickness won't stand a chance against the ice pack–Sprite tag team."

Harry's breath was already returning to normal when he

took the frosty can of pop from me. I wrapped my hand around the ice pack and pressed it more firmly on his neck. "Better?"

He took a sip, then followed it up with a relieved sigh. "So much." He took another sip, then opened his eyes. He smiled at me and, abandoning my no-smiles-allowed policy when our parents were around, I smiled, too. "Thanks, Phoenix. Thanks for always having my back."

My smile crept higher. Part of Harry's quest to become his own ten-year-old man was picking up a few choice words and phrases he'd heard from my friends. *Sick* and *having my back* were two of the many. There were a couple of others I'd had to bribe him to forget. "Thanks for always having mine."

He extended his fist toward me. I bumped it with mine and winked. The Ainsworth family's one redeeming quality was my brother. How this little ball of optimism and loyalty could have been spawned from my parents was the eighth wonder of the world.

If there was one reason to not start exploring escape options the moment I set foot in Camp GatesOfHell, it was so I wouldn't abandon my little brother with two people bent on driving their own lives off a cliff.

I checked Harry over again. His skin was normal, along with his breathing. Crisis averted.

"Tell Emerson hey for me." He glanced at my phone and chugged the last of his Sprite before unleashing a burp that would not end.

"Harrison . . . ," Mom warned in *that* tone. The one that basically implied she and her kind didn't burp, fart, poop, or pick boogers.

"Sorry, Mom," he said, grinning at me like he'd just gotten away with stealing an armored truck's worth of *Minecraft* games and ice cream sandwiches.

I'd tilted my phone just enough so Harry could read Emerson's name at the top. He loved Emerson. As in wanted to marry her. He had good taste in girls—I had to give him that—and she was just crazy enough she might actually consider it one day.

"We're here," Dad announced, finally easing off the gas as we passed under a gleaming wood sign hanging between two more—big surprise—trees. No more trees. For the love of God. This wasn't natural.

CAMP KISMET was carved in big letters that looked as if a kid wielding a melon baller had done it. I hadn't been too far off with the *Camp KissMyButt* name.

Harry's face was hanging out the window, taking it all in, pointing at so many things his arm was a blur. Dad rolled down his window and hung his elbow out. Even Mom had opened her eyes and stopped drilling at her temples long enough to inspect the approaching camp.

Me, though? No way. Slumping down further into my seat, I plunked my dark sunglasses into place, put one of the songs we played at track meets on repeat, jacked up the volume, and sent another text to Emerson. *I hate my life.*

Of course that was when I went from three bars to no bars, trapping her reply in no-reception limbo.

"This is going to be the best summer ever!" Harry shouted as log cabins came into view. Great. I'd be spending my summer learning about how the pioneers had lived back in the day.

Crossing my arms, I slumped as low as I could into the seat. I wasn't holding my breath for this to be the best summer ever—I was crossing my fingers, hoping it wouldn't be the worst.

TWO

There was running water in the cabin. And electricity. And walls that divided rooms and doors that closed. So I had it a little better than the Pilgrims did four hundred years ago.

Ever since rolling up to Cabin #13—yeah, really—I'd been trying to focus on counting the positive things instead of zeroing in on the negative . . . because there was a heap of them. My parents kept getting into one of their typical arguments about God knows what. I walked through a spiderweb as I climbed the few steps to the front door. There were only two bedrooms, which meant I'd be sharing a small space with a ten-year-old boy. So, pretty much, the downsides were stacked at ten to one when compared to the upsides.

When I stepped inside the minuscule bathroom and was welcomed by the stink of rotten fish, I realized I was being generous with those ten-to-one ratios.

I yanked my third load of luggage from the car while my dad wrestled his laptop open at the kitchen table. Mom disappeared into the trout-stenched bathroom. Rounding into the "Lil' Campers" bedroom, I found Harry staring at the top bunk. He'd begged my parents for a set of bunk beds since his fifth birthday, but they'd rallied against his pleas, declaring he'd surely fall from the top bunk and break his neck. To a boy who'd be heading into fifth grade next year, bunk beds were like living the dream. For a seventeen-year-old girl who was ready for her freedom, this was like living the nightmare.

But this summer wasn't about me. This summer was about Harry.

"I bet you're thinking I'm going to put dibs on that top bunk, aren't you?" I said as I dropped Harry's and my suitcases onto the old plank floorboards.

"Aren't you?" Harry asked, not blinking as his stare-a-thon continued with the top bunk.

"Nah. I'm more a bottom-bunk type of girl." I rolled my purple suitcase the rest of the way across the floor before heaving it onto the mattress.

"Really? You want the bottom one?" Harry stepped toward the ladder at the end of the bunk.

"Totally. This way if I have to get up in the middle of the night, I don't have to worry about tripping down the ladder."

Harry nodded, his small hands curling around one of the ladder rails. "You *are* a bit clumsy. It probably would be safer for us both if I took the top."

"I prefer the term 'gracefully impaired,' and thanks for the favor." I mussed his hair as he started climbing the ladder. "My potentially cracked skull and bruised shins are in your debt."

As soon as Harry reached the top, he leaped onto the mattress. "Woo-hoo!" he shrieked as a plume of dust erupted from the underside of his mattress, raining down onto what was to be my bed. So I wasn't sleeping in this thing until it was dusted and disinfected. Twice.

"Yeah, keep it down up there unless you want to alert the warden."

Almost instantly, Harry stopped laughing and hooting, knowing our mom would put an end to his top-bunk dreams if she marched in to see what all the "racket" was about. If we kept it quiet and flew under the standard parental radar, I knew from experience neither of them would step foot in our room this summer.

Harry's lips might have stayed sealed, but he kept up the bouncing. More dust swirled down onto my mattress and suitcase.

"Hey, Phoenix?" Harry's bouncing came to a stop. His head poked over the edge of the bunk, his wide eyes blinking down at me.

"Hey, Harry?" I answered.

"Are we going to be okay?"

My fingers froze in the middle of unzipping my suitcase. "What do you mean?" I said, keeping my tone light and my expression the same.

"I might only be ten, but I know something's wrong."

"Nothing's wrong. And you better stop leaning over the edge of the bunk like that."

"Come on. I know you know what's going on." He sighed, flopping back on the mattress.

"Maybe I do. Maybe I don't." I shrugged.

"Why does everyone in this family treat me like I'm a child?"

I started lining my shoes up beneath the lower bunk. The whole four pairs I'd packed. "Eh, because you *are* a child."

Another grumble fired off from the top bunk. "According to my aptitude scores, I've got the brain of a thirteen-year-old, which is pretty much like saying I'm a teenager, which is pretty much an adult. I might be ten according to the calendar, but I'm *not* a child."

After lining up my shoes in descending height order—running shoes, everyday sneakers, sandals—I pulled open the top drawer of the dresser shoved next to the wall beside the bunk. I winced in anticipation of what I'd find, but other than a clean, empty drawer and the faint scent of cedar, no plumes of dust or eau de trout erupted in my face.

"You're a child in the eyes of the law," I said.

A snort echoed in the room. "Whatever." Then Harry's head popped over the side of the bunk again. "Are Dad and Mom going to get a divorce?"

"Of course they're not. Why would you even ask a question like that?" I restacked my shirts to give myself something to focus on. I arranged them in order of color, dark to light, with charcoal being on top and cream being on the bottom.

"Because they act like they hate each other now."

"They don't hate each other. They're just dealing with some things. . . . It will get better. Don't worry about it, 'kay?" I hustled over to my suitcase, grabbing another stack of tees. I rarely did tanks, I occasionally did sweatshirts, but I *lived* in tees. They were comfortable, familiar, a piece of home I could take with me wherever I went.

"Are we going to get kicked out of our house?"

After the initial shock of the first question, now I was prepared for the rest that would follow. I'd been bracing myself for them. "Of course not. People don't just get kicked out of houses."

"What about the Holloways? They got kicked out of their house last year, and I heard that Sawyer didn't even get to pack his Legos before they got the boot. If that's what's going to happen to us, I don't want to leave my Legos behind. I want to make sure all my stuff's packed and ready to go before we get the boot."

"No one's getting the boot."

"I don't want to leave my Legos behind, Phoenix."

"No one's leaving their Legos behind!"

I hadn't meant to shout. I wasn't upset at Harry. I wasn't even irritated with his questions. I was angry at our parents.

For screwing up and dragging Harry and me into it. As far as I was concerned, they'd dug their hole all by themselves. Why did Harry and I have to fall into it with them? It wasn't fair.

"I'm sorry I shouted. I'm not mad at you. It was just a long drive up here, and I'd rather be home with my friends instead of trapped at Camp . . . whatever it's called. I didn't mean to take it all out on you, Harry. Forgiven?"

He nodded. "Forgiven," he said in a grown-up voice. "But at least you managed to get a job as a counselor so you could make some serious money. I bet by the end of the summer, you'll be able to buy a Lamborghini or something sweet like that!"

"For being such a smart kid, you sure don't understand the concept of money." I smashed a small spider as it scrambled across the floor plank in front of me. Another item to add to the Camp Kismet *con* pile—arachnids in my bedroom. "I'd probably have to work summers for the rest of my life to be able to put a down payment on a car like that, but I might be able to scrounge together enough for a nineties Accord with half a million miles on it. Hopefully," I added. I wanted a car bad. No, I *needed* a car bad.

"So you can leave for college." Harry reined in his sigh, but it was written all over his face.

I felt the familiar stab of guilt dig right into my side. I'd been experiencing lots of those lately. "More like so I can come home and visit you all the time."

The corners of Harry's mouth twitched. "Really?"

I nodded. "Really."

Harry's smile tilted from happy to the relieved spectrum. He wasn't thrilled with the idea of being stuck alone with my parents for a solid eight years—not that anyone would be unless they were into living with things like misery.

"Hey, just for the record, I'm with Emerson."

What wasn't he with my best friend on? "In what way specifically?"

"Keats is a douche-burger with a side of scum sauce." Harry formed his mouth into a sneer.

"Did you hack into my phone again?" I tried giving him the mom look. I didn't really have a knack for it.

Harry's shoulders bobbed. "It's so easy I figured you wouldn't mind."

"Why would I mind my little brother snooping through my phone?" Rolling my eyes, I threw my thumb over my shoulder. "I'm going to get the rest of the luggage. Be right back."

"I'll help!" Harry shouted as he scrambled down the ladder. I paused when I heard what sounded like more of a fall than a successful descent. But when I saw Harry rush into the hall after me, I knew no permanent damage had been done.

"Hey there, Mr. Graceful." I mussed his hair again when he jogged up beside me.

He swiped my hand away, fretting with his hair to get it back into place. He gave me an irritated look, but I knew he secretly liked it when I messed up his hair. Once, after a six-day break, he practically promised to do my chores for the next year if I'd just get back to messing up his hair.

If that didn't scream *affection-starved*, I was nominating my parents for dad and mom of the year.

I shoved through the screen door, Harry shadowing me, and headed for the Range Rover. Parental units were MIA, because it wasn't like an entire vehicle needed to be unloaded or anything.

I shuffled through what was left of the luggage in the car, gauging what would be the lightest item to hand Harry. "Here, you can carry this in." I snagged one of the reusable grocery bags my mom had packed with enough sunscreen, bug spray, and aloe vera to supply a team of hockey players forced to spend a summer running around the desert, and scooted it toward Harry.

Mom might have missed the carsick memo with Harry, but she wasn't blind to the paleness of his skin. Might have been because the poor kid seemed to reflect sunlight whenever he stepped into it.

"Harry?" I shook the handles of the bag I was holding for him, but he was too busy focusing on a band of boys around his own age. As they marched in our direction, I froze for a fraction of a second. Harry went with the opposite. After adjusting his glasses and patting down his hair, he approached the boys.

That was when I unthawed. Hopping out of the Range Rover, I lunged up beside him. There were more than I was used to dealing with when it came to Harry, but if I couldn't manage to scare off five prepubescent boys, then I didn't deserve the title of overprotective older sister.

When the boys stopped in front of us, Harry adjusted his glasses again.

"Did you just get here?" one of the smaller kids of the pack asked Harry, seemingly oblivious to the fact I was even there.

"Yeah, we got here about"—Harry lifted the wrist his watch was on—"eleven minutes ago. Give or take fifteen seconds or so."

I shifted in place. This was usually the point where things got messy. If insults hadn't been firing right from the start, the teasing and laughing typically came after Harry started rattling off random facts or bits of knowledge that pegged him more as a shut-in academic five times his age.

"Yeah, we all just got here, too. But more like a few hours ago," the same boy continued, tipping his head at the other boys around him. "Give or take fifteen seconds." One of the other kids checked his own watch strapped to his wrist. The electronic display was blank, though, and from the look of the wear and tear on the band, they'd probably stopped making batteries for it last century.

"How long are you going to be here?" the "round" boy of the bunch asked Harry.

Harry shrugged. "I don't know. A while, I think." When he looked up at me for confirmation, I added my own shrug.

"Give or take fifteen seconds."

That made Harry and the other boys all snicker. They were laughing. They were *all* laughing. I felt my shoulders start to relax.

"We're heading down to the stream to see if we can catch a giant toad. Wanna come?" one of the boys asked.

Harry froze for a moment. I stayed that way for a few more. He was already following them when he glanced over at me. "Would you tell Mom I'm catching toads?" The words came out sounding unsure almost, like he was trying a foreign language for the first time.

"Who should I tell her you're catching toads with?" I shouted after him. He was already loping across the campgrounds with the other kids, but he must have heard me.

His head tipped, but before he could answer, one of the other boys fired off a response. "His friends. Tell her he's catching toads with his friends."

"His friends," I repeated as I watched him run away, rattling off a few random facts about the genus *Bufo* to his fellow amphibian catchers.

We hadn't been here for ten minutes and Harry had already made five friends. That might have been the reason I was smiling as I loaded myself up with luggage and started for the cabin.

As I was heading through the door, my mom was just coming through it. The top two buttons of her cobalt cardigan were undone and she'd slipped her loafers off. "Oh, Phoenix." She looked over my shoulders, concern creasing the corners of her eyes when she didn't find what she was looking for. "Where's Harrison?"

"Off catching toads. With his friends." Now it was me sounding like I was butchering a new language for the first time.

Mom checked behind me again, her gaze shifting to the Range Rover like she was expecting to find Harry tucked into the back, hiding. "Friends?"

I stared off in the direction the boys had disappeared and flashed my hands. "Friends."

Mom started to smile, the kind I remembered as a little girl. "Maybe when we get home, he'll be able to make a few friends there. Wouldn't that be nice?"

It seemed like she was phrasing the question to herself, but I jumped in with my own thoughts. "Yeah, it would be great, Mom. When and if we return *home*."

I moved to pass by her and drop the suitcases inside the cabin before my arms gave out when she turned to me. Nothing on her face gave anything away, but her eyes were wider than normal. "What do you mean? Of course we'll be going home at the end of the summer."

Like her eyes, her voice was just a bit off, too.

"I didn't mean anything, Mom. Just forget I mentioned it." After dropping the bags onto the round kitchen table, I debated my next move. I'd planned on emptying the rest of the car and then exploring what was to be home base for the summer, but that would require passing by my mom again. Locking myself up in the dusty bedroom seemed like the most appealing option given the alternatives.

I'd just made my first step in that direction when a sharp pounding sounded across the room. It was my dad beating down on his laptop. "Ben told me there was Wi-Fi up here. He promised me." My dad's fingers tore through his hair, making him look like some kind of mad scientist when he was done. He shoved his laptop away from him, as if its mere presence was offensive.

I watched my dad throw his arms around a few more times, my mom stuck in place, too, watching him how I was: like we barely recognized the person losing his cool in front of us.

Neither of us seemed eager to speak up, but someone had to say something before he lost any more of his marbles. "If Ben told you there's Wi-Fi, there's Wi-Fi, Dad." Instead of continuing toward the bedroom, I turned and headed for the screen door again. "You probably just need a password or something. I'll go see if I can find out what it is."

If he'd heard me, he didn't acknowledge it. He was too busy cursing at the screen in front of him. Where had the fun, confident dad with a smile plastered on his face gone?

"Phoenix?" Mom's voice carried after me.

I paused but didn't stop. "Yeah?"

"Would you mind seeing if there's some kind of sack lunch the kitchen might have for us? With us missing lunch here and your dad not wanting to stop for anything on the drive, I'm sure Harrison and you have got to be hungry. Maybe they'll have something to tide you two over until dinner."

"I'm okay, but I'll find something for Harry." My feet were moving, carrying me away. Why they stopped, I didn't know, but I'd been experiencing a lot of that lately: half of me wanting to go one direction while the other half wanted to go the other way. "Do you want me to grab something for you, too? Do you need anything?"

She took a moment to answer. "I'm okay," she said, except everything about her seemed the opposite.

I knew the feeling.

23

THREE

I'd been all set to hate camp. That was my plan.

It became harder to keep to it once I started to explore the place. The camp might have been covered by trees, and the cabins might have been leaning hard toward the rustic side, and it might have felt like it was an entire world apart from California, but it wasn't so bad.

Not as bad as I'd imagined when the words *family camp* and *summer break* slipped from my parents' mouths in the same sentence.

I'd only been wandering for a few minutes—I didn't want my dad to go totally ape-poop waiting for his precious Wi-Fi password—but it was enough for me to realize that Camp SomethingOrOther could have been a lot worse.

Not that that was an endorsement for spending an extra hour past what we had planned, but at least my outlook on the place had improved from *worst summer ever* to just *worst summer this decade.*

After weaving around the outskirts of the camp, I meandered down one of the paths that looked like it headed toward the center of camp. The place seemed to be arranged like a bike wheel—one large circle of cabins tucked into the trees, with numerous trails connecting the cabins to the hub of the camp.

Once I'd moved past the circle of cabins, the grounds thinned out and a blanket of grass covered the center of camp. It was the kind that made me want to kick my sandals off and walk barefoot through it, wiggling my toes and letting the blades tickle them. I missed grass. California and its drought situation made grass ancient history.

I would have been happy just to lie down and take a nap since I'd slept a total of three hours last night. As I trudged across the lawn, I noticed a large group of campers clustered outside the big building ahead.

One problem, though—the main, if not only, entrance to the dining hall was right behind the campers sprawled on the lawn and listening to what looked to be some kind of lesson on paddling.

I skirted as far around the group of campers as I could, hoping I could sneak into the dining hall without anyone noticing. As I got closer, I could hear someone talking to the campers. It must have been one of the counselors, but he was kind of hidden from view. All I could see was one foot sporting a muddy hiking boot, and his forearm when a bright yellow paddle would circle into view every few seconds.

I slowed my pace and adjusted my path so I was closer to the group on the lawn and tuned in to what was being said. It only took a few seconds to figure out nothing more thrilling than paddling was being discussed. He was talking about what to do if you fell from the raft into the river—"just go with the flow," whatever that meant.

I kept moving toward the dining hall. I didn't make it far.

Since I was still trying to check out Instructor Paddle

Stroke, I missed the step leading to the porch. Well, my eyes missed it, but the toe of my sandal did not.

I went down hard. And loud. Just great, Her Gracefulness has arrived.

I didn't need to check across the lawn to wonder if anyone had noticed my wipeout. The sudden quiet was all the confirmation I needed—nothing like easing myself into camp life and flying under the radar.

My knees and hands were stinging like someone had just scrubbed them raw with sandpaper, but I ignored them. Just as I was about to hoist myself up, an arm extended my way.

"You okay?"

I dusted off my knees and palms. "Yeah, I'm okay," I replied before glancing up, which was a good thing since once I looked at him, my tongue tied into those knot thingies I'd heard about.

Hello . . .

Instructor Paddle Stroke was towering in front of me, holding out his hand like he was waiting for me to take it. Under normal circumstances, I would have let him give me a lift up, but this wasn't a normal circumstance because this guy wasn't, well . . . normal. In a good way.

That sounded bad, but I didn't know how else to describe him. I couldn't look away, but it wasn't because he fit the hot-guy mold with, you know, the hair and the smile and the jaw thing. He was the *other* type. The one with enough quirks to make him interesting to look at—the kind with just enough imperfections to make him attractive.

His hair was messy in the unstyled way, and while he had clear skin, his face was marked with two largish scars—a smooth one traced across part of his upper lip and a rougher one running down his temple. From the small bump at the top of his nose, it looked like he'd broken it—at least once.

So he'd broken some bones and earned some scars—good for him. I had my own—they just weren't as obvious.

I couldn't tell if his eyes were more brown or green, kind of like his hair couldn't decide if it was more blond or brown. Even his body seemed to be in some kind of tug-of-war between bulky and lanky.

"Are you sure you're okay?" The skin between his brows creased when I stayed frozen, still staring at him like the idiot I was.

Get a grip, Phoenix. This isn't exactly the first guy you've ever pasted your eyes on.

I had to force myself to look away before I could reply. "I'm sure I'm not *not* okay."

"Well, that's a start." I could hear the smile in his voice, which made me want to look. Yeah, his smile was just as great as it sounded. Kinda crooked, his eyes grinning, too. "You can work on the rest later."

That made me smile back. Again, like the idiot I was.

I didn't do boy-crazy, I reminded myself. I didn't do weak-kneed and tongue-tied and starry-eyed. I did Miss Independent. I did my own thing. I did guys-were-a-nice-perk-but-not-the-pinnacle. That was my MO.

So why in the hell was I acting like my own personal guy-stupid nightmare, grinning like a moron at this guy? Especially when I was fresh out of a failed relationship?

"Are you busy?" he asked suddenly, glancing at the group on the lawn.

Yeah, I'm busy. Checking you out . . . and berating myself for doing it.

"No," I said, forgetting all about what I'd been "busy" doing before my tumble heard around the camp.

"Would you mind helping me with something?"

"No," I said, realizing one word too late I had no idea what I'd just agreed to.

"I'm going to need your help over there." He tipped his head toward the lawn and campers. When he lowered his hand again, waiting, I shoved off the porch and lifted myself up. I could barely look at the guy—game over if I actually touched him.

He started heading for the lawn, checking over his shoulder to make sure I was following.

"What exactly do you need my help with?" I asked, trying not to check out the way his hips moved when he walked . . . or the way his butt looked in action.

I needed an intervention. A reality-check bitch-slap. I needed to stop noticing all that was so right about this guy, and latch on to whatever I could dig up that was wrong. I started repeating the phrase *If it looks too good to be true, it probably is* through my head.

"I'm going to use you to show everyone how to fit a life jacket." He held a giant orange life jacket in the air, waving me forward with his other hand.

Too good to be true. Too good to be true, I hummed to myself as I walked up to him.

The cluster of campers gave a courtesy round of applause for the victim-slash-volunteer. He joined in and clapped with them.

I gave a little curtsy and reminded myself I'd made a vow to keep this summer complication- and boy-free. I had enough to deal with already.

He didn't hesitate as he slipped behind me and stuffed my arms through the life jacket's armholes. "To kill time, let's play a Camp Kismet favorite, the Getting to Know You game."

I swallowed. I would have rather walked on hot coals. With my face.

"Don't worry. I'll keep it painless." His head poked out from behind me like he'd known I'd be panicking over the idea of exposing my soul to a bunch of strangers.

"Where are you from?" he asked as he came around in front of me to start snapping the life jacket into place.

I exhaled. Painless. "California."

A few hoots shot through the group.

"A fellow Californian." He nodded at me like we shared some kind of bond now. I nodded like I knew exactly what he meant. "What part?"

"Santa Monica," I answered.

He gave a low whistle as he snapped one of the life jacket's buckles. "Must be nice over there. All that sand and ocean."

I couldn't tell if he was teasing me or being serious. His face told me he was teasing, but his voice sounded serious. "What part are *you* from?"

There. Now it was a *fair* game of Getting to Know You.

"The part where we don't have sand and ocean."

When he fastened the next strap around my chest, I cleared my throat. He must have thought I was calling him out on his vague answer instead. That worked.

"Inglewood," he said. "Home sweet home."

"Oh," I said, kind of surprised. Not that I spent a lot of time there or knew a lot of people from Inglewood, but he didn't dress or talk like the few I did know.

"How old are you, Santa Monica?"

"Seventeen—almost eighteen." When he finished buckling the last strap, I took a breath. I'd been holding it the whole time. "How about you? Inglewood?"

"Just turned eighteen. It was a good year to be born." He tipped his head at me again, like we shared yet some other bond. I tipped my head, still not getting it. God, I was a wreck.

A quiet round of laughter circled through the campers who

I'd forgotten were there for all of three and a half seconds. I shook my head and gave myself the proverbial kick in the butt to pull my head out of the same spot.

"So we know where you're from now. Maybe we should know your name, too." He punched the shoulders of the life jacket down into place. Hard. He wasn't treating me like I was a delicate flower. Part of me liked that. The other part wasn't so sure.

"Phoenix," I said. Was I supposed to be speaking to him or the group? Just to be safe, I spoke loud enough that most of the campers should have been able to hear me.

"The mythical bird that rises from the ashes." He flashed his hands at the life jacket and looked at the campers like he was suggesting this was the time for questions if there were any. I never realized putting on a life jacket required an in-depth demonstration. Seemed kind of self-explanatory. "My mom says our names are symbolic of the kind of people we become. Do you think she's right?"

"That's a loaded question," I replied.

"Why's it loaded?"

From the smirk he flashed me, he knew why. "Because if I answer one way, I'll be admitting I'm an ashy bird, but if I answer the other way, I'll be insulting your mom."

He tested the tightness of my jacket by giving it a few hard tugs, followed by a series of harsh shakes. "It's not a loaded question, I swear. Just one of those normal ones."

I was having a conversation with a cute guy in front of a couple dozen people while wearing a giant orange life jacket. Yeah, this was a first. And hopefully a last. "Well, I wasn't a mythical bird the last time I checked, so I guess that answers your question."

The corners of his eyes lined. "Are you saying my mom's wrong? That she's a liar?"

My shoulders sagged beneath the life jacket. Great. And now I'd offended him. From wiping out, to ogling, to offending. I don't think I'd ever bombed a first impression worse than this one.

"What? No. Of course not. I just meant . . ."

He held his devastated expression for another second, right before it disappeared behind a smile that took up half his face. And then he laughed. "I'm just messing with you."

I wanted to punch him in the arm. I wanted to shake off the life jacket and storm away. Instead, I stayed in place and let him finish laughing. How was that for calm under pressure?

"Don't let him get to you, honey!" an older woman shouted, patting her hand in the air like she was patting my back instead. "Over time, you'll eventually build up an immunity to Callum."

"How many summers have you been coming to Camp Kismet, Mary Jo?" *Callum* asked, squinting his eyes as he looked, since the sun was blasting into his face from that angle.

"Twelve, honey."

"And when did you finally build up your 'immunity' to me? Taking into account I've only been coming to camp for the past eight years."

Mary Jo nudged the man beside her, who I guessed was her husband since they were rocking the same style of tracksuits, hers shocking purple and his fluorescent orange. They shared a look and a laugh. "Toward the end of last summer."

Callum lifted a shoulder at me. "See? All you have to do is hang around me for eight summers and then you can build up your own immunity to me. Whatever that even means . . ." Callum shot a look at Mary Jo and her husband and grumbled. "I like to think of myself as having an infectious personality instead of one a person needs to build an immunity to."

For a second, the campers were all quiet, looking among

31

one another like they couldn't believe their ears. Then they all started busting up.

"Yeah, yeah, I hope you're all paying attention to this life jacket demonstration," Callum growled at the crowd good-naturedly. "Your lives depend on it."

The campers kept laughing. These people loved this guy. There was also a group of girls around my age who looked like they *loved* him. Or at least the part of him I'd been admiring when he'd been walking in front of me. Fine ass alert, as Emerson would have announced.

"What's your biggest fear, Phoenix?" Callum asked, picking a paddle up from the ground and moving it through the air again like he was instructing.

"Huh?" I asked.

"Your biggest fear?" he repeated slowly. "We're playing the Getting to Know You game in case you forgot. Or have a short-term-memory issue."

"Oh," I said, thinking. It was a personal question. A little too personal to just announce to a crowd of strangers, so I kept it vague. "Failing. I guess that's my biggest fear."

He kept slicing the paddle through the air. "Failing what?"

I took some time to think again. I didn't need it, though. "Anything." He moved closer, probably about to drop another question, so I beat him to it. "What's your biggest fear?"

If he was surprised by me firing his question back at him, he didn't show it. His paddle stroke stayed smooth and even, not even a wobble. "Failing."

I narrowed my eyes in a question of *Really?* He shrugged in an answer of *Really*.

"Failing what?" I asked.

"Everything." This time, his paddle wobbled. Just for a sec-ond, and no one else probably even noticed, but I didn't miss it. I'd been watching for it. Like me, he had something specific he was afraid of failing. I knew what mine was, but I couldn't begin to imagine what his could have been. Was he afraid of failing a little brother of his own, too? Failing someone else important? Failing *himself*? Failing physics? Failing a driving test? Failing his principles?

When it came to failing, the possibilities were endless.

"So what does *your* name mean, Callum?" Mary Jo's husband called. I had to shake my head and take a few steps away to clear my mind. All I'd needed to find was a Wi-Fi password and a sack lunch—instead I'd stumbled on everything besides those two things.

Callum answered the guy's question by clamping his mouth shut.

"You spilled the meaning about her name and made her confirm or deny if it was accurate. In front of a whole group of strangers." The man in the orange running suit opened his arms up. "Seems only fair you do the same in return."

Callum kept paddling. "I'm instructing."

"The life jacket demonstration's done and you've pounded proper paddle stroke and 'going with the flow' into our brains." He circled his finger around the group. "We're waiting." Orange Jogging Suit lifted his shaggy gray brows and demonstrated just how ready he was to wait.

A few more shouts of support circled the group, but Callum didn't look close to caving. At least until he glanced over at me and I crossed my arms over the bulky life jacket. I probably looked like an escaped mental patient in an orange straitjacket.

He shook his head at me, smiling the whole time, before shouting into the crowd, "Dove!"

"I didn't see it," shouted one middle-aged camper with the

biggest set of binoculars I'd ever seen strung around his neck, his head shooting up toward the sky.

"There are no doves in this part of the country," added another camper, who had a not-quite-so-impressive set of binoculars around his own neck.

Callum settled his hands on his hips and stared at the group like he couldn't believe his ears. "My name," he said slowly. "The meaning of it is 'dove.' And you're wrong about them not being in this part of the country. Doves are a hardy, adaptable breed. They can thrive in *any* part of the country."

"Dove?" I felt my forehead pinch together. *Callum* didn't sound like it meant "dove" to me.

His expression was of the deadly brand of serious. "Dove." He shrugged his shoulders. "You know, the common bird that's associated with the pigeon family that people consider an all-around nuisance and pest?" Callum motioned his hands at himself like he was proving something. "So yeah, totally prophetic for the person I grew into."

This time when the group laughed, I joined them.

It took me by surprise—the laugh. Until this moment, I'd been convinced I'd spend the summer on a laughter strike. An hour into day one and I was already disproving that whole theory.

I could tell he was trying not to laugh, but one slipped out. It was a nice sound. One of the nicest sounds I'd heard in a long time. It wasn't the fake kind or the dialed-down kind; it was the *real* kind.

"So I guess we're just a couple of birds." I smiled at him, wondering if at the end of the summer, I'd leave this place with more than just enough money for a beater car. Maybe I'd leave with a new friend. Callum had friend material taped all over him: didn't seem to take himself seriously, had a *decent*

34

sense of humor, laughed more than he groaned, and he had the whole upfront and honest thing down. A friend. No complications, no added drama, no romance to mess things up . . . just what I needed. A friend to make the summer more bearable.

Maybe I didn't need to focus on finding something wrong with him—maybe I could find something right instead. Yes, he was attractive, and sure, he seemed interesting, and hells yeah, I loved the way he laughed, but that didn't mean I had to either want to hook up with him or pretend he didn't exist. A friend. I think I could manage that.

Returning my smile, he unsnapped the top strap of my life jacket. He repeated the same with the other two. "Yeah, but you're a phoenix. I'm a pigeon with a fancy name."

FOUR

I didn't feel like a phoenix. At least not the mythical-bird kind. Rising from the ashes? Yeah, right. I was still dizzy from the fall. No thanks to my parents and with no way to "rise up" from the ashes.

When someone else was responsible for the fall, weren't they the only ones who knew the way back?

Okay, enough brooding. People were starting to stare, and Harry was watching me. He hadn't touched his dinner yet, and most of the other campers were already halfway done. A few were already scraping the last few morsels from their trays into the garbage cans before sorting their silverware and cups into the appropriate bus bin.

"If you're keeping your fingers crossed that this feast is going to taste better cold, you're going to be disappointed." I waved my fork at Harry's tin tray before lowering it to my own. I poked around at the mashed potatoes, but I wasn't hungry.

"I'm waiting for Dad and Mom." He sat up straighter on the bench seat, his gaze flickering to the doorway.

"They're not coming, Harry. Eat your dinner." I crumpled the napkin in my lap between my fist. I was tired of dishing

36

harsh reality after harsh reality to my little brother in the name of not wanting to fire false hope instead. I was tired of filling the role of parental figure in addition to the one of big sister I already performed with top marks.

"Fine," he grumbled before stuffing a heaping bite into his mouth. "Mmmm," he practically moaned. "Good."

Harry had never been a big eater. Not even a mediocre one. He'd been the kid people had to coax and encourage and practically bribe to get down a few bites. When he was a toddler, it had been like holding hostage negotiations—three hours later and the kid might have rewarded the efforts with a puny bite of his peas.

Tonight, though? He could have kept pace with the football players back home when they started the season pulling daily doubles and inhaling everything in their path.

"Hey, just because they're mashed doesn't mean you can't choke on them." I clinked my fork against his.

"I'm starving, Phoenix," Harry mumbled. Hard to articulate with a mouthful of food.

"Clearly." It only took a small nibble to confirm that he was right—they weren't bad. I'd been expecting them to be of the powdered, school-cafeteria variety, but these tasted like the real deal. You know, the kind your grandma makes at Thanksgiving—oozing in yellow pools of butter and thick with cream. My next bite wasn't a nibble.

"See?" He moved on to one of the ribs he'd stacked on his plate. They were charred, clearly fired on a grill, and dripping with thick caramel-brown barbecue sauce.

"Not bad," I allowed, trying not to smile as Harry went to work on his first rib. We didn't do "caveman" meat in the Ainsworth household. You know, the kind that came with sticky fingers, messy faces, and chunks of bone left on china plates.

Mom preferred her protein to come in the form of rich-in-omega-3 salmon fillets or tasteless roast chicken breast.

"Why are you so hungry all of a sudden? You've gone ten years of your life on some kind of hunger strike and tonight you suddenly decide to make like an American and eat like there's no tomorrow?" I set my fork down and moved on to the roll at the top of my tray. Still warm from the oven, the roll pulled apart in flaky layers.

"Do you know how much I did today? I'm starving. I *need* food. I *need* sustenance. So I can do it all again tomorrow." Harry was waving his rib around, which made a few drops of sauce fly onto the table and his pale blue polo shirt . . . joining the half-dozen other stains already there from what looked to be mud, grass, and who knows what else.

"If you played that hard, then you'd better eat mine, too." I shoved my tray across the table to him, saving half the roll for myself because it was just that good. I hadn't tormented toads and snakes all day, but I'd unpacked an entire car, gotten a cabin arranged, and given a highly ineffective demonstration on how to put on a life jacket. That was enough to earn me half a roll.

"Can I go sit with my friends?" Harry's arm stabbed into the air, waving.

The same pack of boys from earlier were flailing their arms at Harry.

I tipped my head at the rowdy table of boys. "Get out of here. Go get into a little trouble."

Harry was in the middle of scrambling out of his seat and picking up his tray when he paused.

"A little," I repeated. "The kind of trouble that's easy to get out of, not the other kind."

Harry gave that half a moment's thought. "Deal."

Bounding across the dining hall as fast as he could without

spilling his tray, he came to a screeching halt. When he looked back at me, his face all creased with concern, I shook my head.

"I'm good," I said, loud enough for him to hear. "Go have fun with your friends. Besides, Mom and Dad will probably show up soon." I waved my fork at the empty table I was seated at, keeping the optimistic look plastered on my face.

He might have only been ten, but he could see right through me. "Phoenix . . ."

"Harry," I said in the firmest tone I had. "Go. Have fun. Play. Carpe diem."

"Seize the day." He smiled, then scurried away toward his friends.

Now that Harry was gone, I picked up my brooding right where I'd left off. Instead of my parents, though, I moved on to someone else. I didn't really know him at all, but I could already tell Callum wasn't your typical guy. I liked that about him. Or I respected that about him, because—I reminded myself—there was nothing I should "like" when it came to Callum.

Like was a word that came loaded with possibilities. *Respect* was far more straightforward.

Yeah, because that made a whole lot of no sense.

Sighing to myself, I started picking at what was left of my roll, pretending that being the one person in the whole hall sitting at a table alone wasn't making me feel like I was under a microscope as it passed from person to person.

I shifted on the bench and took a look around. Empty across the table. Empty on the left. Empty on the right. So much for a family camp. Not that I cared, but still . . . if my parents weren't planning on actually participating, why didn't we just stay back home where my friends were and I was used to sitting alone at the table?

"Mind if I join you?" A big guy wearing a Camp Kismet

shirt took the seat Harry had just slid out of. This shirt wasn't in the same sky blue or sunny yellow or grass green I'd seen earlier, though; this one was tie-dyed and, from the looks of it, had been washed half a thousand times and was paper-thin. It was the kind of shirt most people would have tossed into the garbage or rag pile several dozen wears ago.

"Go ahead," I finally said, though he'd made it clear that he was taking a seat whether I invited him or not. At least I wasn't sitting as the lone camper anymore, though when I gave the guy across from me a quick inspection, I wasn't sure this was a much better alternative.

Middle-aged, his hair pulled into a low ponytail, and a row of leather bracelets running from his wrist a third of the way up his forearm—I wondered if I'd just come face-to-face with a hippie for the first time. The real kind, not the wannabe kind that California was overrun with.

"I'm glad you and your family finally made it up here, Phoenix. You don't know how long I've been trying to get your dad up to my mountain." His voice matched his appearance, kind of rough upfront, but gentle around the edges.

I didn't have to read the name stitched into his shirt to realize who was sitting across from me. "Ben?" My voice sounded as surprised as I felt. I was a little girl the last time I saw him, but the man across from me didn't look anything like the one I remembered, who used to favor power suits and flashy cars and almost always seemed to have a cell phone to his ear.

"Yeah, I know I look exactly the same as the last time you saw me, right?" He pinched at his shirt and shook his head enough to make his ponytail flick side to side.

I took a bite of my roll. "Why did you leave California and your job in the first place? Dad never really said much about it," I asked. Actually, Dad had said plenty about it—starting and ending with how mental Ben must have been to go from rolling in seven-figure-income kind of dough to barely scraping by at some family camp in the middle of Nowhere, USA.

Ben looked around the dining hall, like that should have been all the answer I needed. Not quite. "Because I realized life isn't a dress rehearsal. Better get it right the first time around because there's no such thing as a do-over."

"Oh" was all I could manage. I didn't get it. At least the part about willingly going from civilization to this . . . whatever Camp Kismet could be classified as.

"Where are your mom and dad?" He spread his arms at the empty table.

"Probably at the cabin." I shrugged and took a sip of my milk.

"Didn't they read any of the brochures I've been sending them for the past decade?" Ben held his arms out again and looked around the buzzing dining hall. "This is a *family* camp. The kind where you come together and behave like a family."

I gave another shrug. Apparently, this was the way our conversation was going to go: He spread his arms; I shrugged. "Actually, this is how we behave as a family." I waved my fork around the empty table and gave yet another shrug. If I kept going at this rate tonight, my shoulders were going to be sore in the morning.

"This might be how the Ainsworths worked as a family in California, but you're here now. Time to change things up."

I felt my eyebrows squeeze together. "What's so magical about this place that makes you think a family who's been used to eating meals in separate rooms at different times will suddenly come together to share a meal of ribs and baked beans?"

This time it was Ben who shrugged. "Because you're at Camp Kismet."

I closed my eyes to keep the eye roll to myself. "Let me guess. The place where our 'destiny awaits'?" I quoted the line I'd seen written on the front page of the brochure Harry had worn down to nothing. That line had *lame* stamped all over it.

Ben watched me for a few moments silently, a small smile on his face. "Our destiny is always waiting for us. It's right in front of us, all the time. Sometimes we just need a place and a time to be reminded of that."

I shifted on the bench. "And what if this *is* my 'destiny'?" My eyes circled the empty table.

Ben leaned forward. His eyes were dark brown, but right then they almost looked light. "What if it isn't?"

I distracted myself by staring at my tray. I probably should have asked my parents the question I was about to ask Ben, but I wasn't sure they'd tell me the truth. "Why are you letting us stay here the whole summer for free?"

Ben clasped his hands in front of him. "Because I want to. Because I can. Because you guys have had a rough go for a while and I figured you were due a breather. Because you're doing me a favor staying in that old cabin so a family of raccoons doesn't move in and take over." He rapped the table a few times, almost like he was knocking on some door, before he stood up. "Besides, I wouldn't say it's totally free, since I managed to get a new counselor out of the deal. You wouldn't believe how hard it is to find enough counselors every summer."

I pulled another chunk from my roll and smashed it flat. "I'm sure it must be really hard to find people willing to get paid to play outside all summer."

Ben managed to keep a straight face. "You have no idea. You're actually the one doing me a favor being here."

I knew who was doing who the favor here, and it wasn't me and my family. But I gave him credit for wanting to make me feel better about the whole thing. This Ben guy was okay. "You got all my paperwork, right? All my first aid and CPR certifications? If something didn't make it, I brought a file with everything in it. I can run to the cabin and grab it for you now. . . ."

Ben lifted his hands when I started to stand. I couldn't jeopardize this job. I needed it to keep busy, as a distraction, and to stow away some money for a car.

"Your paperwork is shipshape." Ben nodded in acknowledgment when a family passed behind him, the dad clapping him on the shoulder, before continuing. "I just wanted to let you know who your trainer will be for the next few weeks."

"Trainer?" I repeated.

"You know, someone who shows you the ropes, gets you comfortable with the job before setting you free on your own?"

I shook my head. He'd misunderstood me. "I know what a trainer is, and that I'd have one since I have a whole zero days of camp counselor experience." I made a big zero with my thumb and index finger. "But I thought that person would be you."

Ben's forehead folded with amusement. I didn't see what was so amusing. "As much as I'd love to spend a couple hundred hours training my best friend's firstborn in the ways of camp counseling, I've got a camp to run." Right then, a shattering sound echoed from the kitchen. "And until the day comes when it learns to run itself, it's three full-time jobs keeping up with this place. It's all needy like that." Another sound spilled from the kitchen, but this one was more splitting in nature.

I cringed right along with the rest of the staff and campers. I hadn't given much thought to how much time and effort it would take to run a several-hundred-acre camp. "Just name the time and place, and I'll be there."

Ben was slowly making his way in the direction of the kitchen. "Tomorrow morning, seven o'clock, on the front lawn. Your first official duty as a counselor-in-training will be to help guide a couple dozen hikers up the Matterhorn."

I swallowed. Just what had I gotten myself into? Early mornings in the summer? Dozens of hikers? Matterhorns? Oh well. Fire walking and stone throwing would have been better options than spending the whole summer trapped in a cabin with my parents.

Before Ben could disappear inside the kitchen, I shot up in my seat. "My trainer? Who am I looking for bright and early tomorrow morning?"

Ben skidded to a stop. His smile tipped a degree higher before he answered. I could have guessed the name before he said it.

"Callum. Callum O'Connor," Ben answered. "I wanted you to learn from the best, and that's him. Oh, and don't take it personally if he seems a little rigid, okay? Callum's tough on the counselors-in-training, but it's only because he wants you guys to know your jobs from the inside out. The campers' safety is in the hands of the counselor."

"He didn't seem so tough to me earlier," I said, recalling how the Callum I'd met seemed more into joking around and laughing than getting down with the serious.

"So you two have already met?"

I nodded. "Earlier this afternoon. I found myself the unfortunate victim of a life jacket demonstration."

Ben's gaze wandered across the dining hall. When his eyes landed on someone, I found my gaze following. I wasn't the only one sitting alone.

His back was to me, but it was his unruly hair that gave him away. Callum. The other two tables were almost spilling over with people, but the one he sat at remained vacant except for him.

I tried to balance the picture before me with the one I had from earlier this afternoon.

"He's tough, but that's what makes him great at his job." Ben lifted his chin at Callum before his gaze flitted in my direction. "You can take him."

FIVE

I shouldn't have slept as well as I did that night.

The mattress wasn't exactly what pleasant dreams were made of, and Harry had always been a heavy breather when he slept. That should have kept me awake. Finding out Callum and I were going to be spending a whole heck of a lot of time together should have kept me awake. The sound of the metal roof pinging when a rainstorm rolled through should have kept me awake.

Nothing about this situation screamed peaceful night of sleep.

I hadn't slept this well in months. Camp Kismet was screwing with me. Big-time.

When my alarm jolted me awake at five-thirty, I forced myself from bed. Not in enough time so that I could sit down for breakfast and make myself somewhat presentable for my first official day as a counselor-in-training, or C.I.T., as Harry informed me, but early enough that I could squeeze in my morning training run.

Cross-country season was only a couple of months from starting, which meant this was go time for training. I ran five days a week, and I cross-trained the other two. I didn't do rest days. I didn't believe in them. Taking a day off to rest was like admitting I was too weak or too lazy to get up and work for it. The other girls I went back and forth with in the top of our division didn't believe in rest days, either.

That was what I reminded myself of as I pried myself from bed when I wanted to hit the snooze button instead. I visualized first-place rankings, college scouts, and scholarships as I tied my shoes. Once I was out the cabin door and had found my stride, I didn't need any more reminders, warnings, or visualizations because I went on autopilot when I was running.

Instinct took over, and in those miles that followed, my mind was quiet because I knew that even though I was questioning a lot of things in life, running wasn't one of them. I was good at it. I loved it. I felt strong when I did it and peaceful in the minutes after a hard run. For those few or many miles, my world was right.

After my run, the time on my phone read 6:45 when I bolted from the bathroom, dressed, hair wet from the shower, and shoes tied. Hustling around a rickety, old cabin so I didn't wake anyone else was a challenge. So instead of searching the cupboards, I snagged a banana from the counter and dashed out the front door.

I'd have to get through the next five hours and six miles until lunch with nothing more than a banana. Awesome start to my first day.

The air was warmer than it had been during my run, but there was just enough chill left in the air to make me wish I'd thrown on a sweatshirt over my North Shore track-and-field tee. I'd have to remember that tomorrow morning when I showed up for my second shift at god-awful o'clock.

The big clearing was quiet when I got to it. Other than a few noisy birds, there wasn't another living thing in sight.

The dew on the grass was evaporating from the sun beating down on the lawn, creating a blanket of fog that moved across the clearing. It felt like I was walking on top of clouds as I crossed the lawn.

I wandered over to the place where Callum and the rafting crew had been yesterday—it seemed to be the congregation point at the camp—but no one was there. Not even my best-of-the-best trainer. My cell phone said it was six-fifty. Ben told me to show up at seven.

When 6:55 flashed on my screen, I started to worry. A little.

Another minute ticked off, and that nervous feeling settled deep in my stomach. Where was Boy Wonder? I wouldn't expect the best camp counselor trainer around to show up late for a shift. I mean, I didn't even have a camp shirt yet.

That was when I noticed someone lumbering toward me from the other side of the campground.

Callum looked tired. Actually, he looked beat, like he might have gotten three minutes of sleep. Even from here I could tell his eyes were bloodshot and his hair was a disaster. It looked like he'd taken a hand beater to his hair and dialed it to the top speed.

A few steps later, he pulled a baseball cap from his pocket and flopped it onto his head. That took care of the hair problem, but not the bloodshot, tired thing. "You," he said. Nothing else followed.

It sounded like an accusation.

"You," I repeated. Mine sounded like more of a confirmation.

"You could have mentioned you were the new counselor yesterday." He kept moving closer, tucking his T-shirt into his pants.

"Someone else was a little busy dominating the conversation or else I might have."

He kept looking at me, like he was waiting for something. I didn't know what. "Have you ever been a counselor before?" he asked.

"Nope."

"Have you *ever* had a job before?"

I shook my head as I tried to figure out how to look at him without *looking* at him. His hair aside, the rest of him looked pretty damn A-okay. He was in a pair of heavy canvas cargo pants, and over his T-shirt, he'd thrown on a heavy flannel shirt that had been washed so many times most of the color had faded from it. Mud-flecked hiking boots completed the Ranger Callum ensemble.

"You're seventeen, right? About to go into your senior year?" His voice was lower this morning, probably from just waking up.

"Yes and yes. Is there something you're getting at?"

"Just that I don't know a lot of people our age who've never worked before."

If his voice had been a bit higher and his expression a smirk, I would have taken that as an insult. "Yeah, well, I know plenty who haven't."

"I bet you do, Santa Monica."

I felt my blood warm. Just because I'd never had an official job didn't mean I hadn't worked my ass off in other areas. "What are you saying, Inglewood?"

He shrugged, then started moving in the direction of a big shed off to the side of the dining hall. "That we've got a lot to go over in the next three weeks. I hope you're a fast learner."

"I am," I fired off, marching after him. "I hope you're a decent teacher."

"I am, but Ben already told you that, right?" He glanced over his shoulder, a smirk shifting into place. "About me being his best?"

"I think the word he used was *tough*. Or maybe it was *hard-ass*. I can't remember."

He kept moving. "If you don't think you can handle me, I bet Ben would be willing to let someone 'nicer' train you. You know, if that's what you're looking for."

This time I huffed, continuing to charge after him. "I've handled way harder than you. Do you think *you* can handle *me*? Or would you rather Ben hire someone more submissive?"

"I've handled way more than you, too, and besides, I'm used to strong women." He stopped outside the shed doors and pulled a set of keys from his pocket.

What had I seen in this guy, again? "Let me guess. Your probation officers?"

His gaze cut my direction. "My mom."

"Oh." I hadn't been expecting that.

"She raised me, so that automatically earns her the strong-woman title. And my brother, which earns her the title of saint, too." The first key he slid into the lock worked. There had to be a few dozen keys on that ring, none of them labeled.

"Older or younger brother?" I asked as he threw open the creaky metal doors.

"Older."

I waited just outside the doors when he ducked into the shed. It was dark and smelled musty. "In age, but you're the older brother of the two, aren't you?"

A giant backpack landed at my feet with a thud. "What makes you say that?" His voice kind of echoed.

I stepped to the side, just in case anything else came flying out, like a sharp projectile. "Personal experience."

"You have an older brother, too?" He dropped another pack beside the big one.

"No, mine's younger, but I just recognize that protective look, you know. I live that look." I moved aside again when he stepped out of the shed. He didn't seem to know (or care) about personal space. "Does your brother still live at home?"

"Nope. He moved out." He closed the doors and locked them.

"Do you still get to see him?"

"Yeah, sure." One shoulder lifted as he pocketed the keys. "Every Saturday during visiting hours at the correctional facility back home." Another shrug, but I could tell from his voice and the way he wouldn't look at me that he wasn't as indifferent as he came off. "Hopefully, you do a better job protecting your brother than I did with mine."

I shifted, not sure what to say. I'd never been in a situation where a person just dropped the my-brother's-in-jail bomb on me. "We all make our own choices," I said.

Callum threw on the bigger pack like it was filled with marshmallows. "Then let's hope your brother makes better choices than mine did."

I grabbed the bag meant for Counselor-in-Training Ainsworth. I watched what he was doing and mirrored it, trying not to act like I didn't have a clue how to fasten one of these beasts. I'd been hiking before, sure, but the kind that went with old school backpacks stuffed with a couple bottles of water, a first aid kit, and a few emergency granola bars. I'd never gone *Hiking*. "What about your dad? What's he like?"

He leaned forward and buckled the hip strap. "I don't know. You'd have to ask him. If you could find him, which neither my mom nor the State of California has been able to do since he bailed on us and decided to do the honorable thing by dodging child support." He said it like he was talking about the last movie he'd seen—totally matter-of-fact. It threw me, learning what I guessed were Callum's dirty little secrets less than twenty-four hours after we'd met.

"That must have sucked," I said, considering kicking my own butt for coming up with such a lame response. "I'm sorry." There. Better. Barely.

Callum's response to that was a shrug. "With a guy like that? We were better off without him. Besides, Mom nailed the parenting thing all on her own." He nudged me. "Ben told me you're here with your family. That must be cool."

I checked his expression twice, sure he must have been joking. "Eh, *cool* isn't the word I'd use to describe it. At all." He glanced over, surprised. "Other than my little brother, Harry, I couldn't imagine a better summer job than one that put me out-of-state and away from my parents. Better yet, out-of-planet."

"So you're saying you guys have a great relationship?" He adjusted his chest strap. His chest was wider than most guys his age had. Not that I'd noticed.

I smiled at the ground. "Off the charts."

"What's the deal, then?" He moved closer when I kept fumbling with my chest strap. He snapped it into place.

"More like what *isn't* the deal." I cleared my throat as he pulled on the shoulder straps. The pack felt a hundred times better once he'd dialed in the straps. Instead of feeling like I was lugging around a gorilla holding on to my shoulder by its pinkies, now it felt more like a koala bear hugging my back.

I needed to change the subject. If I talked about my family, I was going to cry, and I'd made it a policy not to cry in front of virtual strangers. "How does some guy from Inglewood wind up a lead counselor at a camp in Flagstaff?"

As soon as he looked at me, he glanced away. After all the

eye contact yesterday, he was struggling today. "His mom brings him and his brother to camp when they're kids and he discovers that there's more to the outdoors than the playground at his school."

"Go, Mom."

"She *is* the best." He unbuttoned the cuffs of his flannel shirt and rolled the sleeves to his elbows, smiling. I didn't know many guys who'd fess up to idolizing their moms for fear of being labeled a mama's boy, but I admired him for not seeming to care.

"Her son didn't come out too bad, either, right?"

He laughed, shaking his head. "Are we having a bonding moment right now? Because I make it a point not to fraternize with the underlings."

I lifted an eyebrow. "I figured that out last night at dinner." I paused, reliving the scene. "Why were you sitting alone?"

"I was in a roomful of two hundred people. I wasn't alone."

I sighed. "Fine. Why were you sitting at a *table* alone?"

He shrugged. "I don't know. Why were *you* sitting at a table alone?" When I didn't answer right away, he settled his hands on his hips. "As fun as the game of Getting to Know You is, we've got to get you trained if you're going to be on your own in a few weeks. Sharing time comes after snack time comes after nap time, cool?"

"Cool."

He backed up a couple of steps. "I'm not sure how much Ben's gone over with you—"

"Not much."

Callum looked out at the lawn in front of the dining hall, where campers were starting to show up for the hike. "Well, campers rotate through in two- and four-week sessions, which means a counselor comes in contact with over a thousand campers every summer. Campers who've been doing this kind of thing their whole lives and campers who wouldn't know how to lace a hiking boot to save their lives. It's important for a counselor to be able to meet each camper where they're at."

My head was swimming. "And how do you do that?"

"Get to know them. Get to know the job. Get really good at the job."

"Sounds intimidating."

He tipped his head toward the campers before heading toward them. "Let's go over." He made sure I followed. "It's easy. Know the plan. Stick to the plan. Have fun. The rest will take care of itself."

I held my arms out. "*So* easy." I didn't hide my sarcasm.

He dropped his hands on my shoulders and lowered his head to my eye level. "One foot in front of the other. That's it. I'll take the lead to set the pace. You'll take up the end, so all you have to do is make sure no one gets left behind. Stay alert, follow my lead, have fun, leave no camper behind," he said, listing each off on his fingers. "I trust you."

My face flattened. "You've known me for two and a half seconds."

"Doesn't matter. In my world, you start out with my trust," He squeezed my shoulders before dropping his hands. "What you do with that is up to you."

"But—"

"No *but*s. This is how you learn, by doing, not by sitting around in some classroom, taking notes." Callum motioned at the campers. "We've got to get this hike started unless we want to eat lunch for dinner. Any more questions?"

I knew he meant *There better not be any more questions*, but I had to ask. "What about a camp counselor T-shirt? Don't I need one so the campers will know who I am?"

Callum gave me a look, one that suggested he was questioning my sanity. Then he cupped his hands around his mouth and turned toward the cluster of campers. "Hey, everyone! Good morning! This is Phoenix, you know, named for the bird that rises from its own ashes." When he threw me an amused look, I elbowed him. Didn't do anything but make him look more amused. "She'll be along on the hike with me, so if you need anything or have a question, feel free to ask either one of us."

I smiled and waved at the crowd. As long as they didn't ask me anything too technical or expect me to splint a cast, I should be able to fill in the shoes of camp-counselor-in-training today. Hopefully.

"We'll be leaving in five minutes. Please take this time to make one last bathroom break, double-check your boots, and recheck your water bottles. The Matterhorn's three miles up and three miles down, well into blister territory if your socks or boots are rubbing at you wrong. Do your feet a favor and double-check."

When he glanced down at my feet and saw what I had on—an old pair of running sneakers—he rolled his eyes. Total confidence booster right there. "And please make sure you packed at least two liters of water with you. It's going to be a warm day, and dehydration's an outdoor enthusiast's worst enemy."

He hadn't finished his little checklist speech, and people were already following his instructions, checking. Most of these people looked to be twice Callum's age, but they listened to him like he was the president of the United States of Camp Kismet.

I was impressed. I couldn't even get my parents to listen to me when I was trying to tell them that someone was on the phone for them.

"You might want to rethink those shoes," Callum said to

me, aiming eye roll number two at my shoes. "You've got five minutes to get to your cabin and change them. Think you can do it?"

"It wouldn't matter if I had twenty minutes because I don't have any other shoes than the ones I have on." I glanced down at my old sneakers. I didn't see what the big deal was. I'd put five hundred training miles on these babies and another couple hundred hiking around the trails or the beach back home. They were tried and true.

"You don't have *any* other shoes than those?"

"Unless flip-flops or sandals are a better option, then no, this is what I've got."

He exhaled through his nose. "Unbelievable. Where did you think you were going? Cheerleading camp?"

I felt a small spark of fire in me. Probably because the girl Keats was two-timing me with was on the cheerleading team. "Thanks for your concern, but I'll be just fine."

Callum lifted his hands and stepped aside. "Your call. Forget I mentioned it." He moved away, in the direction of a camper who was wrestling with one of his boots. "Just be ready to head out in five."

I checked my shoes again. They didn't seem so unfit for the task of a six-mile hike. Why was Camp Counselor America making such a fuss?

As I scanned the other campers' feet, I saw a trend emerging. One I was not in on. All of them were in high-top, serious-looking hiking boots. The kind that looked like a person could make a trek around the world in. Either everyone else on this hike had come way overprepared or I'd come seriously underprepared.

My eyes latched onto something familiar—a pair of small hiking boots that had been recently purchased at the giant outdoor warehouse store just off the new highway back home.

Harry, hiding behind the group of hikers.

Neither of our parents was here, and if he was hiding, that meant neither of them knew he was here, either.

I rushed over to him, keeping Callum in my sights so I could handle the Harry situation before he came over to see what was up.

"What are you doing here?" I whispered, grabbing Harry's arm and pulling him aside.

If his expression didn't give away that he'd been caught, his voice did. "Hiking."

"And Dad and Mom know you're heading on a six-mile hike this morning?" I already knew the answer, but I wanted Harry to say it himself.

"They . . . *will,*" he started, rubbing the back of his head. "At least when they get up and read the note on the fridge."

My eyes went wide. "Harry? Seriously? How do you think that's going to go over?"

Harry's nose crinkled. "Hopefully good?"

"Probably not." I rubbed my forehead and thought on the fly.

Harry had been the only one who'd actually seemed excited about coming to camp this summer. He'd made friends on his first day. Plus, I looked after him. Our parents relied on me to look after Harry most of the time anyway, so why should this time be any different?

I pretended to think it over, but my decision had been made the moment he'd looked at me with those big, begging eyes of his. "Stay toward the back, where I'll be." Harry's face lit up like he'd just learned he'd get to captain the next space-ship to Mars.

"I will. I promise." He threw his arms around me and smashed the side of his head into my stomach. "Thanks, Phoenix."

"For helping you deceive and possibly royally piss off our parents?" I mumbled, returning his hug. "Sure. Anytime."

Someone moved up beside us. "And this must be the little brother I've heard so much about." Callum's voice was warm as he crouched down in front of Harry.

"That's me, Harry." He stuck out his hand, and Callum shook it without hesitating. "Who are you?"

Callum looked insulted. "You mean Phoenix doesn't talk about me to you as much as she talks about you to me?"

Harry shook his head. "Nope. Phoenix hasn't told me about any friends she's made here yet. She doesn't like it here. She didn't want to come."

When it looked like Harry was going to keep on spilling my secrets, I stepped in. "And how about that hike we should be getting to?"

Callum and Harry ignored me.

"So you're telling me your sister didn't want to come here?" Callum sounded disbelieving. "That she doesn't *like* it here? The best place in the whole world?"

Harry sighed all solemn-like. "Not even a little bit."

"That's a bummer." Callum slid a bit closer to Harry, angling himself so both he and my brother could look up at me. "Maybe if she'd give this place a chance, she might actually find she likes it."

Harry lifted one shoulder. "Maybe."

Callum and Harry exchanged a look before Callum stood up.

Callum's attention moved from me to Harry. "Are your parents here?" He didn't look around, because he already knew.

Harry and I swallowed at the same time. He shook his head. "No."

"Did they sign the permission slip that says you can participate in activities at camp without them?" Callum looked Harry in the eye, man-to-man. Harry's throat bobbed, his eyes widened, and right before he answered, he looked at me. I wasn't sure why.

I went with my gut. "They signed it," I jumped in. "He's good to go."

SIX

Two and a half miles into the hike up the Matterhorn, I knew I was in over my head. And I also knew why they called this hike the Matterhorn—because it was insanely steep.

The trail itself was well groomed and mostly rock and root free, but what it lacked in tripping hazards it more than made up for in elevation gain. My butt was on fire, and my heart rate was nearing the jacked zone. And I considered myself physically fit. Or I had until this hike.

Callum was keeping a nice slow and steady pace at the front, and I was doing my best to keep one eye on the hikers in front of me and the other on Harry. He would have rather been up front with Callum Almighty, who'd apparently filled in the superhero slot in Harry's life, but he knew better than to ask. I would have said no, and since I'd already lied for him, he owed me.

"How are you doing?" I asked Harry, tapping his arm as we kept climbing the trail. We were close to the last half mile, and Callum had been calling down promises that it would start to level off here. He'd better not have been exaggerating.

"You've asked me that . . . fifty times already . . . Phoenix."

Harry had to pause every few words to suck in a breath. Poor kid sounded close to hyperventilating. "Ask me one more time . . . and I'm going to scream."

I tapped his arm again. "How are you doing?"

Instead of screaming, he went with something else.

"Ugh, Harry, gross." I pinched my nose and made a face. "You said you'd scream, not drop a stink bomb on me."

He'd already been laughing over the whole fart thing, but when he saw my face and me waving to clear the air, he really started letting loose. He stopped paying any attention to the trail, and, two steps later, he went down, knees and palms first.

"Harry!" I cried, rushing toward him.

He was already pushing himself up from the ground. I dusted off his knees while he took care of his palms.

"Are you okay?"

"I just wiped out climbing the Matterhorn and didn't even cry." Harry's face lit up. "I'm phenomenal!" He dusted his palms a few more times. "Although it would have made for a better story if I'd drawn some blood."

"You got lucky."

Harry adjusted his glasses and shrugged, before continuing along the trail again. He was getting tired and going slower. Maybe this hadn't been such a great idea, I thought as I watched his smile fall into a frown.

After a few more minutes of what felt like vertical hiking, Harry's legs gave out beneath him. He crashed, hard.

Rushing forward, I skidded down beside him to see what was the matter. "What is it?" I asked, lifting his arms and checking his legs again. "What hurts?"

He wouldn't look at me. He was too occupied with staring at the ground. Actually, he was glaring at it. "Nothing," he grumbled. And then he sniffed.

"Harry . . ." I lowered my head so I could look into his face. It was hard to tell how dusty his face had gotten from the hike, but I noticed a few clear streaks winding down his face. Lines that only could have been drawn by tears. "What's the matter?"

"Nothing." He kicked the ground with the heel of his boot.

"No one in the history of the world has cried over nothing. There's got to be something." I dropped my hand to his shoulder and gave it a squeeze. "Tell me."

Harry kicked out both legs in front of him and glared at them like they were traitors. "I can't do it. What are my friends going to think when I tell them I couldn't do it?" He sniffed and tossed a pebble into the trees.

"Um, that you gave it your best and that you're only ten years old and almost finished the climb up the Matterhorn. A hike every single one of these people have been heaving and grunting their own way up." I found a decent-size rock on the side of the trail and handed it to Harry to toss. I was a fan of letting off steam in constructive ways, chucking rocks into the forest included.

He heaved it deep into the woods, surprising for a kid who'd apparently reached his I'm-beat level. "Not Callum. I've been watching him, and he hasn't once looked like this is hard for him."

"That's because he's probably done this hike dozens of times before." Harry made a face, clearly not pacified by my explanation. "And I have a strong suspicion he could be one of those mutants with crazy-insane powers."

"Why do you think that?"

The line of hikers had almost disappeared from view when I noticed something moving so fast it didn't seem natural. Harry whipped around to see what I was staring at.

"Whoa . . ."

My nonverbalized word exactly.

Callum was bounding down the trail with speed and precision, two things that didn't seem to go together when it came to a trail like this. Going up, it took grit, but coming down, at that pace, took some serious guts.

He skidded to a stop, kneeling beside Harry. "What happened?" he asked, his voice even, his breathing steady.

"He's tired," I answered. "I'm not sure if he can make it the rest of the way up."

Callum nodded once. "Anything hurt?"

Harry sighed. "Everything hurts," he confessed with another sigh. "But nothing's broken."

Callum scooted closer, a smile settling into place. "That's my definition of a good day's hike." He patted Harry's back a few times before checking up the trail. "You gave it your best— that's something to be proud of."

"My best didn't get me to the top. I failed."

"You made it two and a half miles up the three-mile climb to the Matterhorn. That's not a failure in my book, and it shouldn't be in yours, either."

Harry sniffed and wiped at his face with the back of his arm.

"Besides, if we succeeded the first time at everything, life would become pretty damn boring."

I shot a look at Callum. He shrugged at me, like *damn* was a perfectly acceptable word to utter in front of an almost fifth grader.

"You have water?" Callum asked me. His voice was more formal—he was in trainer mode.

"Yeah, we're good."

"Here, just in case." He unclipped one of his water bottles and gave it to me. "I'll try to hurry them through their lunches, so hopefully we'll be able to meet up with you in an hour. Two at the most."

I wasn't thrilled that Harry and I would be trapped here alone, but there wasn't any other option. "We'll be here."

Callum gave a brisk nod. "Are you okay?"

Something about Callum asking if I was okay made my heart squeeze. "My little brother's body is refusing to cooperate, we're trapped in the middle of the steepest piece of trail I've ever seen, and I'm pretty sure I just failed my first task as a camp counselor since not every camper completed the hike."

Before he replied, I beat him to it. "Let me guess, you're about to give me a pep talk about only failing if that's what I tell myself, right?"

"Oh no. You definitely failed your first task," Callum called as he started climbing the trail.

"But you just said—"

"I just said that to a camper. You're a counselor. The rules are different." He raced up the trail.

"You suck at pep talks! *Boss!*" I hollered, but he was already out of sight.

From up above, a low laugh echoed down the trail. At least he had a sense of humor while he was on the clock.

"What are you doing?" Harry asked as I started unbuckling my pack.

"Getting you up this damn trail."

Harry's brows hit his hairline.

"Oh, sure, so when Super Callum says it, no big deal, but when I say it, you look at me like I just committed a felony." I shrugged out of the pack and perched it up against a tree, where it would be easy to find on the way down. I rolled my shoulders and flexed my back, feeling so light I could have flown. Crouching down beside him, I waited. "Well? Come on. Climb aboard the Phoenix Express."

Harry finally registered what I was suggesting. "No way. I weigh too much. This trail's sick without me strapped to your back." Harry's eyes wandered up the trail—it wasn't just steep at this point; it was vertical.

"We're doing this, no matter how long you sit here making up your mind. Climb on now or later, whatever, but you're getting to the top of this thing."

He held out for another ten seconds before he started crawling toward me. When he wound his arms around my neck, I braced myself and stood up, hooking my arms beneath his legs.

"Don't worry. I've got you. We won't fall." I looked over my shoulder and gave him a smile.

He had the most unconcerned look on his face I'd ever seen. He beamed at the trail. "I know. I trust you."

SEVEN

I felt like I'd just scaled an entire mountain with a person strapped to my back . . . instead of what I'd really done— walked the last half mile of a flattening trail with a ten-year-old riding piggyback. A *small* ten-year-old.

"Wow, Phoenix. Check it out." Harry's breathing was back to normal as he squirmed around until I let him go.

My breaths sounded more like I'd spent the past six hours blowing up air mattresses and beach balls. "It's . . ." One shallow breath in. One sharp pant out. Repeat. ". . . great." One shallow breath in. One sharp pant out. Repeat. Repeat again.

"I can see everything from up here!" Harry sprinted across the meadow, his legs bounding through the grasses and weeds and wildflowers.

"You made it."

I'd been too busy overworking my lungs and watching Harry to notice someone had crept up beside me.

I didn't trust that any words would come out clear, so I went with the classic thumbs-up.

"Hungry?" Callum shook a couple of paper lunch sacks,

giving me what I guessed was a concerned look. I went with another thumbs-up. I wasn't hungry—I'd probably throw up whatever I tried to get down right now—but I guessed Harry would be. That is, once he stopped tearing through the field like he'd just been hooked up to a sugar-caffeine drip.

"Do you . . . you know . . . need anything?" Callum looked like he wasn't sure what to do. Probably a first since he was the guy with all the answers and seemed to know everything about everything.

Since my thumbs-up wasn't going to work in this situation, I made myself put some words together.

"I'm . . . good." Progress. At least I'd gotten those two gems out in one breath instead of the five it would have taken a few minutes ago. "Thanks." Another thumbs-up. Dammit. What was the matter with me?

"Yeah, Phoenix, you don't look like you're 'good.'" Callum leaned down a little, the skin between his brows still pinched.

Finally, I felt my heartbeat slowing, enough so that I could inhale through my nose instead of sucking in lungfuls of air through my mouth. "I'm okay." Inhale through the nose, exhale through the mouth. "Thanks for checking."

"Okay." Callum bobbed his head from side to side, considering that. "Now, see, that I believe. *Good* was a stretch. *Okay* is more like the truth."

He'd lost the flannel, but while it had been too big, his T-shirt seemed to be too small. It pulled at his chest and arms, even a little on his upper back. I pretended not to notice. I pretended again that if I had noticed, I didn't like it.

I sucked at pretending.

"Glad you two made it." He gave me another one of those infuriating nudges that made me feel like my insides were liquefying, before heading for a group of campers snapping photos of themselves doing handstands with the view behind them. He didn't make it far before he was intercepted.

One of the campers was holding Callum's radio, and just from his face I could tell something was wrong.

I moved a little closer, but I couldn't hear what was being said. Callum started talking into the radio, that line between his brows going deep. A few seconds later, his face went from worried to something else. That was when his eyes narrowed on me.

Firing off a few more words into the radio, he lowered it at his side and started marching in my direction.

"What's up?" I asked, sliding a step back when he stopped right in front of me.

"There's a kid missing at camp." His voice matched his expression—pissed off.

"Really? Who?" I took another step back because I'd guessed where this was going.

He took another step closer. He was trying to make me uncomfortable. It was working. Then he threw his arm in the direction of Harry, who was still hustling circles around the meadow. "Your little brother."

EIGHT

Busted.

Big-time. Those permission slips were kind of a big deal. Especially when the note Harry had taped to the fridge had fallen and gotten wedged underneath before our parents found it.

How two of the most self-absorbed beings on the planet noticed that their son was missing and practically sent out an Amber Alert was beyond me.

Once everyone figured out where Harry was, it was cool. My parents signed the slip so Harry could take part in "safe" activities on his own and disappeared into Cabin #13 before we made it back from the hike. Their concern was overwhelming.

So the 'rents had moved past it, just like everyone else at camp had, save for one person. My trainer. I'd let him down and I knew it. . . . I just didn't know how to make it right.

When we made it into camp by afternoon, Callum kept with the whole silent treatment he'd been dishing my way ever since the meadow incident, and other than a shake of a head when I asked him if he needed help with anything else, that was all the response I got from him. I didn't know when my next shift was or what kind of adventure I'd be tackling. I wasn't even sure if I still had a job after what I'd done.

So I was a little distracted all day. That was no different in the dinner line. I noticed with a groan when I looked down at my tray and saw a couple of barbecued drumsticks, a sweet potato wrapped in foil, a grilled ear of corn, and another roll. A few problems with all that: I didn't eat dark meat, sweet potatoes were an insult to the potato family, and I was against corn on all levels based on the evidence that it had little to zilch in the nutritional value category. Looked like dinner was going to consist of a roll tonight.

Luckily, I wasn't really hungry.

It was kind of hard to feel anything but gut-wrenching shame after the day I'd had.

"Hey, Phoenix. You want to come sit with me and my friends?" Harry had been in front of me in line, and he'd started for one table while I'd absently moved toward the one we'd sat at the night before.

I glanced in the direction of his friends' table. It was a long one—the boys clustered together in the middle while who I guessed were their families were staggered on the ends. I wasn't sure where I'd fit into that equation.

"Thanks for the invitation, but I'm going to park myself here tonight." I set my tray down on the empty table and gave Harry a smile. It was strange—him looking after me. It might have only been an invitation to come sit with him and his friends, but I knew why he was doing it—he didn't want me to be alone.

"Ya sure? I don't mind, and my friends would be cool with it, too."

I cleared my throat to keep from smiling. Our roles in the looking-after department might be shifting. "I'm sure, but thanks."

He gave me a good look, probably doing what I did to him and assessing if what I'd said was more a truth or a fabrication, before nodding. "Okay, but I'll come back when Mom shows up."

I bit the inside of my cheek. "I thought we'd settled that last night."

"Yeah, but she said she was really coming tonight. For sure this time."

Instead of arguing with him, I changed the subject.

"Go have fun with your friends. You know where to find me if you need me." I waved at him as I slid into my seat. By the time I looked up a half second later, Harry was already across the dining hall.

I didn't know how long I'd watched him mixing it up like the social butterfly I hadn't known he was, when someone slipped into the seat across from me and set her tray down.

"Sorry I'm late. I was waiting for your dad . . . hoping he'd want to . . ." Mom's voice trailed off as she distracted herself by looking around the hall for Harry.

I would have pointed at where he was if I wasn't so shocked at her presence.

When she was still searching the room a minute later, her forehead folded with concern, I pointed in Harry's direction. "He's over there. With that big group of barbarians looking and sounding like they're having some kind of burp-off."

Mom found Harry just as he stood up on his seat, chugged a can of soda, and let out a belch that echoed through the room.

I smiled as I picked at my roll. He totally owned that burp-off.

"Harrison?" she whispered, like she couldn't process the boy waving his arms in the air in victory across the cafeteria with the boy she'd spent the past ten years pretending to raise.

When Mom looked like she was about to go stop him,

I grabbed her hand. "Don't. Please. He's having fun. Just let him, okay?"

Mom looked down at where my hand was clutching hers. Something I couldn't read settled into her face. I couldn't remember the last time I'd touched my mom. I couldn't recall the last time she'd touched me back.

"I wasn't going to go ruin his fun, Phoenix. As hard as I know you find it to believe, I'm not the fun police all the time." She must have noticed my reaction, because she added, "Okay, fine. Just *most* of the time." Was she smiling?

"Other than your brother going missing"—she cleared her throat—"how was the rest of your day?" She picked up her fork and lowered it to her baked beans. "It was your first day as an official camp counselor, right? How was it?"

"Eh, yeah. It was." I picked another hunk of my roll to pieces and crumbled them over my drumsticks.

Mom set her fork down. "It was a bad day, then."

I wondered why now, when I wanted to forget about the whole thing, she'd decided to pick up the concerned-parent baton again.

"It wasn't a great one, that's for sure," I mumbled.

"What happened?" She gave me the Mom Brow.

"Other than my parents going nutso looking for Harry when they should have known he was with me . . . and lying to my trainer, Callum, about you guys signing Harry's permission slip for camp?" I mumbled around a sigh. "That didn't go over so well."

Mom was quiet for a minute, watching me. "You made a mistake. One you'll hopefully learn from. And thankfully Harrison turned up and was okay. That's what matters." She picked her fork up, but it stayed frozen above her tray again. "Who's Callum?"

It took me a minute to catch up. I didn't want to talk about

Callum with her, but I *really* didn't want her to know I didn't want to talk about him with her. "He's just another camp counselor here. He's the one Ben assigned to train me for the next few weeks."

She nodded, but I knew—she could tell I was hiding something. Moms were especially skilled in this area.

"Where's he sitting?" Mom casually scanned the hall.

"I'm not sure," I started, searching the hall like she was, pretending I didn't have a clue where he was. "Probably with the other camp counselors." I waved my finger at the tables reserved for the counselors. Two tables were packed and noisy with conversation, and the third quiet and empty except for one.

"Which one is he?"

"Huh?"

"Callum. Which one is Callum?" When she looked at me, I knew she'd seen right through my whole Huh?-I-forgot-who-we-were-talking-about act.

Tucking my leg beneath me, I pointed at him. "That's Callum."

She studied him for a moment, then turned her attention back to me. "Have you heard much from your friends?"

Yes. And no. They were busy enjoying their summers. I was busy *pretending* to enjoy mine.

"Emerson and I have been texting, but you know, everyone's busy, and I've only been gone for two days." I stabbed at my potato, almost like it was a voodoo doll and my fork was the pin. It was surprisingly therapeutic.

Mom nodded. "Well, I'm sure everyone's thinking of you."

"I'm sure."

How much longer was she going to sit here and grill me? How much longer should I sit here before I could bail without being too obvious?

"I know we haven't gotten much of a chance to talk about this . . . but how are you doing with the whole Keats thing?"

Okay, Mom bringing up the ex topic? A wince didn't even begin to cover just how not okay this was.

"The *Keats thing?*" I shoved my tray away. "By *thing,* do you mean his way of breaking up with me? Because I don't know your definition of a *thing,* but what happened was more than that to me."

"Phoenix—" Mom reached her arm across the table, almost like she was trying to calm me down or something, but I'd had it. Too much parental interference for one night.

"You know what, Mom? You have my permission, blessing, and encouragement to pretend to parent when it comes to Harry. He's young and still innocent enough to not see this whole mother-of-the-year thing for the act it is." I flew out of my seat. "I made it through the past two years without a mother pretending to care. I can make it one more year before I'm out, so save it for Harry. I've believed enough of your and Dad's lies for one lifetime."

Her face remained calm, eerily calm. Her eyes didn't even flicker in anger. Other than the way her chest was moving faster now, there was nothing that gave away that she was getting lectured by her teen daughter in front of a room full of people.

Instead of getting up and walking away, Mom looked me in the eye. "I know," she said, and then she finally took a bite of her dinner.

NINE

I'd failed my first assignment as a counselor-in-training on yesterday's hike. I didn't want to carry that trend into day two—rafting.

I woke up before my alarm went off at five that morning, images of campers falling from rafts and being pulled down rivers racing through my head. I couldn't erase Callum's voice, either—the words he'd said to the campers on the lawn the afternoon I'd arrived, instructing what to do if and when disaster struck.

That nervous pit opened up in my stomach the longer I lay in bed thinking about it, so, early or not, I threw the covers off and headed out for my morning run.

I might have messed up yesterday, but I wasn't going to repeat that today. Nope, I learned from my mistakes, and I was going to be the best damn counselor-in-training Camp Kismet had ever seen.

I was supposed to "rendezvous" with the other counselors behind the dining hall at seven. The campers would show up an hour later once we'd had time to get all the rafts and equipment ready. The schedule was planned like it was some Navy Seal mission, which did nothing to calm my nerves.

When Dad had brought up Ben's offer, I'd pictured a camp counselor leading songs around a campfire and making beaded bracelets and taking kids on snipe hunts. If I'd known what it was really like, I might not have jumped at the job how I had. Being responsible for people's lives was more than I'd bargained for, all while trying to learn the ins and outs of the job.

Like yesterday morning, I showed up ten minutes early, my wet hair steaming in the cool morning air and my bare legs covered in goose bumps. Okay, so I'd really needed to steal my mom's blow-dryer in the morning and throw on my fleece jacket, because this was the second morning in a row I'd spent shivering.

"Layers. You should give them a try." His voice surprised me right before an object sailed through the air toward me. An oversized, heavy flannel, a lot like the one he'd worn yesterday morning, landed in my arms. It was soft—the kind that could only be achieved from being washed a few hundred times.

This time when I shivered, it wasn't from the cold. "Thanks?" I said as he came closer, looking every bit as blurry-eyed and messy-haired as he had the morning before.

"Don't mention it." His voice was the same cool, removed one I'd quickly gotten used to, making me wonder if I had made up the fun, light side of Callum.

"Are you sure you don't want to wear it? I'll be okay."

He didn't look up at me while adjusting the Velcro straps of his sandals, but he tensed when I moved in his direction. Yeah, so he pretty much hated me. From making jokes one morning to certifiable loathing the next—way to go, Phoenix. Way. To. Go.

"If I wasn't sure, I wouldn't have given it to you." He stood up and started for an old truck that had a trailer stacked with four rafts hitched to it.

"Do you need any help?" I had to jog to keep up with him.

When he didn't answer, keeping his back to me as he double-checked the straps tying down the rafts, I cleared my throat. "What do you need me to do?"

Callum kept moving around the rafts. "Just stay out of my way."

I sighed to myself—clearly he wasn't the "forgive, forget, and move on" type. Not that I couldn't identify . . .

"Okay, why don't you just say what you need to say and get it over with?" I held my arms out. "Let me have it."

I followed him around to the other side of the trailer and watched him check and tighten the straps over there. "You lied to me. You looked me in the face and lied." He gave a hard yank on the strap he was working on. "What else is left to say?"

"Don't you think 'lied' is a bit harsh?"

That earned me a sideways look. Well, a sideways glare. "What would you call it? Fudging the truth?"

"I didn't tell you my parents signed the waiver to betray your trust, but to keep Harry's."

He spun toward me, his eyes aiming directly at mine. "Well, that plan backfired."

"Obviously." I looked him straight on. "What's your point? Besides me being a terrible person for making a bad decision in a tough situation?"

"If I can't trust you, you might as well just hand in your notice now." He didn't blink.

"Yeah, well, maybe I will. Especially if this is the way you're going to treat me every time I mess up."

He yanked a little harder than necessary on the next strap. "Listen, there are rules for a reason. For *good* reasons. If you can't follow them, then, yeah, you should quit."

The more he kept telling me to quit, the more I wanted to keep my job. "You're telling me a signed permission slip is that important?"

I noticed the way his throat moved when he swallowed—like he was trying to swallow a whole apple. He was trying to be patient with me. I was trying to return the favor. "Keeps us from getting sued, keeps parents from losing their shit when they can't figure out where their kid disappeared to, and lets us be ready if that kid has any special medical concerns. Like asthma. Or a life-threatening allergy." His eyes cut to mine. "So, yeah, that permission slip is *that* important. Along with all the other rules we have here."

I stalled just long enough to give myself a second to think. "Oh."

"Oh," he echoed, looking at me like he knew what he'd said had clicked.

"I'm sorry." I bit my lip, feeling like a terrible person. I'd really screwed up—without even trying to. "I didn't think. I didn't get why it was so important."

"You had my trust yesterday. Today you're in the red," he said. "What are you going to do about that?"

I shifted. "Earn it back?"

He studied me for a second. I studied him back. This morning, in this kind of light, his eyes looked more green than brown. "Okay, then. Lucky for you I believe in second chances." He waved at a pile of paddles leaning against the shed. "Why don't you load those paddles into the bed of the truck?"

"On it," I said, going into action. Had he really just let me off the hook? Was he really willing to just take my word for it and hand out a redo? I wasn't going to hang around for him to change his mind.

There were at least a few dozen paddles to get loaded up, so I got started. I'd barely grabbed the first one and the entire stack of them clattered to the ground. Great.

"Why does camp hate me?" I groaned, wondering if Callum

was right and I should just hand in my notice now. I couldn't seem to do anything right anyway.

I was expecting some kind of sigh or lecture from him when I heard something else. Laughter.

Was he laughing at me? When I turned around to check, I found him covering his mouth like he was trying to hide it. "You're a jerk for laughing," I hollered back at him.

"I know." He kept laughing.

The sound of crunching gravel caught my attention. Callum lost the smile.

"Is everything okay over here? I thought I heard laughter," someone shouted.

"Or cries of torture," a different someone replied.

Callum nodded at the others coming toward us. Their shirts gave them away as fellow counselors. "Same difference."

"What do you say, New Girl? Is it a laugh or a cry of torture? Is a cry of torture a laugh?" one of the two guys asked, nudging the third counselor, a girl who was almost as red-eyed and tired-looking as Callum.

"I'm going to play it safe and plead the fifth," I said, tugging at one of the straps like I knew what I was doing.

"Stop giving her a hard time, guys," the girl said around a yawn and a stretch. "She answers one way, she pisses off her boss; if she answers the other way, she's going to alienate herself from us. Give her a break. It's barely seven in the morning." She shot me a tired smile, like we'd somehow wound up on the same side. "I'm Naomi, by the way. And this guy, who was beat with the ugly stick so many times it actually broke, is Evan, and the even uglier one beside him is Ethan."

Naomi was one of those boho-chic girls. The kind who looked like she was planning on saving the world by day and walking the catwalk by night—striking hair, striking smile, striking everything . . . but not in an in-your-face kind of way. I liked her already.

I did a double take of the guys. . . . They were twins. They might not have dressed the same—one dressed more prep-cool and the other one went straight-jock, and the prepster's hair had clearly been carefully and craftily sculpted, while super-jock's was cut closer to his head—but their faces were identical: flawless tan skin, wide-set blue eyes with a serious fan of lashes, and prominent cheekbones. It was a good thing they were both built like a couple of gladiators to balance out those pretty faces.

"Hey," I said at last, while Callum continued shuffling things around in the truck. I wondered why he didn't holler at the four of us to pitch in.

Ethan/Evan leaned in my direction. His smile was something else. Something else that had no doubt killed it with countless girls before . . . just not this girl. "Pick a side, New Girl."

I was unfazed. I knew his type. California was chock-full of them. I also knew the sooner I made my point that I was not interested now or ever, the sooner he'd move on to the next female thing on legs. "I'd rather ride the fence."

"New Girl's smart," the jock twin said, elbowing his brother.

"New Girl's hot." Bold and Brazen Brother elbowed his twin back.

"New Girl's got a name," I said, noticing Callum stick his head out from the canopy.

"I'd be a fool to think otherwise," Ethan or Evan said. "What is it?"

I frowned. "Not Interested."

One brother laughed, shoving his twin. The other one

looked like he'd just been issued his first reality check ever. "Funny. What is it really?"

From the truck, I could tell Callum was watching us, listening, but he didn't seem interested in contributing anything to the conversation. "As far as you're concerned?" I said, blinking. "Really Not Interested."

The twin holding the grand name inquisition covered his chest with his hands. "I think I'm in love."

His brother grunted. "She hates you, so *of course* you are."

Smitten Brother's smile didn't dim. "Unhealthy relationships are my specialty."

Naomi leaned in to me and whispered, "More like his Achilles' heel."

She and I shared a grin right before Callum leaped from the truck. "Time to head out," he said. Stiff voice, stiff walk, stiff shoulders.

That was the camp-counselor-on-duty Callum I knew. Fun, considerate, mellow . . . that was the camp-counselor-off-duty Callum I thought I knew. Total opposites. North pole, south pole. Right, left. Heads, tails. Dr. Jekyll, Mr. Hyde.

Who was Callum when he wasn't here at Camp Kismet? What was he like back home? Why did I care? Why did I want to find out?

Questions: in abundance. Answers: nil.

"I will find out your name before the morning is done," Relentless Twin stated.

"You already know my name," I replied.

"It's probably something that starts with a *J*," he went on like he hadn't heard what I'd just said. "Jamie or Jessie or Julie. Yeah, definitely a *J*."

"Give it a rest already, Ethan. New Girl isn't picking up on your game, so call it and move on." Evan crawled over

81

the front seat of the truck and pretty much crashed into the backseat.

Callum had the driver's side door open and waved me into the front seat. I got the feeling sitting in the front was less of a privilege and more of a punishment.

"Thanks," I said to Callum, crawling across the old cloth interior of the front seat to the passenger side. He wasn't smiling in the way most people noticed, but his eyes were. Glad he found this all so amusing.

"Welcome" was all he said.

Ethan loped toward the truck, looking like he hadn't just been rejected—repeatedly. As I buckled up, I could tell he was watching me, that smile still in place. Right before he started to crawl into the back, he opened his mouth, no doubt taking his first jab in Round 5 of trying to TKO my better judgment.

"Ethan?" Callum said in the tone that would have made the president sit up straighter in his seat. "Shut the hell up."

TEN

He didn't say a single word to me the entire drive to the river. He didn't say a single word to the other three, either, so at least I didn't have to obsess over why he was singling me out in the silent-treatment department.

The three in the backseat, however, didn't shut up. Not once. Not even for a fraction of a fraction of a second. It was irritating, but I had to give them credit for creativity in their conversation topics: from which adolescent campers were getting it on with other adolescent campers, to supported theories on if Ben was a boxers or briefs kind of guy, to whose college mascot would come out the victor if they were thrown together in some sort of to-the-death match.

Naomi, Ethan, and Evan were all heading off to college in the fall, and from the sounds of it, they'd peaked out at peeing-their-pants levels of excitement. If nothing else, I could relate. I still had another year plus a few months before I'd be riding the freedom express, and I already had a daily countdown going.

When we arrived at the parking lot, the three of them teamed up carrying down rafts, leaving Callum and me to tag-team the other equipment. Even after the rafts and paddles and life jackets and the rest of the heavy, cumbersome crap Callum had shoved into the canopy had been hauled down to the river's edge, the three of them worked together getting everything laid out.

I didn't get the feeling that they'd divided themselves off from Callum and now me because they were being mean . . . but more out of familiarity. They were used to Callum doing his thing while they did theirs. I was fast learning that Callum kept to himself while the other counselors hung out together, which led me to wonder why I was laying out paddles beside him right now. Was it more a matter of me not taking a hint that he liked to fly solo? Or more an issue of him tolerating me . . . in the twisted, confusing way he did?

More questions, I thought with a grumble. No more questions. Not until I wrangled up some answers. I was already so filled with unknowns I was about to rip apart at the seams.

I was in the middle of counting life jackets, making sure that number matched the number of paddles in the raft in front of me, when a burst of laughter exploded from down where the other three were.

"Dude! It totally looks like I just pissed my pants!" Ethan was thrusting his arms in the direction of his crotch area, where a very prominent dark stain was splattered across his light blue shorts.

"You wet the bed until you were ten. Just giving New Girl a little vindication that she totally snubbed a bed-wetter." Evan laughed, pointing at his twin's shorts like it was the funniest damn thing he'd ever seen.

"We're twins, asshole!" Ethan threw back.

"What's your point, pant-pisser?" Evan nudged Naomi, who was trying so hard not to laugh she was turning purple.

"We've done everything the same since Mom tells the story of us shitting our first diaper within a half second of each other. *Including* wetting the bed until we were ten."

Evan's laughter rolled to a pause. "Yeah, but you're older. Which means you pissed the bed longer than I did."

"Older by twenty-three seconds, buttmunch." Ethan pinched his shorts in the water-stained area, shaking to dry them.

When Callum caught me watching them instead of counting the next raft's life jackets and paddles, I braced myself for what I expected to be a get-back-to-work warning or at least the dreaded raised brow. Instead, he stayed quiet, continuing to work on what he was doing.

I cleared my throat. "Wow. Great group." Right then, Ethan splashed his brother's shorts, returning the favor. There. Now they both looked like juveniles with idiotic tendencies.

Callum glanced their way before getting back to checking the raft next to me. "They're great at what they do. Acting their age and charming the pants off the opposite sex aren't requirements of the job." It almost looked like he was about to smile, but it never quite got there.

"That's good. Otherwise those guys would be out of a job."

"Those guys never would have gotten their jobs in the first place if those were the requirements."

When I glanced over at him this time, it was definitely a smile. Not a big one, but one that qualified. That might have been why I asked him the question I had no intention of asking him ever.

"Why don't the other camp counselors like you?"

Instead of disappearing, his smile grew. "*Other* camp counselors?"

He'd caught me off guard. I'd been expecting him to argue it or deny it or play the indignant card, but I hadn't expected him to answer my question with a question of his own—*that* question especially.

"I don't know what you mean. . . ."

"You asked why the other camp counselors don't like me, meaning one of them does." He didn't have to look up from the knot he was tying to get his point across.

"Yeah, and the other *one* I was talking about was you." I grinned victoriously over at him. Nice try, but he couldn't dissect and twist my words until I was too turned around to remember where I'd started.

"Oh, then I'm afraid you're wrong." He paused, no doubt for dramatic effect, before adding, "Because I don't like myself. Not even a little."

I huffed. "Why do I find that hard to believe?"

"Because it isn't true." Callum popped up from the rocky river's edge he'd been kneeling on and held his arms out at his sides. "Because I'm the shit."

I was going for another huff when a laugh burst free instead. "More like full of it."

Callum laughed a few beats of his own before a shout rolled down the river at us. "The cries of torture again! What's the deal? Is New Girl killing you down there, Big Kahuna?"

We both ignored him.

"So?" I pressed.

Callum lifted a shoulder, moving down to the next raft to check it over. "I don't know if it's that they outright hate me—"

"That's not what I meant," I interrupted, because it was clear they didn't hate him. They just kept their distance.

"It's just a weird position to be in. I'm the person they report to, but also a peer. It's easy to blur the lines in that kind of a situation, so I just choose to draw a thick, uncrossable one instead. Makes it easier for them."

That wasn't the explanation I'd been expecting to hear from him. I'd been more expecting half the honesty and a quarter of the words. "But not easier for you. Right?"

He shrugged the other shoulder and kept working. "Ben doesn't like giving lectures or talking-tos or pointing fingers. He doesn't like dealing with the downsides to running a business—he'd rather pretend the world is all blue skies and rainbows—so I take some of that burden off of him when it comes to the counselors."

I nodded. "That can't be easy for you."

"Yeah, well, I don't map my life around what's going to be easy, so it's not a big deal." Callum's attention moved up to the parking lot, where a brightly colored bus with the Camp Kismet logo painted onto the grille was pulling into the parking lot. For the first time that morning, I felt nervous. "Besides, if I'm not busy working, I'm busy with other things. I don't have time for a social calendar."

I thought of the past two mornings and the way he'd shown up looking like he'd spent the night any other way than asleep. What was keeping him so busy he didn't have time to hang with the other counselors after he'd punched out?

I was trying to be all composed-looking, but either I was failing or he could sense it, because before he started for the parking lot, he strolled up beside me and gave me a gentle nudge. "It's okay. You'll be fine."

"But what if something bad happens?" My throat was dry, making my voice sound all high and pitchy.

"What if it does?" he replied, heading for the bus. "What's going to happen is going to happen. It's your choice if you sink or swim."

ELEVEN

Cynthia Ainsworth was rafting. *Mom* was rafting, down a river, with a paddle in hand, getting sprayed by water, and instead of crying out in horror that her hair and silk blouse were ruined, she was laughing. Not nearly as loud or often as Harry was beside her, but it had been a long time since I'd heard my mom laugh. I wondered where Dad was, although I supposed I could make an educated guess—glued in front of his laptop, hiding inside the cabin.

They were in a different raft than the one Callum and I were in, which I knew was intentional because Callum had straight-up told me it was. He said he thought I'd be better off if they were in a different raft so I wouldn't be hovering over them and ignoring the other rafters. He had a point. I might not have liked it, but he had one.

Although it wasn't like I wasn't *not* focused on them because they were in another raft, being guided down the river by Naomi. Every few strokes of my paddle, every couple of checks of the six campers in our raft, I'd find myself checking to make sure they were both still smiling and, most important, still firmly in the raft.

Mom had made it pretty clear before coming to camp that she wasn't going to sign off on Harry participating in these types of things. You know, types of things that ten-year-old boys lived for. Like rafting. It was cool of her to change her mind—on this activity, at least.

"We're getting close to the take-out point," Callum announced from the back of the raft, that ever-calm and resolute look on his face. The river hadn't exactly been what I'd call a serious adrenaline rush—I'd heard someone say the rapids were considered class two—but the water was fast, moving with just enough whitewater to make my stomach drop.

I wasn't sure how many times he'd rafted this section of the river, but from the way he seemed to know every bend up ahead and memorized every rock jutting out of the water, he could have spent the last decade of summers rafting this river every single day. He wasn't just good at his job—he was great.

He wasn't the only one, either. He'd been right about the other three counselors being pretty great at what they did, too. After this morning, I wouldn't have guessed any of them were capable of taking something seriously, but I'd been wrong. They might not have had Callum's same level of familiarity on the river, but they definitely knew what they were doing.

"Did you four have to get some kind of special training or certification to do this?" I asked Callum when we hit a nice, smooth stretch of water. Like the five hundred times before, a chorus of disappointed groans circled the rafts. From the way they made it sound, it was like they were all a bunch of adrenaline junkies who couldn't wait a whole five minutes for their next fix.

"Yeah. We all had to go to some special training camp and pay for the certifications." Taking advantage of the calm water, Callum used his shirt to wipe off the water spray dotting his face. And no, it totally wasn't distracting that while he was doing this, half his stomach was exposed. "Well, Ben paid for the camp and certifications, but it was pretty hard-core."

The experience of rafting was "hard-core," so I could only imagine the training. "Are all the counselors able to guide a raft down the river?" I asked.

He shook his head, his eyes intent on the river ahead. "No, just the four of us. It would be a waste of time and money for Ben to get every counselor trained, so he picks the regular returners to get certified."

"How many summers have those three been counseling?" I glanced at the other rafts, waving at Harry for the millionth time, but he was too busy pointing down or up the river.

"This is their third year." Callum's gaze moved from the river to circle the rafters in our boat. It was quick and thorough at the same time, before his eyes flickered back to the river.

"Will they be back next summer?"

"Maybe. Some of the counselors who leave for college come back and some don't."

I stroked with my paddle gently, inspecting the rafters like Callum did.

"How many summers have you been counseling?" I asked him.

"This is my third summer."

This time when I waved over at Harry, he noticed. He whipped his arm back and forth like he was flagging a 747. Mom smiled at me and waved the dignified version.

"Will you return next summer?"

"Probably," he answered without a pause.

"The summer after that? The one after your first year of college?"

This time there was a pause. A long-enough one I looked

over my shoulder at him. His eyes were still focused down the river, but they were somewhere else. "Probably," he said. I didn't think he was going to say anything, but that was when he added, "But I'm not sure about college."

"What do you mean, you're not sure?"

"Exactly that. I'm not sure."

I did another scan of the raft. These campers were like the rafting equivalent of teacher's pets. They were the rafting guide's dream: followed directions, seemed to value their lives, and oohed and aahed in all the right places.

"Like you're not sure which ones you want to apply to?" I asked after I was satisfied everyone was safe. For the moment.

"Like if I want to go at all."

I glanced at him to see if he was being serious. I hadn't quite figured out his humor yet, and when he was pulling my leg or being dead serious. Made it harder to know when it seemed like I was dealing with two personalities in a constant battle of tug-of-war.

"Really?" I said after taking a guess that he was serious.

"You sound like this is going to make the world news or something." He adjusted the bill of his ball cap a bit lower to shield his eyes from the sun . . . or to shield them from me. One or the other.

"Well, no, I'm just surprised."

"Why? I wouldn't be the first person to take a pass on college."

"I get that, but, I don't know . . . you just seem so . . ." I paused. *What is the right word?* "Driven."

"And there's more to being driven than just taking a couple of standardized tests and filling out a few applications and four years later coming out the other end with a piece of paper and a hundred grand in debt."

I didn't know why—his face and voice were the same as they always were—but I got the impression that this was a sensitive topic for him. One that a person would rather have run naked through a maze of cacti than talk about.

Of course that only made me want to talk about it that much more. Callum seemed like both the guy who could have had no secrets and one who could have had a million.

"So yeah, there's more to being driven than going to college. . . ." He nodded in response, like the topic was closed. Not even. "But do you want to go?"

He exhaled. "I don't know."

"You don't know." I gave him a look. "Most people know. They might not know if they'll have the right grades or get the right amount of financial aid or if they'll get the right scores on the SAT, but most high school juniors know if they at least want to try to go to college or if there's no way in hell."

He fired off a shrug. "Well, I guess you just met one of the rare few who doesn't know what he wants to do yet, so would you mind dropping it? Talking circles around it with you isn't going to help me make my mind up any faster."

I turned around and while I was giving the rafters another inspection, I added, "Well, I want to go to college."

"And this is supposed to make me think I should want to go, too?"

This time I was able to tell this was his way of being funny. Progress. If only in snail scoots. "No, it's my way of telling you something personal about me."

"Good for you," he said.

"Which is generally reciprocated by the other person," I continued like he hadn't said anything at all.

"Which won't be reciprocated by *this* person." He pasted on a grin and lifted a brow. "So you can feel free to share all you want, but just because you showed me yours doesn't mean I'll show you mine."

I dipped my hand in the water and flicked some water at him. "You're twisted, you know that?"

"Oh, I know that. Thanks for the confirmation, though." His fake grin started to shift into something almost genuine as he wiped the water off his face.

I was ready to splash him again when he sat up straighter. "Okay, everyone," he announced to the raft. "We're about to hit the last stretch of whitewater before the take-out spot, and we've saved the best for last."

That was when we came around the bend in the river and I could see what he was talking about. Up ahead, the river seemed to go from this glassy dark blue to frothy white. It was definitely the "whitest" of the whitewater we'd rafted today, and it had me and the rest of the rafters clutching our paddles a little tighter.

From Naomi's raft, I heard Harry give off an excited yelp. Beside him, Mom looked more like they were marching toward the gallows.

"Just remember to paddle, stay calm, and listen to what I'm saying, and this will be one hell of a ride," Callum instructed.

When I glanced at him, I caught the faintest glimmer of excitement in his eyes. He winked and gave me a nod of encouragement because I could only imagine what I must have looked like right then. "It'll be okay. Take it down a few hundred notches there."

I bobbed my head, but I don't think he really got it. I wasn't freaking out because I was worried about myself, but because Harry and my mom were drifting down this river, too, along with the six rafters in our boat I was responsible for. All of a sudden, I got this sense that I was a little kid tasked with saving the world from certain destruction. Who was I to think I could do this? Who was I to be pretending I knew what I was doing and could be responsible for the lives of others when most days I felt like I was barely scraping by being responsible for myself?

"Okay, everyone!" He had to shout now since the white-water was so loud. The water looked almost like big soap bubbles breaking around the rocks, so that was what I was going to imagine: a bubble bath. A nice, relaxing bubble bath that—

The instant we hit the first section of rapids and the nose of the raft thrust down right before bursting up again, nice and relaxing were the farthest things from my mind.

"Paddle!" Callum yelled as spray broke around us. Why were the other rafters laughing? Why were they hooting and hollering like they were riding Space Mountain? Why were they smiling and leaning forward like they were eagerly anticipating what was coming next?

Leaning forward? No leaning forward. That was a definite way to get one thrown from the raft. I knew I needed to keep paddling with the others, but I needed to remind all of them to stay low and balanced in their places, because clearly they'd forgotten and Captain Adrenaline back there was too busy steering the raft to make sure we didn't bash into the maze of boulders jutting up from the river.

"Marylynn!" I shouted at the woman right in front of me. Maybe if I could get her attention, she could pass the message to Mike in front of her and he could pass it on to Cole beside him, so on and so forth. And yeah, I had memorized the first and last names of everyone on our individual raft, along with their blood types and allergies. You know, just in case.

Marylynn didn't hear me, not that that was a big surprise. I could barely hear myself screaming.

I chanced a look over at Naomi's raft, and, like Callum, she was navigating the river with the same calm and ease he was. Why were these people so chill when we were skipping like a stone down a river? Were they the crazy ones, or was I for not acting like this was the best thing ever?

Harry was squealing with delight, moving his little arms so fast that his paddle was a blur. Beside him, Mom looked like they were about to walk the plank. So I wasn't totally alone in my panic. Mom and I were feeling the same thing. Not that I was so sure how I felt about that . . . Mom and me on the same page? Not exactly the life story I was hoping to write.

"Marylynn!" I cried again, this time so loud it hurt my throat. Still, nothing.

If I didn't get these lunatics to sit back, they were all going to fly out of this thing. Keeping the paddle in my hands and managing to still move it mostly in time with everyone else, I slid up closer behind her, crawling on my knees in quick, tiny slides.

I was so close I could have reached up and tapped her on the arm, but I wanted to get just a bit closer.

"Phoenix! Heads up!" I heard his shout, and I even listened, but I was about one second too late for putting my head up to see what was coming. The raft took a serious dip right before taking an even more serious pop back up, successfully managing to trampoline me right up . . . and out of the raft.

I hit the water and went under, the icy-cold river issuing me a serious reality check.

The current clawed at me, pulling me under at the same time it seemed like it was trying to pull me apart. I froze. For one awful moment, my whole body went frozen, my brain suffering the same condition.

It wasn't until my head broke through the surface—thank

god, goddess, and whatever else for life jackets—that I came back and my fight-or-flight response powered on full charge. My arms and legs went into action, whipping around, left and right, up and down, as the frothy white water surged around me.

I couldn't see the rafts. Not at first. It wasn't until I got spun around by a current that I saw them. They were a little ways behind me and it looked like everyone was yelling something at me. Other than the roar of the river, I couldn't hear anything, not even my heartbeat pounding in my ears.

It was just long enough for me to make out Harry and my mom, both still safely in their rafts, before the current thrust me around again. My body raced through the water in whatever way and direction the river wanted me to go. It didn't matter how hard I fought to head toward the shore or how much I tried to fight—I was stuck.

When I swept past a boulder jutting out in the middle of the river, I tried to grab on to it, but the river was too strong. It bounced me against the boulder as it swept me out again.

This was where I hit panic mode, totally consumed by adrenaline. I was going to die. This was it. The river was going to suck me under, and I'd spend eternity in some underwater grave. Harry. All I could think about was what this would do to him, watching his sister drown right in front of him at summer camp. Talk about leaving some serious scars.

The river swept me around again, and this time there was one raft that had pulled in front of the others—the same one I'd just somersaulted out of. It was only a few seconds before the current twisted me around, but it was long enough to catch a glimpse of Callum. Unlike the looks on the other rafters' faces, his wasn't tipping the worried scale. Instead, he was giving me a look that was easy to read, probably because I'd seen it aimed at me a handful of times already. The one that said, *What in the hell are you doing?*

It took being thrown against a rock wall—literally—for me to get it. He was gaping at me like I should have known what to do because I *did* know what to do.

Don't fight it, just go with the flow.

His words chimed in my head, repeating over and over until I was finally able to calm down a hot second.

My arms stopped flailing around, and my legs stopped kicking against the current. I forced my whole body to relax, took in a deep breath, and let the river do its thing.

Immediately, it stopped feeling like the current was trying to suck me under or that the waves crashing around me were trying to split me open. Instead of feeling like I was fighting for my life, it felt more like I was having the ride of my life.

All too soon, the whitewater came to an abrupt end, spitting me into a calm stretch of the river. I waved at the rafts to let everyone know I was okay before making my way to the sandy patch of beach Callum had pointed to before the rafts turned in that direction.

It was amazing how easy it was to swim in the calmer water. I could still feel the slight pull of the current tugging at my legs, but it was easy to fight it. Even though my muscles felt cramped and sore, I made it to the shore before the rafts.

I plopped down onto a warm patch of sand and thought about catching my breath. I didn't get a chance before I got tackled from the side by one ten-year-old whose strength had apparently doubled since we'd come to camp.

"Oh my gosh, Phoenix, that was crazy. Are you okay?" Harry's arms tightened around me like a boa constrictor. "I was freaking out."

Harry had managed to knock me over so half my face was planted in the sand. I wrestled an arm free and wrapped it around him. "Ease up there, Hercules. Contrary to popular belief, I'm not made of solid steel."

His arms loosened. A little. "Sorry. I was just so worried. If something happened to you . . ."

I gave him a hard squeeze. One that made him grunt. "I'm okay, really."

His response to that was hugging me harder. This time it was me who huffed a sharp grunt. What had this place been feeding this kid? "Hey, Harry?"

"Yeah?"

"Can you let me up now? I'm going numb."

He shot back, pulling me up with him. Sure enough, I could feel a thick layer of sand sticking to half my face. "Sorry about that."

"Don't sweat it. It's nice to know that someone would miss me if I kicked the bucket." I mussed his already-messy hair and tried wiping the sand from my face. At least I was exfoliating my skin.

"Phoenix Elizabeth Ainsworth." Mom came up behind Harry, arms crossed, but she was biting at her lip anxiously. "What happened back there?"

Harry plopped down on the sand beside me and slung his arm around my neck. Apparently, he wasn't letting me out of arm's reach anytime soon.

"I fell in," I answered her with a shrug.

"More like you cartwheeled in," Harry added with a grin. Now that he knew I was safe, he could make jokes. Maybe I should have played the in-shock card a little longer.

Mom was still chewing on her lip. "Why did you fall in?" Translation: *Nobody else fell in, so why did you?*

"I was trying to get a rafter's attention. I guess the river kind of took me by surprise."

"Harrison tried to jump in to help you." Even though Harry and I had clearly moved on from the incident, Mom had not.

"Only after you tried to jump in first," Harry piped up with a defensive look on his face.

Say what? I blinked up at my mom. "You were going to jump in and save me?"

She lifted a shoulder. "I was going to try."

"You were really going to jump in after me?" I finally noticed how different Mom looked. Her hair was drenched and pasted to one half of her face. Her mascara was streaked and running down her cheeks. Her life jacket dripped buckets. Her linen pants and blouse were so wet they were sticking to her. My mom was a mess. A total, undeniable mess . . . and she'd tried leaping into a raging river to come help me.

It was a weird mix of emotions I felt then, foreign things that swirled in my stomach and messed with my head.

She reached out and patted my leg. "You're my daughter. I'd walk through fire for you, so of course I'd jump into some silly little river to save you."

TWELVE

I was still in a state of parental-concern shock when Callum made his way toward me. After helping the rafters out and herding them to the beach. After securing the rafts up onshore. After doing a count of everyone to make sure we hadn't lost anyone. And after making sure the sack lunches were handed out and everyone got their veggie or BLT sandwiches.

I had to practically force Harry and Mom to go grab their lunches after trying to convince them that I was fine—no permanent physical or mental injuries. They'd finally wandered off, promising to bring me a sack lunch.

I had barely recovered from what my mom had just said before Callum crouched down in front of me. He wasn't quite, but he was almost smirking at me.

"Nice swim?" he asked, keeping a straight face.

"Nice of you to leap in and save me," I replied as he unzipped a small red nylon bag in his hands. "*Lead* Counselor."

My attempt at guilt-tripping him was clearly failing. Instead of looking guilty, he smiled. "Let's say I had jumped in to 'save' you. How do you think that would have gone down?"

I paused, wondering where he was taking this. "Heroically?"

His smile spread as he tore open what looked like an alcohol wipe. Was that a first aid kit he was holding? What did he need one of those for? It wasn't until he starting wiping at my shins with the pad, which stung something fierce, before I realized I was bleeding. In more than one place. Those damn river rocks had drawn some serious blood.

"*Heroic* wouldn't be my term for it," he said.

"What would be your term for it?" I curled my fists into the sand, bracing myself, as he tore open another alcohol wipe for the other shin.

"Stupid," he said bluntly.

"So you're saying my *heroic* is your *stupid*?"

He didn't pause. "Pretty much, yeah."

"I was just thrown from a raft and the river decided to play a game of pinball with my body. Everyone else has been coming up and asking if I'm okay or giving me a nice pat on the back. Why are you lecturing me on what is and isn't heroic?"

Callum dropped the bloody alcohol wipe into the same small plastic bag as the other one and then grabbed a tube of antiseptic ointment. "Because we all need someone in our lives who shoots straight instead of shoveling bullshit, right?"

"I'm not sure I want to answer that."

"Why not? Because the truth is harsh or because you're one of those girls who prefer the bullshitters?" His tone wasn't argumentative, just casual—sincere, even.

"I'm not sure I want to answer that, either." I braced myself as he started smearing gobs of ointment onto each of the cuts running down my shins, but this didn't sting. It actually felt pretty good, especially with how gentle he was being every time he touched me.

"Let's say I had jumped in after you." He paused to rip open one of those giant beige bandages. "What do you think would have happened to the rest of the rafters in our boat? What would have happened to them when their guide bailed?" He waited a few seconds to let that set in before moving on. "Let's say I dived in for you and somehow managed to catch up to you. What was I supposed to do to help? I couldn't shove you back into a raft. I couldn't swim you to shore. You saw what happens when you try swimming sideways in the middle of a section of whitewater." After placing the bandage over one of the bigger cuts on my left shin, he glanced up at me. His hair was wet and hanging over his forehead and eyes, but I didn't miss the raised brow hiding behind his hair. "I guess I could have held your hand and said something sappy, like *Don't worry, I'm here with you,* or something encouraging, like *We'll do this together,* or something macho, like *I'll save you,* but it doesn't matter because I couldn't have left that raft in the first place." He tore open another bandage and carefully smoothed it over the next cut on my shin. "But I promise that when and if you *really* need my help and I'm around to give it, I've got you covered."

He was probably just saying that to be nice, but it made me shift in the sand. He didn't sound like he was just saying it. He didn't look like it, either.

"I fell in once, too. My first summer here with my mom and brother." He glanced up to make sure I was still with him.

I tipped my head to the side. "You, outdoorsman extraordinaire, fell out of the raft and into the river? Say it isn't so."

"Oh, it's so."

"What happened?" I asked, trying not to notice the way his fingers felt grazing my skin or the way the warmth from them seemed to make its way inside and pool in my stomach.

"My brother shoved me in. That's how I got this." He traced his thumb down the crooked scar at his temple. "I face-planted into the side of one of those boulders back there."

Callum zipped his first aid kit up and sat down on the sand across from me. "I was a kid that summer I fell into the river. You thought you were panicked? You should have seen me." He shook his head as he looked at the river. "I'd only learned how to swim the summer before that and wasn't exactly comfortable in the water yet. Especially that kind of water. I didn't remember what the counselor had taught us about falling in or anything. I just eventually ran out of steam. That's my claim to fame—I beat the river by *accidentally* going with the flow."

I touched several of the bandages dotting my legs. He hadn't missed a single cut, scratch, or gash. They'd all been taken care of. The pool of warmth in my stomach swelled. "I feel like there's probably some moral to the story you're wanting me to catch."

He toed at the sand. "No moral to the story. That was my attempt at relating your traumatic experience with one of my own. Of sharing something personal about myself with you." He fired a quick wink before rising. "Now that you're bandaged up like a mummy from the knees down, my job here is done."

"Let me guess. Campers to check on. Paddles and life jackets to account for?"

He spread his arms wide. "What can I say? A lead counselor's job is never done."

"Thanks for the mummification," I called after him.

He didn't make it far before he stopped. As he glanced at me over his shoulder, the look on his face made me swallow. "You know what I remember most about that day, though?" He waited, so I shook my head. "Realizing that no matter what came at me, I could face it. I'd come out okay on the other side. Come hell or whitewater"—he paused long enough to shrug—"I could save myself."

I swept my arm in a lavish motion. "At last, the moral of the story is revealed."

His brows came together as he tried to fake a serious look. "I don't know what you're talking about."

I lifted my eyes to the sky. "Sure ya don't."

Callum looked like he was about to come back at me with something when a shadow rolled over me. Ethan. "Hey, New Girl. You know what they say, don't you?"

I sighed. Now that he wasn't responsible for guiding six lives down a treacherous river, he could jump back into his favorite role of camp charmer.

Ethan's eyes ran up me, landing on my dripping-wet ponytail. "When it comes to rafting—actually, when it comes to anything in life . . ." He bounced his brows a few times. "The wetter, the better."

My nose curled. "Could have done without that little Ethan-ism, but thanks for dropping that one on me before I ate my lunch."

"I can swing back around after lunch and drop another Ethan-ism on you," he offered.

"Actually, I'm one of those girls who prefer to keep her food down. Thanks anyway."

Ethan's face went flat. It was like I was the first girl who'd turned him down.

"You've got really beautiful eyes," he said, putting on a strange expression that I guessed was his version of something sexy.

It looked more like he had something in his eye and had to add some fiber to his diet. "Ah, gee, thanks. And let me guess what's coming next." I worked up a wide smile that was all teeth. "I've got a really nice smile?"

His eyes narrowed. "New Girl? What's your deal?"

Why he was being so persistent was beyond me. I wasn't the obviously pretty girl who stuck out in every crowd. I wasn't even the "naturally" pretty one. On my best days, I suppose I could qualify for the cute category, but Ethan didn't strike me as the kind of guy who swam in cute waters that often, if ever. Why was he all over me like white on rice?

Glancing around at the campers, I knew I had my answer. The only reason he was hitting on me was because of low supply and chart-topping horny demand. That might have been the reason I snapped my response. "My 'deal,' Ethan, is that I'd rather make out with a marmot than you. My 'deal' is that I'm not looking to get mixed up in a summer romance today, tomorrow, or ever. Now, will you please leave me alone?"

Instead of walking away, shoulders slumped and ego in the gutter, he shrugged. "Who said anything about romance?"

I groaned. Talk about a person who could spot a silver lining.

I hadn't realized Callum was still close by until he cleared his throat. "Hey, Ethan?" He waited for Ethan to acknowledge him with a tip of the head. "Shut the hell up."

THIRTEEN

At the start of summer, my life had made sense. In a messed-up, dysfunctional sort of way, but it was predictable. I could count on the same things to happen each day and for people to act the same way.

Camp Kismet had blown the whole life-making-sense thing out of the water, though. In barely a week.

My world felt as if it had been flipped upside down, and people were not behaving the way I'd expected they should. All except for me . . . and you could also lump my dad into that pile. Great. Now I was lumped into the same pile as my dad. This summer was just made of win.

My mom was still acting all different and strange, like the old version, who specialized in nighttime snuggles and napkin notes tucked into lunch boxes. Part of me wanted to believe the old mom was making a comeback, but most of me wasn't going to get my hopes up.

Then there was Harry. Sure, he was still the same good, thoughtful kid who was more likely the spawn of Einstein than Preston and Cynthia Ainsworth, but he'd gone and turned over a new leaf, too. He was a pint-size daredevil, a miniature Evel Knievel, a featherweight adrenaline junkie.

In addition to the packed activity schedule he handpicked each and every day, Harry had his own posse of friends now. By the way these boys talked, a person would have thought they'd been to war and bled together.

So that was how the first week of camp went. Mom became a . . . *mom* again. Harry became Mr. Popularity with a taste for living life on the edge. And I was making like Dad and holding on, white-knuckled and all, to the way things were and had been and would likely go back to when we packed up and left here at the end of the summer.

And then there were the boy issues. Not Ethan—though it wasn't for a lack of trying to become an "issue"—but Callum. I couldn't figure the guy out. One minute he was making jokes and grinning; a split second later he was practically snapping at me about tying sloppy knots. One second he seemed to like me; the next he barely managed to tolerate me.

He was absolutely, positively a modern-day Jekyll and Hyde, and that wasn't even the most troubling part of that revelation. It was realizing that I wasn't sure which one I was more drawn to: benevolent Jekyll or malevolent Hyde.

So yeah, I had some shit to figure out. The sooner the better.

That might have been the reason for my sprint this morning. I was scheduled to run a fartlek workout today, but it had turned into more of a let's-pretend-we're-running-for-our-lives session.

It was therapeutic, and shin splints could be fixed with a couple of bags of ice.

When I hit the Y in the trail that would send me back to camp in one mile if I went left or three miles if I went right, I hung a right. I don't know why. I'd gone six miles and hadn't planned on pushing anything higher than seven today, but I'd already pushed the speed way beyond, why not throw the rest of the plan out the window while I was at it?

I was so in the zone when I was pushing this kind of speed a cargo plane probably could have flown a hundred feet over my head and I wouldn't have heard it. That was probably why I didn't notice someone else fly up the trail behind me. I didn't hear him at all. I didn't see him until he started to pull in front of me.

Actually, I was surprised that he was able to keep up with me. Okay, I admit, it looked like he could have flown past me. And yeah, I was more than just a little competitive when it came to running.

"What in the world are you doing out here, running like you're being chased by the cops, when you could be asleep?" Callum sounded a little winded, but not as much as I was. I wasn't pushing a pace that made conversation comfortable, or even possible.

"Being chased by the cops?" There. That sounded relatively normal—not like I was sucking air by the lungful.

"Just something my brother and I used to say when we'd train together. This was our run-like-we're-being-chased-by-pit-bulls pace, faster than run-like-we're-being-chased-by-the-cops pace, but slower than run-like-we're-being-chased-by-our-mom."

How was he able to get all that out at this speed? We were holding sub-seven-minute miles. Breathing was a chore.

"You and your brother used to run together?" I asked, suddenly self-conscious about how sweaty I was. At least I wasn't the only one—most of his shirt was wet.

"Right up until he really did run from the cops, but you know, they have these handy things called cruisers. They go really fast, too."

I nodded as he tore up the trail in front of us. That was the hard thing about being a runner, and a competitive one at that—no matter how fast I got, someone was always faster. "Did you guys run cross-country?"

"Track," he said as we both ducked under a low-hanging branch cutting across the trail. "He ran the one and two hundred, and I ran the four and eight hundred."

Well, that explained why Callum was so dang fast, but after watching him this past week, I wasn't sure there was anything that he wasn't good or fast at. "So he was faster, but you could—"

"Run faster longer." I could feel his smile aimed my way. "In case you hadn't noticed." I huffed and kept my eyes forward. The sweaty, smiling image of him was stuck in my head. I'd barely glanced at him for half a second, and that brief flash was embedded in my brain.

"What do you run?" he asked, his breathing almost sounding normal. I *knew* he'd pulled back when he came up beside me. God, I hated knowing his heartbeat was practically normal when mine felt close to bursting through my chest.

"I run cross-country in the fall and track in the spring."

"What events in track?"

I took a few seconds before answering, to catch my breath from my last answer. "The four and eight hundred. Sometimes the sixteen hundred, too."

Even though we were bounding down a trail, he managed to nudge me with his elbow. "The four and eight. So we're both masochists?"

I didn't answer him, since it was pretty much common knowledge in the track circle that people didn't normally gravitate to those events. Track coaches often had to beg, bribe, and plead with runners to get them to train and compete in these events. But I didn't have to ask Callum if his arm had been twisted to the point of breaking to persuade him to run them, or if he'd volunteered for the punishment. He liked a challenge. The bigger, the better. It was one of the areas where we were alike.

"Why are you a runner?" he asked. "Running from something or toward something?"

There wasn't anything in my path, but I almost tripped. "Neither," I stated.

"Okay, so both. Good to know."

His tone was infuriating. The look on his face probably was, too. Not that I was going to glance over to confirm it.

"Why are *you* a runner?" I threw back, trying to match his voice. "Running from something or toward something?"

"Neither." I could hear the grin in his voice.

"Okay, so both. Good to know." I had to swing to the side to avoid a chunk of rock sticking out of the trail, which made me bump into Callum. My bare arm against his bare arm.

"Aren't you going to ask me what my PRs are?" he asked.

I checked my watch. Only a mile and a half left before we were at camp. I could manage another ten minutes of running next to a sweaty Callum O'Connor at speed Insane. Hopefully. "No, because from the way I can tell you're dying for me to ask"—I took the briefest pause to catch my breath—"you must think your personal records are pretty hot stuff."

"Oh, they are."

"Then that's all I need to know."

"Yeah, more fun to leave it to your imagination, right?" He nudged me again. My skin experienced that same sparking, surging thing.

I scooted over a bit farther on the trail, reminding myself this guy was my trainer, probably split-personality, and irritated me as much as, if not more than, he intrigued me. Not that any of that mattered anyway, because I was a no-go for the summer romance thing. No how, no way. I didn't need any other complications in my life.

"Aren't you going to ask me what mine are?" I asked,

kicking the pace up a notch when we crossed the last-mile threshold.

"Sure. What are they?"

I felt the burn start to fire in my legs, but I pushed through it. I didn't slow down when things got uncomfortable; I kept charging forward. "More fun to leave it to the imagination, don't you think?"

He grunted and matched my pace. His chest was moving a bit faster now, but not like mine was. I think I took two breaths to his one. "College scholarship good?"

I smiled. "College scholarship good."

"Full-ride good?"

"If I can keep doing well in school, yeah, I think so."

Callum nodded at me, impressed. "Aren't you just an all-around overachiever?"

"What about you? Are *your* times college scholarship good?"

Callum shrugged. "That depends on who you ask."

"I'm asking you."

He gave his neck a quick roll. "Yeah, my times are solid enough to get some kind of college scholarship."

"Full-ride good?"

He was quiet for a few seconds. "If I manage to *not* keep my grades where they've been and somehow manage to score in the genius category on the SATs, then yeah, maybe."

"Is that your way of saying your grades suck?"

"That's my way of saying my grades aren't full-ride good, no matter how fast I can run."

We were close enough to the camp that I could just make out some of the cabins. "I'm not used to you being so vague."

"I'm not used to you being so specific."

Callum wasn't dumb, not by a long shot. He also didn't strike me as the slacker type. Maybe he was one of those kids who got a B once in their life and thought it was the end of the world and, worst of all, their grade point average.

"So what is it? Your GPA?" I asked.

He huffed. "I think it's more fun to leave it to the imagination."

"Really?"

"Really." He picked up the pace the last hundred meters to camp. It was all I could do to keep up.

I didn't push him any further, but when we broke to a stop once we'd charged into the big grass clearing, he hung his hands on his hips, caught his breath, then said, "Let's just say I've got two years of making up to do, and even if I kill it in my classes this year like I did last, the best I can come out with is a so-so GPA."

I was walking slow circles in the grass to cool down, my arms wrapped around my head as I struggled to catch my breath. "For someone who is totally undecided in the college department"—exhale, inhale—"you've sure put a lot of time into thinking about this."

He bobbed his shoulders. "Just because I'm undecided doesn't mean I haven't looked into my options."

My breath was getting back to normal, and the burn had almost left my legs. "Want to meet here in ten and grab some breakfast?"

I didn't know I was going to ask him until I'd asked him. Like the first couple of dinners I'd seen him at, Callum had eaten all his meals since then in the same way: alone. I wasn't sure if it was a choice or a circumstance—maybe I shouldn't have asked, but I was getting a little tired of flying meals solo. Mom had joined in for a few, and Harry always hung close by for a few minutes before beelining for the table where his team of troublemakers sat, and despite the enigma Callum O'Connor was, I liked him.

He shook his head, making drops of sweat fling from the ends of his damp hair. "Hey, thanks for the offer, but I've got to show up for my shift in an hour."

I grabbed my foot behind my back to stretch my quads. "Which should be plenty of time to shower and eat."

"Showering and eating comes lower on the hierarchy of needs than sleep does," he said around a yawn. He'd just torn up who knows how many miles of trail, was still sweaty from the effort, and he was yawning? He was tired after that adrenaline punch?

I felt the opposite after a run. Almost like I could take on the whole world with my fists tied behind my back.

"Didn't you get any sleep last night?" I asked when he yawned again and started moving in the direction of the staff cabins.

"No. Did you?" He waved and kept moving. "Thanks for the run, Phoenix. I like being challenged."

"Yeah, me too," I called after him. "Though that wasn't much of a challenge. For me, at least."

He chuckled, his eyes telling me he was calling my bluff. "Same time tomorrow, then?"

I smiled. "Don't be late."

FOURTEEN

Two days later. He'd gotten me a pair of hiking boots. *Nice* ones.

They'd been waiting on the cabin's porch when I got back after breakfast with the words *To Mythical Bird, From Glorified Pigeon* scratched onto the box. Thankfully, I'd found them before my parents or Harry had. Wasn't eager to explain the boots or the note.

They weren't wrapped. There wasn't a card attached. Not a receipt so I'd know how much to pay him back. Just a box of boots that made me wonder what kind of agenda or expectations were attached to them. If any at all. He was eighteen. He should know by now that a guy couldn't leave a random gift for a girl without some kind of explanation. There were rules against playing those kinds of head games.

I was trying to figure out something witty and confusing to "thank" him with while I ate breakfast later that morning.

I had the day off because Ben had made it a point to not schedule me when a family day was on the docket. If he would have checked with me first, I would have informed him that those were the days I wanted to work overtime.

He hadn't given up on the idea of reuniting the Ainsworth family like I had, but he had to eventually. There was no way a person could observe the way we functioned and hold on to hope that we'd all just work it out.

Today's prescribed dose of family torture included the ropes course, which was appropriate since I'd probably want to hang myself by the end of it.

I'd done a ropes course a couple of years ago as part of a team-building activity with my cross-country team, and it had been fun and, go figure, team building. However, what brought other people together would do the opposite for our family. I knew this from experience. Christmas, birthday parties, events that required gathering around the dinner table . . . what most of the world viewed as relatively pleasant encounters were considered rare and cruel forms of torture in my family lately.

After we made the trek to the ropes course, everyone started gathering around Callum as he demonstrated how to put a harness on. Once he was done, Callum separated us into three groups. Harry and I got lumped into his group. I wondered if it had been intentional. I wondered if it had been the luck of the draw. I wondered why I was wondering about those things in the first place.

"Phoenix?" After fist-bumping his friends, Harry wandered up to me.

I fought the urge to pull him into a hug. I'd missed the kid. He'd been so busy with his new friends, and I was doing my best to not play the role of dejected sister.

"Harry?" I replied.

"I like Callum," he said, waving up at him like he was hailing Zeus.

"Good for you." I tried to keep a straight face for two reasons. One, I didn't want him to think I was making fun of him for hero-worshipping Callum, and two, I didn't want him to catch on that I might have kind of liked Callum, too.

"Do you like him?"

Of course he'd ask that question. Why not?

"I don't *not* like him," I replied.

"But that doesn't mean you *do* like him."

I glanced down at him. "No, it means I don't really feel like answering your question."

"What question don't you really feel like answering?"

I almost jumped out of my brand-new boots when I heard his voice. He was right behind me—two feet behind me.

"Nothing," I spat out.

Right before I could fire a warning look Harry's way, he shrugged. "The question if Phoenix likes you or not."

Callum snorted, looking as if he was trying to swallow a laugh. Then he glanced down at my feet and smiled. "So? What's your answer?"

"No comment," I muttered before holding my foot up since he was still looking at the new boots. "Thank you, by the way, for picking these up for me. How much do I owe you?"

"They were a gift."

"It isn't my birthday."

"It doesn't have to be for someone to give you a gift."

I worked my tongue into my cheek. He was as stubborn as someone else I knew. "I'd like to pay you back."

"And I'd like a twelve-inch meatball sub in my mitts right this minute, but sometimes we just have to live with our disappointment."

Harry's head was whipping between us, every few turns lowering to my new boots.

My arms folded over my stomach. "You're difficult."

His smile went wide. "Thank you. I love a good compliment."

Then he crouched down beside Harry. "Getting back to the topic . . . what do you think, Harry?" He paused, no doubt for dramatic value. "Does Phoenix like me? Or does she hate my guts?"

Harry lifted his hand and tilted it back and forth. "I don't know. I don't think she even knows," he answered, shoving his glasses higher on his nose as he peeked up at me. My face was one giant warning sign. "But even if she did or one day figures it out, I couldn't tell you."

Callum shrugged. "Why not?"

"Because she's my sister and she's got my back." He motioned up at me like I was sitting on some kind of jewel-studded throne. "And I've got her back, too."

I had this strange feeling watching my little brother stick up for me to a guy almost twice his age. Had the switch happened here at camp? Or had he been this way for a while, and it had taken Camp Kismet for me to notice?

"I respect a man who looks after his family." Callum clapped his hand on Harry's shoulder. "You're one of the good ones, my man. Don't change."

"Oh, I'm planning on growing at least another thirteen inches and looking into contact lenses one day, and who knows? I might even grow a beard." Harry drew a beard coming off his chin with his thumb and index finger pinched together. I had to keep biting my lip.

"Change that stuff all you want. Just don't change the important stuff."

Harry blinked. "Like my theory on whether the chicken or the egg came first? Because I'm certain which one did. I've got an entire notebook of evidence proving it, too."

Callum gave me a quick look. I shrugged. Harry really did have a notebook full of research and documentation on the topic. "No need to change that since you clearly feel so passionately about it, but I was *specifically* talking about your loyalty and courage. Hang on to those no matter what."

Harry nodded all solemn-like.

"Now, if you guys will excuse me, duty calls." Callum lifted his hand in front of Harry for a high five. Harry didn't hesitate to give it a solid smack. A month ago, he would have stared blankly at someone if they'd lifted their hand in front of him like that.

Harry and I followed Callum and the other campers down another short stretch of trail. It was only a minute before the Beam came into view and I could see what the hype was about. From our vantage point on the ground, with that giant log suspended a good twenty feet in the air, it didn't just look ominous; it looked like one of my worst nightmares.

Harry squealed beside me, clasping my hand and giving it a hard squeeze. Of course my dread was his thrill. I was what some people would describe as having an issue with heights.

I didn't like heights.

Heights didn't like me.

"We get to climb up to that thing and walk across it, *twice*, before getting to climb back down?" Harry was still squealing, about to cut the circulation off to my left hand. "Pinch me." When I stayed frozen beside him, Harry nudged me. "Pinch me so I know if I'm dreaming or not."

"How about I slap you over the back of the head instead?"

Up front, Callum was talking to the group. The Beam was hanging between two large trees, which climbers would scale by using these small metal "steps" that were sticking out of the tree. To get to the top, a person would have to leap from step to step up the tree.

Super. Just effing super.

Of course, once—*if*—a person made it to the top, they

actually had to balance themselves across the tightrope-thin beam, turn around, and balance back before making the return journey down the stairway to hell.

I wondered if it was too late to disappear. Would anyone notice if Harry and I vanished? Maybe I could fake a sudden stomachache.

"Okay, so who's going to take on the Beam first?" Callum shouted over to the cluster of campers as he clipped a big colorful rope to his harness.

"Anyone?" Callum said. "I promise, it's been years since we lost anyone to the Beam." He shot a grin around, but my stomach was too busy convulsing to laugh with everyone else.

Beside me, an arm shot up into the air. For one moment, I was relieved someone else had volunteered. Then I realized whose hand had shot up.

"Harry Ainsworth. Confirming my courage theory all day long." Callum winked at my foolish, knocking-on-death's-door little brother. But then Callum shook his head. "I'm sorry but I suppose I should have mentioned that you have to be a certain height and weight. I should have figured you'd want to be the first to tackle the Beam."

My whole body sighed in relief. Harry's whole body sagged in dismay.

The other campers around us gave him sympathetic smiles, and a couple of the dads patted his shoulders. I could tell Callum felt bad. Genuinely bad. After a moment, he called for another volunteer.

"Harry . . . ," I started

"It's okay, Phoenix. Rules are rules." He sniffed. "I get it."

"Really?" I asked. He sighed, but when he looked up, I could see he hadn't been crying. "That's really . . . *mature* of you," I said, pulling him into a sideways hug.

"I learned it by watching you."

"Learned what?" I asked. How to not cry when you wanted to? How to fake one emotion for another?

"How to be mature," he answered, returning the hug.

"Oh. Wow. I'm not sure how to take that, but thanks." I was in the middle of mussing his hair when someone came up beside us.

"Sorry I'm late. What did I miss?" Mom sounded almost out of breath. Like she'd rushed to get here. Her hair was pulled into a ponytail and her face was mostly makeup free.

"Harry being the first volunteer to walk across that thing," I answered, lifting my eyes to the Beam where it seemed to hover a hundred feet above. Forget whatever Callum had said about twenty feet.

When Mom's eyes followed mine, she swallowed. "Please don't tell me . . ."

"Don't worry. He's not big enough to do it yet," I said.

Her shoulders relaxed.

"But I will be next summer," Harry chimed in, stretching to his four-foot-eight frame. "So can we come back? Puh-lease? So I can walk the Beam?"

Mom paused.

I leaned in closer. "Don't make any promises you can't keep."

For a moment, she looked at me the way she might look at another adult. Wrapping her hand around my wrist, she gave it a soft squeeze as she smiled down at Harry. "Okay, sweetheart. If you love it so much, we'll return next year." Harry leaped up into the air as if he'd sprouted a springing tail like Tigger. "*That* doesn't mean I'm agreeing to let you walk the plank . . . beam . . . whatever," she piped up, "but we can come back."

Harry threw his arms around her and kept bouncing. "And maybe we can get the same cabin, and maybe Phoenix can be a counselor again, too." His jumping stopped abruptly when he looked over at me. "You'll come back, too, won't you, Phoenix?"

I hesitated. I was worried that this whole new Mom act was too good to be true. "I don't know, Harry. It will depend on the college I wind up going to and when school starts."

"Maybe if you get into Northwestern you won't start until the end of September. You could totally be a counselor again next summer."

"Northwestern?" Mom's head whipped in my direction. Great. Busted. "I thought you'd narrowed it down to UCLA and Cal Poly. Northwestern is on the other side of the country." Her voice was different, too high, borderline panicked. *Weird.*

"Well, now I'm considering Northwestern, too."

"It sounds as if you're doing a little more than just considering it." Mom steered us away from the other campers. She didn't appreciate having family "talks" with others in earshot. You know, messed with the whole keeping-up-appearances thing.

"It's my top pick."

That surprised her enough to shut her up for two seconds. "And you told Harrison about your change in college plans before you told your father and me?"

The first camper had just walked the Beam and was getting unclipped by Callum. I could tell Callum was watching us, but he wasn't making it obvious. The only reason I knew was because it took him five tries to unclip a carabiner.

"Harry found the application lying on my desk one day. What could I do? It wasn't like I wanted to lie to him." I wondered if I was still talking about the college application or the foreclosure notice I'd stumbled across on Dad's desk. Was I mad because she was all put out I hadn't told them about my change in college plans? Or was I mad because they'd lied about the house and their marriage and Dad's job and who only knew what else?

"Besides, I probably won't get in anyway. That's why I haven't told you guys yet. Because I was hoping to avoid this fuss if nothing became of it."

"You lied."

"I omitted the truth," I fired off.

"You lied." She said it more softly this time, but it didn't matter. She was accusing me of lying? Yeah, not quite.

"Well, you're the expert on that topic," I said before turning my back and walking away.

If only I could keep walking all the way home to California.

FIFTEEN

I was a glutton for punishment. It was official. That was the only explanation for why I'd let Harry coax me into joining the last part of the family trust- (torture-) building day.

It wasn't until I actually saw Dad with my own two eyes, a few feet down the bench from Mom, that I wondered if I'd accidentally stumbled into some alternate reality. Or had finally dropped off the ledge of sanity.

"Is that really him? Or the twin brother we never knew he had?" I whispered over at Harry.

"I think it's really him," Harry replied, waving at a few of his friends as we passed. "But he's scruffier than I remember."

I almost smiled. From the looks of him tonight, he hadn't shaved in days, and his hair hadn't seen the business side of a comb for just as long. Even his clothes looked disheveled. I couldn't decide if it looked like he'd just been attacked by a werewolf or was becoming one. I'd been so caught up in Callum and making sure Harry was having a good time, I'd missed the effect camp was having on Dad.

"Listen, Harry," I started, slowing our pace so I could say this before we got to Them. "About earlier. I'm sorry. I didn't mean to just bail on you, but I couldn't stand there and let Mom accuse me of lying. . . ."

"But you did kind of lie about college, you know."

"I didn't lie. I just didn't tell them about changing my mind." As we roamed through the room, I found myself searching it for someone. When I realized who that someone was, I stopped looking. But not before I'd found him, at the front of the dining hall, talking to a few campers.

"I didn't lie to her about anything, and if I had, I would have fessed up because when you lie to someone, you lose that person's trust. I take that seriously."

Harry was staring up at me with that you're-older-but-I'm-wiser expression. "Really? One lie and good-bye, trust is gone?"

I looked down at him with the I'm-older-*and*-wiser look. "Really."

"So you're saying you don't think Dad and Mom should trust you anymore because you lied about college?"

"I didn't lie about college."

Harry rolled his eyes. "Fine, so let's say they lied about something. You'd never trust them again?"

I lifted a shoulder. "If the lie was big enough . . . no, probably not."

"That's messed up."

"According to a ten-year-old," I fired back.

"What if *I* lied to you about something? Are you saying you'd never trust me again? Never?" He nudged me, like he knew better.

"And this conversation is officially over," I muttered as we closed in on our parents. Mom smiled when she saw us. Dad didn't seem to notice us.

"There you two are. Good timing. They're just about to get started." Mom scooted farther down the bench from Dad and patted the space between. Harry darted into the spot beside Mom. Leaving me with the spot beside the Walking Dead formerly known as Dad.

"Have they told us what we're doing tonight?" Harry shoved his glasses higher on his nose.

"Your guess is as good as mine," Mom answered him, leaning forward so she could see me. "About earlier, Phoenix . . ." She shifted in her seat. "I'm sorry."

Come again? Had my mom, the authority on all things all the time, just apologized? To me?

It was only when I noticed Harry's face doing the same shocked and awed thing as mine that I knew I hadn't heard her wrong.

"It's okay," I started, sounding like a robot. "I'm sorry, too."

World-stopping moment, take two. Had I just apologized to my mom?

Life, stop messing with me and get back to making sense, already.

"How's being a camp counselor going, Phoenix?" It had been a few days since I'd heard my dad's voice directed at me in something other than a shushing or groaning kind of way.

"It's okay," I said, going with the same response I'd given Mom. Best to keep things simple and uniform when dealing with these two.

"So you're not enjoying it?" Dad's foot was tapping like crazy, but the rest of him was so still he could have been a statue. His head stayed facing forward as he talked to me.

"No . . ." I scanned the room, wishing they'd get this thing going. "It's okay."

"So you do like it?"

I sighed. Why, of all the questions he could have asked me, had he glommed on to the camp counselor thing?

"It's o-kay," I said slowly, hoping he'd get the picture and stop asking.

Dad was quiet for a moment, other than his foot tapping. Then he asked, "Have you made any friends yet? It sounds like Harry's already made enough to last a lifetime."

I glanced over at Harry. He was watching our dad with something that resembled curiosity, because we were *so used* to having these kinds of casual conversations with our dad lately. Oh wait.

"Not really," I said. "I've been pretty busy considering stuff, studying for the SATs, and keeping up with my training, so I haven't exactly been a social butterfly."

"Callum's your friend," Harry chimed in.

I ground my teeth together. Callum was exactly the reason I didn't want to get into the camp counselor thing with my dad. So much for Little Brother Interference—LBI.

"Who's Callum?" Dad asked.

I squirmed in my seat, feeling like I was having the same conversation with him I'd had with my mom the second night at camp.

Just then, the shrill whine of the mic filled the room. Saved by the family trust-building activity . . .

"That's Callum," Harry whispered over at my dad as Callum moved to the front of the room beside Ben and the malfunctioning mic.

"*That's* Callum." Dad's brows came together. "Isn't he a little too old to be your *friend*, Phoenix?"

I wanted to die. I wanted the earth to open up so I could swan-dive in. "We're both going to be seniors in the fall, Dad. Chill."

Callum took the mic from Ben, made a few adjustments, then handed it back to Ben. The whining sound stopped.

"Well, he's too old for you where it counts."

I felt heat fan my face. Dad had never met Callum. He didn't know a thing about him other than what he looked like and what Harry had told him about us being friends. Maybe Callum was complicated, but I knew he cared about others, was hardworking, and had a sense of adventure. When I looked at Callum, I saw a good person.

"Callum's the one training me, Dad. It's not exactly like I can just avoid him."

"Phoenix . . ." There was a note of warning in his voice.

"And if you want to be my parent, that means you have to actually parent. You know, it's a twenty-four-seven gig, not a ten-minutes-every-couple-of-months job." I never used to talk to my parents like this, and here I'd gone off on them both on the same day.

A shadow of irritation fired on his face. "I am your father. You will not talk to me that way," Dad snapped at me.

Heat fanned my face again. "You're my father in title alone, *Dad,*" I tacked on with acid in my voice. "You stopped meeting the actual job requirements of the title a while ago, so don't expect me to fulfill the daughter ones when you're not holding up your end of the deal."

Just as suddenly, Dad's anger disappeared. Watching my dad's face fall apart brought on a serious case of guilt, along with wishing I could get a do-over for the past thirty seconds.

Why I was feeling bad for him after everything, I didn't know, but I was. He already had enough on his Fail plate—I didn't need to add *failure as a father* to the mix beside *unemployed* and *soon-to-be homeless.*

He looked as if he was going to say something right when Ben's voice echoed through the room.

"Love and light and peace, fellow campers!" Ben was

shouting. Kind of made the mic pointless. A chorus of greetings echoed through the room. No one from our bench joined in, though. We were all too busy being pissed, confused, and hurt by one another to even pretend to be happy to be here.

"I hope you've enjoyed the day so far and felt like your family was able to take some valuable lessons away from it." Around us, a bunch of heads bobbed in agreement as arms wound around shoulders. The four Ainsworths shifted in their seats. The only new lessons I'd learned about my family today was that my mom thought I was a liar and my dad could be gutted by a few heated words from me. Probably not the lessons Ben had in mind.

"Tonight we have a real treat in store for you all—the king of trust builders. I'm going to have a few of our wonderful counselors demonstrate what you'll be doing before setting your families off on your trust-building journey." Ben waved a few counselors up to join Callum, grinning like today was the best day of his life and sporting his standard Camp Kismet tie-dyed shirt.

Ben lined up the counselors, two wide and two long, turned his back to them and closed his eyes, and then he did the stupidest thing I'd ever watched another person do.

So, yeah. *Trust-building exercise* was code word for "voluntary sacrifice."

The point of this gruesome exercise was for each person to take a turn being the victim. Ben had used another term, but *victim* was more fitting. The victim had their back to the rest of their family, closed their eyes, called out something lame, like *Can I trust you?* and when the rest of the family answered with a *You can trust us,* said victim was supposed to fall and trust that the members of their family would catch them before they flopped onto the not-soft-at-all floor.

This wasn't just a bad idea. There hadn't been a word devised for just how bad an idea this was.

"Let me know when you guys are ready, okay?" I said as I turned around, my back to them. I didn't get a reply. Not comforting considering I was about to fall backward into the arms of two people I didn't trust to keep a gerbil safe, let alone yours truly. I knew Harry would have my back, because he always did. The problem was, he was small.

Maybe if I just grabbed Harry and we quickly and all stealth-like slipped away, no one would notice.

That was when Ben shouted through the mic again. "Just in case any of you are thinking of taking a pass in Can I Trust You? no one gets to eat until everyone's had a turn. So take your time if you want. We'll all thank you when dinner is served at midnight."

Sucking in a deep breath, I crossed my arms in front of my chest like Ben had done, closed my eyes, and called out, "Can I trust you?"

My parents said something. Just not the something I thought they had.

My body crashed right through my parents' weak hold on each other, and just as I was bracing myself for the impact of the hardwood floor, I stopped. My eyes were squeezed shut and I could feel the grimace cemented on my face, but I hadn't slammed into the floor. Someone had caught me.

I could feel four hands holding me in place, bracing me from falling. Two small, familiar ones . . . and two large, strong ones.

My parents' shrieks were the first thing I heard, followed by my mom blaming Dad for not holding on tight enough, followed by him accusing her of having her head in the clouds. The argument continued, but I tuned it out.

Opening my eyes, the first thing I saw was Harry. His face was creased with concentration, but his eyes were worried. He started to smile when I opened my eyes.

"Thanks for saving me, little man. I've always told you you're my hero."

His smile spread into a grin.

The second thing I saw was him. Callum, totally calm. Like he was used to swooping in and saving the day. "Nice fall," he said, his large hands giving me a hoist so I could stand up.

"Nice catch," I replied, my back feeling warm and tingly from where his hands had just been.

Callum stuffed his hands into his pockets and shrugged. "I told you I'd be there for you when you really needed it. I couldn't go and renege on my promise. What kind of person would that make me?"

Behind me, I could still hear my parents arguing. "Normal," I answered him. "But thank you."

"Welcome," Callum said with a nod.

"You okay, Phoenix?" Harry asked, looking me over.

"I'm okay. Thanks to you two." I might have said the last part louder than necessary, hoping my parents might have heard. They were too busy hollering at each other to hear anyone else, though.

"Do you mind if I go hang out with Matt and Carter?" Harry asked, pointing across the dining hall. "Their family's done and no one suffered any fractured skulls or vertebrae. I'd rather have their family catch me if I really have to do this."

I messed his hair up good and wild. "Go for it. I don't blame you." I checked over my shoulder when Callum stayed in front of me, watching me. My parents hadn't noticed their youngest child taking off. They sure weren't going to miss me if I bailed.

"You want to get out of here?" Callum asked abruptly.

"You read minds now, too?"

Callum tipped his head for the door and waited for me to take the first step. He shouldered up beside me when I started to move. "Not minds. Just people."

SIXTEEN

"You drove that from California to here and lived to tell the story?" I was standing outside one of the staff cabins, gaping at Callum's "ride."

"True story," he answered, handing me a matte-black helmet that was scratched and beat up.

"My parents will freak." I took the helmet, but I didn't drop it over my head.

"Your parents who just let you fall and almost crack your skull open? Those parents?" Callum smiled as he buttoned up his heavy flannel shirt.

I rolled my eyes. He had a point. "They don't like me getting in cars or, similarly, getting onto the back of motorcycles with random guys."

"I'm not some random guy. I'm the one who just saved you. I didn't go all out of my way to do that to let you go splat across the highway half an hour later." He waved at the helmet in my hand, and after I slipped it on, he walked over to one of the clothes-drying lines and pulled off another flannel shirt. "It's going to get cold tonight, and it's only colder on the back of this thing. I know it's five sizes too big, but it's warm." Callum held up his shirt for me.

When I reached to take it, he kept hold of it, sighed, then held it open.

He was putting it on for me? What the . . . ?

When I spun around, he slid the flannel shirt onto my arms and up around my shoulders. It smelled like laundry soap, sunshine, and him. A combination I shouldn't have approved of as much as I did.

"There," he said, turning me around and fastening the top collar button. He looked like he was thinking about buttoning the rest, but he stopped himself. "Ready to get out of here?"

"Where are we going?" I asked.

"Somewhere great."

"Somewhere that has a name?" I pressed as he threw his leg over the side of his motorcycle and scooted forward to give me room.

"Somewhere that needs to be experienced, not described."

"You're kind of mysterious, you know that?"

"That's a relief, because that's my number one goal in life. To be a mystery, an enigma, a question mark." His face flattened as he glanced behind him, waiting. "Ready whenever you are."

"You don't exactly strike me as the motorcycle type." I moved closer and hesitantly swung my leg over the seat of the bike. I knew my parents would go all Mount St. Helens on me if they found out, but Callum was right. He'd saved me when they hadn't. He'd proven himself more capable of protecting me than they had lately.

"I'm *not* the motorcycle type. Whatever that is." Callum turned his head over his shoulder. "This thing just happened to be the cheapest, most reliable hunk of junk I could find. Plus, it comes in handy when it's rush hour in Los Angeles."

I glanced down at my feet. "And now I feel even worse about accepting these boots since they probably cost as much as this thing."

He rolled his shoulders and fired up the engine. I stumbled back a few steps. The motorcycle sounded more like it had a bad case of indigestion than other motorcycles I'd heard zooming down the highways did. Callum's didn't purr, roar, or rev. It sputtered.

"Where's your helmet?" I shouted above the noise.

"On your head," he shouted. "How's that for proving to your parents I'm safety conscious?"

"Probably not that stellar given your gulliver is exposed and just ready for your brains to splat all over the asphalt."

Callum chuckled. "Well, at least it would be my splatted brains and not yours. You're the one destined for college greatness."

When the motorcycle started to pull away, my arms wound around him as quickly and tightly as they could move. "I might be wrong on this, but just because you're undecided when it comes to college doesn't mean you won't still need a brain for whatever you decide to do instead."

"Not if I find myself one of those brainless jobs I keep hearing about." He drove down the road that led right past the dining hall. I held my breath the entire time, sure that would be the moment one of my parents would pop out of there. Callum didn't say anything else as we sped down the long, winding road toward Flagstaff. I'd never been on a motorcycle before, but it was kind of great. I felt free, alive, like the whole world was waiting for me at the end of this road, wherever it led.

It felt like hardly any time had passed at all before the bike slowed when we made it into Flagstaff. Callum took a sudden turn that led away from the main part of the city, and we weren't on that road long before it opened up into a parking lot.

My arms tightened around him when I scanned the parking

lot. Other than the bike's headlight, I couldn't make out anything else.

"Okay, we're stopped now. Think you could ease up your death grip on me before you crush my liver?" He parked the bike and turned off the engine.

It was so quiet out here. Scary quiet. "Where are we?" I loosened my grip, but I didn't let go.

He glanced at me over his shoulder. "Don't you like a surprise?"

"Not when I'm in the middle of some dark parking lot late at night."

Callum fought a smile. "It's barely eight. Not quite the witching hour."

An owl hooted from somewhere in the woods. I jumped. "Where the hell are we?"

He stopped fighting his smile. "The Lowell Observatory. Perfectly safe and nonthreatening, I swear."

"What are we observing?"

Callum waited for my arms to drop at my sides before sliding off the bike. "Pretty much anything you want to up there." He tipped his head and looked up at the sky.

My head followed. "The stars? That's what we're going to be looking at?"

"Stars, moons, planets. Take your pick." He helped me undo the helmet's chin strap after I fought with it on my own for a few seconds. "This is one of my favorite places."

"In Arizona?"

"Anywhere," he answered, pulling a small flashlight from his pocket and turning it on. He pointed it in the direction of a sidewalk and started toward it, making sure I was close beside him.

"How many times have you been here?" I asked.

"I come a few times every summer, more when I was coming here with my family."

I kept my focus on the light in front of us. With that bright beam, the black didn't seem so thick around us.

"So are you into astronomy?" I asked.

"You could say that." When another owl hooted, I didn't leap out of my boots. This time I barely flinched. Callum's presence calmed me. "But I didn't know it the first time I came. I only started getting into astronomy a few years ago."

"Why did you first start coming here?" We were getting closer to what I guessed was the observatory, but nothing about it screamed tourist attraction.

"It was Ben's idea, I guess. He knew about the trouble my brother was getting into at home and that I was following in his footsteps. He has this freaky way of looking at a person and knowing what they're feeling or what they're thinking. Those first couple of summers at camp he used to be able to take one look at me and know when I was about to do something I'd probably regret." He paused and shook his head. "I really hated Ben at first."

"And now you love him." I nudged him as we approached a doorway.

"And now I respect him. I appreciate what he's doing and why he does it." He turned off the flashlight and held open the door for me.

"So your mom would bring you here to look up at the sky and your problems were solved?"

He chuckled softly. "That's what Ben tried to sell. He said there was nothing like looking up at the universe to make my problems shrivel into nonexistence."

"Is that doubt I'm detecting in your voice?"

"That's I-know-better-from-experience in my voice." Callum

waved at a lady sitting behind a counter at the front and led me inside. It was dark in here, too, which made me shift a bit closer to Callum. "Ben tried really hard to sell me on the perspective thing, but, I don't know, looking up at the stars or thinking about the size of the universe didn't make my issues seem any smaller or less significant. They were still the exact same size when I walked out of this place."

"Then why did you keep coming back?" I asked as he stopped behind the biggest telescope I'd seen in real life.

"Because it got me out of my head, you know?" he answered immediately. "It got me to focus on something else for a while, and even though I'd leave here with the same problems I walked in with, they felt more manageable. More like I could handle them."

I hadn't expected him to open up like that. That was becoming a trend when it came to Callum. One minute he came off as the most closed-off person I'd ever met, and the next he could spill his guts. "And then you fell in love with the stars," I said, watching him as he looked through the telescope, making a few adjustments on the dials.

"And then I did." He made one last adjustment before motioning me to look. Even though it was dark, his eyes were glowing. I'd seen him in his element this summer, but never like this. If this wasn't passion, I wasn't sure I'd ever seen it.

"So you're saying this place has played a totally insignificant role in your life?" I smiled at him as I moved up to the telescope.

"Completely insignificant." He stepped aside to give me room to look.

I wound my hair around one shoulder, closed one eye, and leaned over so I could peek through the eyepiece. I could have been looking at a star just as easily as I could have been looking at a planet or a moon. I didn't feel my problems drifting away from me by the masses, disappearing into the Milky Way, but just like Callum had said, somehow they felt less overwhelming. Less powerful.

The longer I stared up there, the stronger I felt down here.

"I get it," I whispered after another minute, feeling like the entire universe was staring back at me as I gazed into it.

He took a step closer. "I knew you would."

SEVENTEEN

"From looking at a million stars to having to choose between a million flavors of ice cream." I tapped my chin as I wandered down the long case for the tenth time. Okay, so there might not have been a million flavors, but close.

"Seemed like a natural progression to me." Callum had already decided what he wanted, but he was waiting for me. He'd already waited five minutes. Thankfully, it was late and Ice Cream Apocalypse wasn't too busy, because I'd be testing the patience of the customers behind us.

"What's your favorite?" I asked him again, but I should have known better. He'd already answered with a solid round of silence, followed by the wise words of listening to my gut when it came to choosing among dozens of flavors I'd never heard of before. Strawberry basil? Bacon and maple syrup? Lemon mint? Wasabi lime?

"What's the least popular flavor?" I asked the employee trudging down the case of ice cream with me. For now, the eleventh time. I could feel her patience unraveling with every footstep.

"Tuna Tartare," she said flatly, stopping behind a bucket of ice cream that I wouldn't have eaten based on its grayish color alone. My stomach rolled. "What's your most popular?"

Camped out in front of the cash register, Callum sighed loud enough for me to hear at the opposite end of the store.

"Vanilla lavender," she answered, managing to flatten her voice even more.

"If you get something with vanilla listed in the flavor after this, I will never let you forget it," he said.

"You told me to go with my gut."

"If your gut is telling you to order vanilla in a place named Ice Cream Apocalypse, you need to get your head checked."

"Don't you mean my gut checked?" I lifted an eyebrow at him and stopped in front of a flavor that had gotten my attention the first pass.

Callum tapped his wallet against the counter, waiting. "That, too."

"I'll have the honey jalapeño, please," I announced proudly because, you know, deciding on an ice cream flavor made the list of top ten proudest moments.

The employee's face read, *Finally.* "Single or double?"

"Or triple?" Callum added, his voice matching the *Finally* tone.

"Double."

"Bowl, sugar, or waffle cone?" the employee asked.

"Or chocolate-sprinkle-dipped waffle cone?" Callum added.

I rolled my eyes at him. For someone pushing me to hurry up and make a decision, he wasn't helping. "Waffle, plain." I waited, just in case she was going to fire off another question, but when she got to work scooping a couple of fist-size balls into a waffle cone, I figured the grand ice cream inquisition was over.

"Happy now?" I said to Callum as another employee handed him his ice cream cone.

"When my blood pressure's recovered, I'll let you know."

"You need to work on your patience," I said, thanking the server when she handed me my ice cream cone. She disappeared quickly after that, before she had to deal with another stream of questions from me.

"You need to work on your decision-making process."

When the other employee rang up the cones, Callum handed over a twenty before I could finish digging in my pocket. "I can get mine."

"Already taken care of." Callum pocketed his change after dropping a tip in the jar, grabbed a few napkins, and waggled his brows at me. "Now you owe me."

After that, we meandered down the sidewalk. Flagstaff was a neat city. Not what a person pictured when they imagined Arizona—no cacti, endless desert, or blistering heat—but more the kind of place a person would imagine in Colorado or Wyoming. Outdoorsy and welcoming.

As much as I'd gotten used to Camp Kismet, it was a relief to be away from it. A relief to not be a counselor or a big sister on call 24-7 or a referee for her parents. It was nice to just be . . . me. Phoenix. Someone who didn't feel like this world and the next one over were resting on my shoulders.

"So it doesn't seem as if your family's embracing the whole come-together spirit of camp," Callum started, glancing over at me to check my reaction.

I exhaled and took a bite of ice cream. Embracing it? Yeah, right, more like repelling it. "You caught that in the dining hall, did ya?"

"I think I caught it, yeah. Literally." He paused in front of a closed coffee shop and turned to face me.

I kept walking. I wanted to keep moving, especially if we were going to start talking about the plague known as the Ainsworths. "Thanks for that, by the way. I didn't have much of a chance to thank you for saving—"

"Your gulliver?"

His abrupt words made me laugh. Never in a million years had I imagined I could laugh when talking about my family. "That and my pride."

"What's the deal with your family, though? I mean, your parents are still together and you guys obviously have money."

"Everything's the 'deal' in my family." Callum caught up to me after a few steps. "My parents probably aren't going to be together much longer, unless divine intervention steps in, and whatever you think we possess is about to be repoed or sold at auction."

It was surreal, having this kind of conversation with a person who'd been a stranger two weeks ago. It had taken me weeks before I could work up the nerve to tell Emerson about what was going down in the domestic home front, and here I was, spilling it to some guy who was my boss slash friend slash question mark.

"I'm sorry. That's got to be rough on you." He offered me his half-eaten cone suddenly, like he should have offered me a taste fifty licks ago.

I don't know why—I'd shared plenty of ice cream cones with plenty of people, germs be damned—but this felt different. Kind of like he was offering me a piece of him, and I couldn't decide if I should take it. Weird.

"Thanks," I said, giving his ice cream a taste. It was just ice cream, not a promise ring. "Not bad. I'd offer you a taste of mine, but I already know honey is too sweet for you."

His nose crinkled when I lifted my cone toward him.

"Thanks anyway." He shook his head and stepped a foot away. "What are you going to do if they get a divorce?"

"Survive. Adapt. Do whatever I have to before I graduate and head off to college."

"Rise from the ashes." I could hear the smirk in his voice, so I elbowed him.

"Or I could crap on the sidewalks. Dove." I elbowed him again.

He gave me a wider berth, laughing. "Sounds like you've got it all figured out."

I wanted to answer, *Hardly.* I stayed quiet, though. Most days, I wondered if I had anything figured out. When the house was foreclosed on, where would we live? Would I still be in the same school district? Would we have to move to a different state? Would I ever see my friends again? And what about Harry and his private school?

"Speaking of having it all planned . . . ," I started, knowing it was time to shift the conversation before I collapsed into a panic attack. "What about you?"

Half his face lifted, like he'd been caught. "I've got everything planned that's important."

"Like your future," I pressed.

He sighed. "You're not subtle, you know that?"

"I know that."

He tossed the last bite of cone into his mouth and crunched it like he had a serious issue with it. "If that's your way of asking me if I've decided on the college issue, no, I haven't. Since I've been tossing the idea around for two years, it's pretty unlikely I'm going to come to a decision in two days."

I stopped in front of an outdoor clothing store. He kept walking. "Come on, I just opened up about my mess of a life. You can't return the favor?"

"I don't know if I'm going to college or not. That's the answer I gave you before, and that's my answer now." He kept walking, but his pace slowed. He was waiting for me to catch up.

"Okay, so you don't know if you're going to college. That's not what I want to know." I jogged up to him and matched his pace. He wouldn't look at me, but at least he wasn't glaring holes into the sidewalk. "But do you *want* to go to college?"

"That's the exact same question," he replied.

"No, it's not."

"They're the same."

I took the last bite of my ice cream. "They're different."

"Same."

"Different."

He groaned and shot a look at me. "You're persistent, too. And annoying."

"Still waiting . . ." I shrugged. "Come on. I shared my story. Sharing is caring."

His body tensed as if he was bracing for an impact. "I want to go to college, sure—I'd be the first in my family to go." His pace slowed to a crawl, like he was pulling a sled holding a family of elephants. "But if I want to go or not is irrelevant since I'm pretty solid on the fact I *won't* be able to go to college."

"Why not?"

He sighed in frustration because, yeah, I'm sure it was so unexpected that I'd ask a follow-up question. "For reasons A, B, and C."

I shoved my hands into my pockets. "So you slacked off the first couple of years of high school. Big deal. Everyone does." Callum shot me a look, not buying the everyone-slacks-off theory. "You worked hard last year, and you'll work hard this year, and you'll wind up with a decent GPA. Plus, you can run a mean four and eight hundred, so that will count for something. Screwing up a few classes isn't a reason to give up on college if you really want to go."

Callum rolled to a stop in front of what looked like an old Catholic church. The kind with lots of wide steps leading up to wooden double doors. It even had a steeple. He collapsed down on one of the lower steps and clasped his hands together. "It was more than a 'few' classes, and that is only reason A."

"What's B and C?" I lowered onto the same stair beside him, keeping a safe distance between us.

"Reason B is I don't want to just bail on my mom. Summers are one thing, but four years is a long time, and I'm all she's got left. My dad . . . my brother . . . they all left her. I couldn't do the same." His hands were clenched so tightly together, veins were starting to pop through the skin.

"But you'd be going to college. You could still visit. Weekends, holidays, et cetera, et cetera. You wouldn't be bailing on her for good like your dad or getting thrown in the slammer like your brother." As I replied, I started to understand why Callum was such an enigma. "I get what you're saying, and I think it's kind of heroic of you to want to take care of your mom, but I can't imagine she'd want you to just give up on your dreams so you could hang around and eat dinners together." When I peeked over at him, he was looking up at the sky.

"It might not be the greatest reason in the world, but there are a lot worse reasons than wanting to take care of my mom."

I nodded. He was right. How hard had I worked to get where I was, and how many times had I contemplated hanging close to home so I could keep an eye on Harry? "So what's reason C?"

The stretch of silence that followed confirmed that this was the big reason.

He clasped his hands together and shrugged. "I bomb tests."

"You bomb tests?" I repeated slowly, wondering if I'd heard him wrong. "What kind of tests? Certain subjects?" I scooted an inch closer.

"*Any* test. *Any* subject."

I paused, thinking. Callum personified calm-under-pressure in every situation I'd seen him in; I couldn't picture him losing his cool when a test got slammed down in front of him.

"Really?" I asked.

He nodded.

"But you said you did well last year. You had to have done well on tests to do that. Junior year was a nightmare."

"I did well last year in comparison to the years before that, but I still bombed when it came to test time. I just had enough teachers who took pity on me and were willing to let me make up tests and give me enough extra-credit assignments that I made it." He lifted the collar of his flannel up around his neck. "High school might be one thing, but I'd be an idiot to expect the same kind of treatment in college. I'd flunk out before midterms of my first semester."

"Aren't you the optimist," I muttered as I rubbed my hands together.

"I'm a realist, Phoenix. If I can't pass a test with any kind of regularity, I'm not going to make it through college, so why shouldn't I save myself the misery and just accept it? There are plenty of things I can do that don't require a college degree."

"I never said there wasn't, but you're the one who admitted you wanted to go to college if you could."

"Which I *can't*." His voice actually sounded less irritated than it had at the start of this college talk. Progress.

"So you've got a few hurdles to jump—big deal." I angled my body toward him.

"What you call hurdles, the rest of the world calls block-ades."

I groaned, kind of wanting to shake some sense into him or out of him. "Even if you did know one hundred percent that you couldn't hack it in college, wouldn't you at least want to try?" I paused to let that sink in good and deep. "Wouldn't you regret it forever if you didn't give it a chance?"

Callum thought about that for a minute. Then he shook his head. "The devil on my shoulder is telling me no."

"What's the angel on the other side telling you?" I nudged the toe of my boot against the toe of his boot.

"That I'm an idiot for even thinking about it."

"Come on. I can help you with this stuff. I'm a pro at tests." I tapped my head, like that was all the proof he needed. If the Lame Police were on duty, they would have come and hauled me away. "You taught me the ins and outs of camp stuff, and I'll show you the ins and outs of owning a test."

I was expecting him to object right away. Instead, he was quiet, like he was actually thinking about it. "You already have to spend all day with me training and running. You really want to spend another minute more than you have to with me?"

I waved him off. "I don't mind. Besides, it will be kind of great getting to boss you around for once. Lecturing you on what to do and what not to do." I rolled my fingers together all cryptic-like. "It will actually be pretty damn cathartic."

He shifted on the step, tilting his head so he could look at me. "You're sure?"

"In case you confused it for my unsure face, this is my sure one." I circled my index finger around my face a few times.

When he looked at me like he wasn't sure, I stuck my tongue out at him.

That got a smile out of him at least.

"So what's life like at home?" I asked, changing the subject because I could tell the test issue made him uncomfortable.

"In Inglewood?" he said, shrugging. "It's pretty nice, actually." I didn't say anything. "I know, right? People hear 'Inglewood' and they think gangs, violent crime, and police brutality, but that's mostly just the media talking. The soul food is legit, it's one of the few cities in California where the crime rate is actually going down, and it's a place a person can afford a mortgage." He shrugged again. "It's home."

"What's your life like?" I scooted closer.

"Different. The same."

"Do people treat you like you're some deity back there, too?"

He chuckled, shaking his head. "That falls into the different category. The much different end of that scale."

"Really?" I couldn't picture Callum any less amazing than how he was here.

"At home, I work, I go to school, I help my mom around the house. Here, I just get to do the things I love, all day, every day." He tipped his head to look up at the sky. He smiled. "Back home, I'm more grunt worker than deity."

"Don't you miss this, though? Not a lot of whitewater to raft or rocks to climb, right?"

"Yeah, not a lot of wide-open spaces in my hood." He held his arms out like this church stoop in quiet Flagstaff was his hood.

"So what do you do when you're stuck in a concrete jungle for ten months every year?"

The corners of his eyes lined. "I'm pretty much a regular at the indoor climbing wall and log a lot of highway miles on the weekends getting out of town and trying to find any patch of earth that has some kind of elevation to it."

I sighed, feeling kind of bad for him. He was supposed to be in the wild, not enclosed in some maze of urban sprawl.

"How do you go from here to there?" I asked.

His forehead creased. "I make a lot of good memories here I take back with me there."

"Like flying down a mountain on a bike at fifty miles an hour or seeing how many class-five rapids you can make your bitch?"

He smiled at me, nodding. "That, or sitting on the steps of some old church and having a crazy-flavored ice cream with some girl who hasn't figured out I'm kind of a pain in the ass."

EIGHTEEN

"You've been gone for almost a month and my life has shriveled into nothingness. When are you escaping that place?" Emerson whined on the other end of the phone.

"It's not that bad. Plus, I'm making decent money, so I'll definitely have a set of wheels by the end of the summer."

"'It's not that bad,'" Emerson repeated. "Okay, where the hell is my best friend, Phoenix, and who are you?"

I rolled my eyes as I stepped outside the cabin. Harry had had a busy day canoeing and learning how to make a tepee, so he'd crashed after dinner. Dad and Mom were locked behind their bedroom door, arguing, so I'd dropped my fancy sound-canceling headphones over his ears before snagging my backpack and bolting for the door.

"You should come visit sometime if you want. That way you can see for yourself why this place doesn't blow like I thought it would. Really."

"Yeah, not happening." Emerson sounded like she was cringing. "Bugs, dirt, snakes, families, singing around a campfire, and a serious shortage of cute boys. There is nothing about that equation that says summer vacation."

"Who said there weren't any cute boys up here?"

Emerson was quiet just long enough that I realized I'd made a fumble. So far, I'd managed to steer clear of the Callum topic with her since I wasn't sure how to explain him to her when I couldn't explain him to myself. Or, at least, I couldn't explain him and me. Did we have something? Did he recognize it or was it pathetically one-sided? If we had something, would anything even become of it? If something did become of it, what would happen at the end of summer? And if, against all the high school romance odds, we managed to make it past senior year, what would happen after? I was off to college; he was deep in undecided land.

"That's it, isn't it?" Emerson hissed. "There's a boy who's come into the picture. Right?"

I winced. I couldn't lie to my best friend, but I wasn't eager to try to explain Callum and me. "Maybe?"

"I knew it," Emerson squealed. "What's his name? How old is he? Where does he live when he's not camped out in some rustic, rodent-ridden cabin in Arizona?"

"The cabins aren't rodent-ridden. They aren't presidential suites, but they're not that bad." I crossed my fingers, hoping she'd roll with the living-space topic detour, but I doubted it.

"And there's that term again. 'Not that bad . . .'" I could almost picture her tapping her chin. "You're not turning into one of those hippies who want to live off the land and go join some wacky cult that makes them eat hemp and kale and brainwashing at every meal before chasing it down with a spiked cup of Kool-Aid, are you?"

I'd held back the other sighs, but not this one. "I don't even like Kool-Aid."

"They don't really care if you like it so long as it goes down the hatch and shuts off all major internal organs."

"Emerson . . ." I'd had a long day. Usually talking to her made the day better, but it was kind of swinging the other direction tonight.

"Phoenix," she fired back, matching my tone. "Come on. Talk to me. That's what best friends do."

"I know," I said, pulling a tiny flashlight from my pocket and turning it on. I didn't want to take a wrong turn and spend the night lost in the woods. "It just feels like there's so much to talk about I don't even know where to begin. Or how to explain most of it." I could feel my eyes thinking about getting watery when I thought about my family and the end of the summer. So much uncertainty.

"Is this about what's going on with your parents?" This time, Emerson's voice was gentle.

"What hasn't been about my parents the past two years of my life?"

There was silence on the other end. "This might not be the right time to mention it, Phoenix, but I swore I'd tell you the next time I talked to you." I braced myself as Emerson went quiet again. "My mom saw something in the paper a few days ago. You know how she is, has to be in everyone's business all the time. She saw your parents' names on a bankruptcy list. . . ."

If Emerson's parents had seen it, so would parents of my other friends. Parents of my not-so-much friends would, too. The whole school would know by the time I walked through the doors the first day of senior year that my family had zip in the bank and zip in most everything else.

"Are you still there?" Emerson asked when I stayed silent. "I know reception up there sucks."

She was trying to make me smile, or at least give me a moment to lighten up. I managed a phony laugh. "I knew things weren't going stellar in the money department for them. I just didn't realize how rock bottom it had gotten."

"So I'm guessing from your surprise they haven't told you yet?" Emerson paused and sighed. "I'm a jerk for bringing it up. My parents said I shouldn't, but I couldn't keep something like that from you."

"No, it's okay. I appreciate you telling me. That's why you're my best friend." I had to stop and lean against one of the trees lining the path. As angry as I tried to convince myself I was, all I wanted to do was curl into a ball and cry. My life was falling apart in front of my eyes, and I couldn't do anything to stop it. "I know it must have been hard telling me. Thank you, Emerson."

"Oh crap, you're crying, aren't you?" Her voice took on a frantic edge.

I sniffed and stomped my sneaker into the soft earth to vent some emotion. It managed to keep my eyes from spilling over. "No, I'm good."

From her pause, I knew what kind of expression was on her face.

"Okay, so maybe I'm not good, but I'm not crying. And I will be good once I let this all settle in." I stomped the ground a few more times before shoving away from the tree.

"So enough with the heavy, then. . . . Who's this guy?"

I rolled my eyes and continued down the path. "Good night, Emerson."

"Come on, just one teeny-tiny, juicy bit?"

"Next time. I'm about to hit my data limit for the month with my phone, and I wouldn't want my parents to have to file for bankruptcy twice."

"You don't have to say a thing. Just snap a picture and send it my way."

"A picture's worth a thousand words?" I said just as the soft glow of lights came into view at the end of the path.

"A picture of a cute boy is worth a million."

"Good night, Emerson," I repeated.

"Good night. Have sweet, cute boy dreams."

The line went dead, but I was pretty sure it had more to do with the spotty reception up here than Emerson hanging up.

I tucked my phone into my pocket and kept moving in the direction of the lights. I'd only visited this end of camp a few times and never at night. This was where the staff was housed, and even though it wasn't off-limits, I didn't really have a good reason to come here. Except tonight I did.

My backpack was heavy with study guides and books. My plans for studying in the cabin had been foiled by my parents' impromptu fight, but I knew there were plenty of picnic tables and benches staggered around the staff cabins.

Of course, there were lots of tables and chairs and benches in the main part of the camp, too, but I didn't want to chance being interrupted by Ben, who was a fan of long conversations, or kids itching to pull a prank on an unsuspecting victim. At least out here, I knew I'd be left alone.

At least I thought I'd be alone, until the first table I noticed was occupied by someone else who was leaned over a handful of open books, rapping a pencil against the table like he was playing a drum solo at a rock concert.

"So you'd rather let an imaginary tutor help you than me. What a compliment." I moved toward the table.

Callum finished reading what it was he was studying, then slowly glanced up at me.

"The imaginary kind says nicer things. Strokes my ego instead of stomping on it." Callum shuffled his stack of open books closer to his side of the table and motioned at the bench across from him.

I slid my backpack off and dropped it onto the table. "That's precious. But you've been avoiding me on this long enough, and I need a study partner." I slid onto the bench and unzipped my bag. "And a light."

"And a cup of coffee?" Callum tapped the ceramic cup in front of him.

"I don't like the taste of it, and caffeine makes me all jumpy," I said before shrugging. "So absolutely."

He smiled and slid off the bench. "One minute," he said, jogging toward the cabin behind us. So that was the one he lived in. The one he slept in.

Not that I cared.

He shoved through the screen door less than a minute later with another cup and the coffeepot. "Round two and three." He lifted the metal pot in his hand before finding an empty spot on the table to set it. "Just in case we need it." When he held out the cup he'd gotten for me, I reached for it, and our fingers brushed together. I don't know if it was just me reading too much into everything, but it felt like he kept his fingers where they were longer than he needed to.

When he finally did let go of the cup, he cleared his throat, sat down, and got back to studying like nothing had happened.

"You're studying SAT books." I waved at all his books before pulling out my own.

"I'm *trying* to study SAT books."

"So why has it taken you this long to ask me for the help I promised I'd give you a couple of weeks ago?"

"Technically, I'm not asking for your help right now. You just showed up and sat down, and you're mooching off my coffee." His pencil was in his mouth, but it couldn't hide his smile.

I took a small sip from the cup and tried not to grimace. "Your coffee sucks, and *technically*"—I matched my tone to his when he'd said it—"I'm a part of the camp staff, so am hereby authorized to use this picnic table."

He took a drink of his coffee and nodded at my bag. "What have you got in that thing? Did you steal the five-gallon tub of lard from the kitchen again?"

I curled my nose at the thought of a tub of lard that size. "I've got the same thing, actually, some of the exact same books as these." I started pulling one study guide after another until I had a tall stack in front of me.

Callum turned the stack so the spines were facing him. "I have or have had every single one of these." He tapped his pencil eraser against a few he had spread around him. "They weren't very helpful."

"Yeah, well, they're helpful to me."

Callum flipped a page in the book he had right in front of him and got back to rapping his pencil against the book. "I'm surprised you haven't already taken the SAT since you're one of those 'decided' types."

I grabbed a pencil from my bag and deliberated on which book to work on—the most challenging one I had. "I already did take the test, but since I can take it again to try to get a better score, why wouldn't I want to?"

Callum glanced up at me like I'd lost it. "Because you value your time and mental health?"

I shook my head and opened my book to the last page I'd worked on. I had it bookmarked and worked out so I'd have gone through it all by the time I took the test in the fall. I wasn't about to let anything like a lack of planning get in the way of what I wanted. "Not nearly as much as I value getting into the college I want to."

Callum continued to pretend to go through his own book, but I could tell I was distracting him. The only reason I was able to tell that was because he was distracting me, too. Now that I was sitting here, across from him, I wasn't so sure this study arrangement was going to work.

"Why have you been avoiding me?" I asked after reading the same problem for the third time.

"We've been working together every day. How is that avoiding you?"

"*Other* than work, why have you been avoiding me?" I pressed. We hadn't "accidentally" run into each other on a morning run, and I swore that at least twice he'd turned and gone the opposite direction when he'd noticed me.

"I've been busy." He leaned over his book a bit more.

"Yeah, busy avoiding me."

"Not avoiding," he said. "Thinking."

"Thinking about what?" When I realized I was tapping my pencil like he was, I tucked it behind my ear.

"Thinking about if I really want to give you a front-row seat to the Callum the Test Bomber Show." He looked up for a moment, and he almost looked embarrassed.

"Listen, if you're uncomfortable with me helping you with this stuff, that's cool. I promise I won't play tutor if you don't want me to. But I do need to study, and if you're doing the same, maybe we can do it together." I bit my lip and paused. Why did I feel so awkward suggesting we study together?

"Because misery loves company?"

I smiled down at my book. "Something like that."

After that, we were quiet. Nothing but the soft hum of the lanterns and the buzz of crickets. I was just starting to work the problem I'd read a record number of five times when Callum groaned.

"Wow. So I never thought studying for this damn test could get any harder, and then you go and sit across from me. . . ." He slammed his book closed.

"Usually one must have the books open in order to study." I threw his book open again.

"If I thought it would help, I'd take your advice, but since nothing short of brain-replacement surgery would help my chances of scoring higher than a twelve hundred on the SAT, I'm not going to waste my time." He slammed his book closed again and moved it out of my reach.

I made myself take a full breath before saying anything. "So what's the problem?"

"The problem is a baboon has a better chance of scoring higher on this thing than I do," he grumbled as he chewed at the end of the eraser. No wonder he had such a tough time with tests—by the time he actually calmed down enough to take it, he'd rapped and chewed his pencil to slivers.

"Come on, Callum. You're smart. There's something else going on besides your brain needing to be surgically replaced." I ignored him when he huffed over the *smart* part.

"Smart people don't set record lows on every test that gets slapped down in front of them."

I rolled my eyes. I wasn't used to him being so defeatist, and I didn't like it. I liked the confident, I-can-save-the-world-and-navigate-class-five-rapids-at-the-same-time version. "What's the equation for the surface area of a cube?" I threw out randomly.

His eyes narrowed in confusion. "What?"

I didn't blink as I repeated, "The surface area of a cube. What is it?"

He didn't blink as he answered, "Six s squared."

"What's the area of a circle?"

He didn't pause. "Pi r squared."

"What's the order of operations?"

"PEMDAS," he fired off with a shrug.

"Huh?"

He exhaled. "Parentheses, exponents, multiplication, division, addition, subtraction."

I was ready to pop off another list of questions, but I stopped. He knew this stuff. He *clearly* knew it. So what was the deal with the test flopping?

"I know," he said like he was reading my mind. "It doesn't make sense. If I know the stuff I'm being tested on, the actual test should be pretty easy, right?"

I answered with a shrug to be polite.

"But it's like when I get in front of a test, I get this tunnel vision or something, and I can't focus on the problems in front of me. Instead, my mind wants to work out everything else besides the problems on the test." He dropped his pencil and scrubbed at his face. "I read the same problem a dozen times and I still can't figure out what it's asking me to do. Sometimes I feel like I'm taking a test written in a different language. Most of the time I just feel like my brain's packed its bags and taken an extended vacation."

I nodded as I listened to him, thinking. "So you know the stuff—you just can't prove that on a test." I paused, not knowing what to do. When I'd offered to help him, I thought it would be by pounding equations into his memory and working through some reading comprehension sections together. I wasn't sure how to help with something like this. "Do you think it's more an issue with you being distracted when you take a test or like just being totally test-phobic or something?"

Callum spread his arms at the stacks of books around him. They were all broken in and worn at the edges from overuse. "Do I look like I've had much success answering that riddle?"

I kept nodding as my brain fired, searching for solutions or, if nothing else, something helpful. "Have you ever tried any deep-breathing techniques?"

"I've never even heard of deep-breathing techniques."

I filed that away as something that might be helpful . . . *somewhat.* "What about positive affirmations when you find yourself getting stuck? Have you ever tried that before?"

"If I knew what"—he crinkled his nose like I'd just suggested dissecting a seal pup—"positive affirmations were, maybe I could have given them a shot."

"Okay, okay." I tapped my pencil against my temple slowly, the wheels inside still turning. "Why don't we run through a quick practice test together and see how it goes?"

"I already know how mine will go."

I lifted an eyebrow at him.

"Down. In a blaze of no glory."

I groaned in frustration. "We really need to get you on the positive-affirmation bandwagon before you get trapped in downer land for the rest of your life."

"I hate bandwagons."

"Yeah, because I hadn't already figured that out from your playlists and hairstyle."

He slid his baseball cap off and shook his head. Half of it was still wet from what I guessed was a shower, and the other half was sticking out in every direction except down. "I don't have a hairstyle."

I clucked my tongue. "Exactly."

After that, I pretended to get back to my practice test. For a minute and a half, at least.

"So that's it? Deep breathing and positive affirmations? That's your answer to me going from an eight hundred to a twelve hundred?"

I sighed to myself and, keeping my eyes on my book, I opened his and slapped my hand down on it. "For now, yeah. I'll look into it when I'm able to get in front of a computer screen, but in the meantime, give deep breathing a try."

Across the table, Callum started inhaling and exhaling so loudly it was like he was in labor.

When he realized I wasn't going to be distracted, he got back to his book. He shifted on the bench thirteen times, sighed seven times, and groaned four times, then rapped his pencil God knows how many hundred times.

"Stop with the spastic pencil drumming, already," I said, snapping my hand down on his pencil. No wonder he couldn't focus—I sure as hell couldn't with that noise.

"It calms me," he said defensively.

"Really?" I set my pencil neatly into the seam of the book. "And this is why you've nailed all your tests?"

His forehead lined. "You're mean."

"Hey, I'm not here to be nice to you. I'm here to help you." I gave him a big smile.

He didn't buy it, though. "And this 'help' requires you to use tough love?"

I tried not to laugh at the irony of him giving me a hard time for tough love. He was the tough love master. I had the emotional wounds to prove it, too. "Do you think Helen Keller learned sign language because Anne Sullivan was all gentle and nice?"

His mouth dropped open. Then he blinked. "Are you comparing me to Helen Keller?"

I had to bite the inside of my cheek to keep from laughing. "No, you are."

He continued to stare at me. "I have no words."

"Well, if you think of any, you can always sign them into my hand."

He shook his head. "No. Words."

"Hey, less talking, more studying." I whacked his book with my hand and took my own advice. If I continued to let him distract me the way I already had, we'd both be bombing the SATs this fall.

He shrugged, giving me a look that suggested I was the one to blame for the talking.

I'd made it through a whole two and a half writing sample questions when one of the cabin doors burst open and Naomi bounced down the stairs like she was a woman on a mission. When she saw us, she smiled and waved. "What's up, you two? Some kind of late-night rendezvous?" She wiggled her eyebrows.

I shifted on the bench, feeling like I'd been caught rounding second base on the principal's desk by the big man himself. Callum finished whatever he'd been reading or *trying* to read, and tapped his study guide. "Try late-night study session."

Naomi shuddered. "Well, if you'd rather do something else, for once"—she was looking at Callum when she said that—"we're all getting together down at the arcade in town to raise some hell."

"As fun as hell-raising sounds, I think I'm gonna take a pass. Make up for my absence." Callum waved and got back to his study guide.

"I don't know why I keep asking." Naomi exchanged a look with me before motioning my way. "You in, Phoenix? Ethan's a TBD, so you may or may not have to ward off his shameless advances."

"Thanks, but I've got to study, too." I smiled in her direction. I liked Naomi. She was a girl who seemed to know what she wanted and didn't feel the need to explain or apologize for any of it. "Have fun, though."

She groaned loud enough the toad that had been croaking stopped. "You two are a couple of fun-mongers."

"I prefer the term *rationer* over *monger*. I don't hoard fun; I portion it out in carefully measured qualities. You know, that way I make sure I don't run out before I hit my expiration date." Callum flipped the page of his book, stone-faced.

This time, I shook my head at Naomi. "And that's my cue to scoot." She fired a wink at me and crunched down the gravel pathway to where the staff's vehicles were parked. She was in heels, and her nails looked freshly painted—hell-raising was definitely on her agenda.

Naomi was one of the only counselors who seemed to go out of her way to try to include Callum. I wasn't sure if this was because she was thoughtful or if she didn't take a hint well or if, perhaps, it had something more to do with a crush of the secret kind. Callum might have been odd sixty ways to Sunday, but in the *Teenage Girl's Bible of Boys,* he was the holy trinity of hot, aloof, and available.

I decided to test my secret-crush theory. "Have you and Naomi, you know . . ." I cleared my throat and tried to look natural. "Did you guys ever date . . . or anything?"

Or anything? Really, Phoenix? Good thing I was studying the English portion of the SAT because my mastery of it was seriously lacking.

Callum looked like he was repeating my question to himself. At first, he looked confused. And then that confusion ironed out into surprise. "What? No." He shook his head. "God, no."

"Why are you acting like going on a date with Naomi would be the highest form of punishment known to Callum-kind?" I asked, hiding my smile.

"Don't pull that taking-words-out-of-my-mouth thing on me. I never said she wasn't date-worthy. I just said she wasn't date-worthy for me." Callum waved his pencil at me like both he and his number two were against me.

"Why not?"

"Because we work together." He flipped another page and shrugged. "And as a personal policy, I like to keep my life as uncomplicated as possible, and girls have a way of doing the opposite." He glanced up from his book. "What about you? Have you found anyone here or back home date-worthy?"

My expression faltered for a second. Mainly because I wondered if his motives for asking me were the same as mine—to assess just how available or unavailable the other person was.

Going back into character, I gave a shrug. "I've recently adopted that personal policy of yours as well."

"Why recently?" he asked. "If it has to do with Ethan, no explanation needed."

"It doesn't have to do with Ethan."

"So if it isn't Ethan, who or what's responsible for the dating policy change?" Callum was trying to make it seem like he was studying, but his eyes weren't moving across the page.

"Oh, you know, after I walked in on my boyfriend hooking up with someone else. Because it would have been so inconvenient if he'd broken up with me first, right?"

Callum grunted and shook his head. "God, what a tool." His jaw clenched first, then his fists. "Your trust issues are really starting to make sense the more I get to know you."

I made a face, not sure how to take that. "Yay?"

Getting back to my books after that, I pretended the reading comprehension paragraph on the growth of the colonies was killing it at eleven o'clock at night while I sat across a picnic bench from the one guy on the planet I might have considered abandoning that no-complications policy for.

I knew he was my boss on paper, and that summer romances never worked, and that I'd just gotten out of a relationship and shouldn't be looking to hop into another one so quickly. I knew he was temperamental at best and unpredictable at worst. I knew he rubbed me in more wrong ways than right ones, and that I probably did the same with him.

But at that moment, sitting across from him, pretending to study for our SATs, I wasn't thinking about the heap of reasons we didn't make sense.

I was only thinking about the reasons we did.

I was just reaching for my cup of coffee at the same time he was reaching for his. Instead of the handles of our cups, our fingers wound up around each other's. I froze, not sure what to do. I'd let him make the call. He could pull away or he could keep his fingers twisted through mine. Either way, I was letting him decide because I needed to know. I'd been pretty obvious—I thought—that I might have sort of been into him. He'd given away nothing.

It was time to find out if Callum felt something for me like I did for him.

At first, he looked almost as frozen as I knew I did, but after a moment, his expression thawed and he got back to studying. His fingers didn't pull away from mine.

I tried to get back to studying. God, I tried. But how was I supposed to focus on a one-page story when I couldn't focus long enough to get through the first sentence? How was I supposed to study for the SATs when we were holding hands . . . or holding fingers or whatever it was we were doing?

The pads of his fingers were rough like his palms looked, but the sides of his fingers were soft and smooth. When I glanced down at our hands, his fingers looked twice the size of mine, which was a big deal since I didn't exactly have dainty hands. His skin was warm, but not so hot it felt searing. It was just right, like pressing my palm into a fresh blanket that had just come from the dryer.

"You're not my trainer anymore, you know?" I said, once I'd accepted that studying was not in the stars for the night. Especially if the hand-slash-finger-holding continued. "Just in case you're worried about that."

I didn't realize Callum had stopped rapping his pencil until he set it down on the table beside him. "That's just one of the million things I'm worried about." He looked at me the whole time he said this, but I could tell it was hard for him to not look away. It was almost like he was ashamed of what he was saying. I wasn't sure why.

"What else?" I pressed, wanting to know.

Callum looked at our hands tied together. The skin at the corners of his eyes creased. "Everything else."

I was about to reply with a *Thanks for being so specific* or something along those lines when the door of the cabin behind us exploded open. A familiar face came loping down the stairs. Ethan didn't miss us at first like Naomi had. Instead, we seemed to be the very first thing he noticed.

"So this is why you've been shooting me down?" Ethan strutted toward us with a tipped smile on his face. Like Naomi, he looked dressed to party, too. "Because your tastes lean more toward the rugged and manly type."

I pretended to focus on studying. "The manly part for sure," I muttered just loud enough for him to hear.

Across the table, Callum laughed silently.

"All right, I'll let you two get back to your 'studying.'" Ethan winked at us. "I'm on the prowl for my future ex-girlfriend."

"Don't let us keep you from destiny." I swept my arm in the direction of the employees' cars.

"Real quick, though, what are you guys 'studying'?" Ethan leaned closer to see what we had sprawled all over the table. He didn't look long before he bounced his brows a few times in my direction. "Chemistry?"

"Good-bye, Ethan," I sighed.

He chuckled as he started backing away. "French?" He fired off next. *"Voulez-vous coucher avec moi? Ce soir?"*

Callum's hand tightened around mine slightly as his jaw went rigid.

"You can go *coucher* yourself," I said to him. *"Ce soir.* And the one after that. And the one after that, too."

"Okay, so not French." Ethan was almost out of sight, but his voice had a way of carrying. "I got it. You're studying . . . human anatomy. Right?"

"Good-bye, Ethan," I half shouted in his direction.

"He's persistent. You have to give him that." Callum finished laughing and picked up his pencil.

"I wish he'd take his persistence somewhere else already." I sighed and scribbled a note down in my study guide that had nothing to do with the actual subject I was studying. I started to reach for my mug.

I didn't make it far.

Callum's fingers tightened around mine and held my hand where it was. I'd forgotten we were holding hands. I'd forgotten we were *still* holding hands.

Callum squeezed my hand gently, continuing to hold it in place. "It calms me" was all he said, before he started working out the first problem on the page.

NINETEEN

I was doing it. Leading my first official activity as a newly minted Camp Kismet counselor. It was a pretty great feeling.

I'd taken the lead and Evan was bringing up the rear, and in the middle were fifteen campers with varying degrees of mountain biking experience. Harry had come along today, not about to miss the first activity I got to lead, and even though he'd become more comfortable on a bike this summer, he was still a bit nervous when it came to the more technical stuff. Sure, everyone was on real mountain bikes and we were pedaling down trails, but the elevation stayed pretty much the same, and other than an occasional root or branch, the trail was impediment-free.

At first, I'd been relieved when Callum told me which trail I'd be leading campers on, but after mile two, I was fighting off a series of yawns.

The first few campers behind me had been whining about it for the last ten minutes and had eventually joined me in the yawning department. I was in the lead, and I had to set the pace to accommodate for the least-skilled rider. Which was Harry. Which meant I was clipping down a flat trail at about the pace my grandma's motorized scooter peaked at.

What felt like five and a half hours later, we hit the mile four marker. Just in time, too, because it looked as if half the campers were about to tumble off their bikes from falling asleep at the handlebar.

The fifteen campers crawled off their bikes and leaned them up against a tree, and most took a seat on the ground. Evan waved down at me, and I was pretty sure I'd seen him more awake at five o'clock in the morning when we had to show for an early activity. I found Harry a few bikes in front of Evan and walked back to see how he was doing.

"How are you doing, Harry?" I asked, moving in to help him position his bike against the tree. He slid in front of me so he could do it himself.

It went against everything in me, but I let him do it on his own.

"Good." He shrugged a shoulder.

"Having a good time?" I fished. If anyone could be relied upon to find something thrilling about today's ride, it would be the sheltered ten-year-old who'd only learned to ride a bike without training wheels two years ago.

"Pretty good." Another shrug.

His back was to me, so I stepped around in front of him. It was just as I'd feared. Even my little brother, the one who I knew to be the least experienced on the ride, looked bored to tears. Actual tears. His eyes were red-rimmed and everything.

"Oh my god. You're bored. You're not having any fun at all, are you?" I groaned and banged my helmet against the tree again. "Is it really that bad? I thought it was . . ." I chewed my lip as I searched for the right word. "Scenic."

"Oh yeah, scenic for sure." Harry unsnapped the buckle of his helmet. "I had plenty of time to take in the scenery."

"Well, excuse me. I didn't know I was talking to a mountain biking pro. Maybe you'd like to lead the rest of the way." I swept my hand up to the front of the trail.

Harry's face lit up. "Really?"

I frowned. "No. Not really." I grumbled the rest of my way up to Evan, who was, yep, snoring. I nudged him in the side with the toe of my sneaker. He didn't move.

"Evan," I said, toeing him a little harder.

Still nothing.

Grabbing his water bottle from the bike cage, I twisted it open and squeezed a stream down on him. It was one thing for campers to be taking a nap, but he was on the clock. No snoozing allowed.

He didn't jerk awake like I thought he would. Instead he groaned, stretched his arms above his head, and opened his eyes. "Thanks. I didn't have time for a shower this morning, so I can check that off the to-do list now." He wiped the water from his face and sat up.

"The campers are bored," I said.

Evan leaned past me and skimmed his eyes down the line. His brows moved into his hairline. "No shit."

"What should I do?" I crouched down beside him, hoping he'd have some magical solution for how to fix this. I couldn't have everyone avoiding my future activities once word spread around camp that I was Counselor Boring. I didn't want to be downgraded to arts and crafts time in the dining hall every afternoon.

"Uh, I don't know . . ." Evan blinked at me. "Not be boring?"

"Have any suggestions?" I asked impatiently.

"Yeah. Stop crawling. There's a tip," Evan said around a yawn.

I resisted the urge to punch him in the arm. I liked Evan. He was a laid-back, chill guy who was always willing to step in and lend a hand. Unlike his brother, he didn't look at me as if I was housed inside a display case.

When he yawned again, I wasn't so sure how much more I liked Evan over Ethan.

"Callum told me to hold to six to seven miles per hour on this ride. That's exactly what I've been doing." I'd checked the speedometer clipped onto my bike so many times over the past four miles I had a neckache.

"And if Callum told you to lead a watching-the-grass-grow activity tomorrow, would you do that, too?" Evan quirked a brow at me.

"Are you suggesting I basically go against what I was told to do?" I felt my forehead line. Evan didn't strike me as a rule breaker. He didn't even come across as much of a rule bender.

"There's a difference between breaking all the rules and making a few adjustments to them." He clucked his tongue. "I'm suggesting you make a few minor adjustments before the troops stage a revolution."

I swallowed and found myself looking at Harry. He was slumped on the ground, kicking at a tree root. He looked like I was forcing him to watch an eighties romance movie marathon—while wearing matching pajamas and fuzzy bunny slippers. "What kind of adjustments?"

"Your call. But good luck getting any of these campers to sign up for whatever activities you're leading on your second and third day on your own." He tipped his head at one of the campers up toward the front who looked like he was napping.

"Because unless you're giving a guided tour through the sleep cycle, you're leading your next mountain bike ride alone."

I popped to a stand. "Aren't you supposed to be here for support?"

"Support, sure. Fanning sunshine up your ass, not so much." He flashed me a wide smile and shrugged. "Hey, where are you going?" he called after me when I started to walk away.

"Off to make a few adjustments," I replied, just loud enough for him to hear as I stormed past the bored or napping campers. Now I was pissed. Evan had pretty much just accused me of being a snoozefest, and every last camper on the ride was showing the same with their expressions or chorus of yawns. I was pissed at Callum, too—for assigning me such a rookie ride for my first trip. I got that he wasn't going to assign me anything like advanced navigating or river kayaking, but come on. This was an activity that had *senior center* stamped all over it.

When I got to my bike, I cupped my hands around my mouth and yelled down the line, "Heading out, everyone! Make sure your tires are good and your helmets are on! We're going to up the pace a little, so be ready!"

One of the guys up front nudged his wife. "From a snail's pace to a turtle's? Can't wait."

I waited for everyone to get their helmets on and give their tires a quick check. Harry was smiling up at me, his eyes excited. It was the first excitement I'd seen since heading out from camp.

"Everyone good?" I called back.

A few verbalized their answers, but most nodded. Reluctantly.

I climbed onto my bike and started down the trail at a slow

pace, waiting for everyone to follow. At the end of the line, Evan fanned his hand over his mouth as he yawned at me. Shooting him a glare, I picked up the speed. Instead of cruising at six to seven miles per hour, I'd just tipped the eight miles per hour threshold.

When I glanced over my shoulder again, unlike the smiles and wide eyes I'd expected to see, I saw a whole lot of the same. What did it take to give these people a thrill, for crying out loud?

I knew there was a Y in the trail ahead. I'd never taken the detour at the upcoming Y, but I knew enough about the rest of this trail to know the first half of the ride had been the "exciting" part.

So when that Y popped out of the trail, faster than I remembered it coming, I took it. The camper right behind me was so surprised by the sudden detour, he almost missed it. I glanced back as long as I dared, just to make sure everyone was following, then turned my attention back on the trail.

Compared with the one we'd been on, this one was narrow. Just wide enough for a bike to wind through, but not wide enough for three to ride side by side like we would on the designated trail. It wasn't just narrow, though—it was winding, too. It felt like as soon as I'd whipped my handlebars one direction, I was forcing them the other direction a second later.

I was just starting to doubt my detour—I'd taken a dozen campers from the bunny hill to the black diamond of mountain bike trails—when I heard the sounds of . . . *excitement* coming from behind me.

They were having fun. They were enjoying the ride.

Day. Saved.

I allowed myself a smile and a pat on the back—I'd managed to troubleshoot a problem on my own on my very first day without having to run it by Callum first. I was a natural camp counselor. . . .

That was when I whipped around the next bend and saw where the trail led next: pretty much straight down.

My smile vanished in the time it took my stomach to lodge into my throat. I had too much speed and momentum to stop before I hit the start of the descent. Even if I had stopped, I would have caused a serious pileup if I came to an abrupt stop without warning the others behind me.

My bike bounced down the trail, and I kept tapping on the brakes just enough to keep my speed from spiraling out of control without locking them up and sending me over the handlebars.

In addition to the trail being steep and winding, it was covered with rocks jutting up from the ground. Most of them were small enough my tires could just roll right over them, but a few were large enough to cause a spill if someone didn't maneuver around them just right.

Once everyone had made it down safely, I was going to stop, pull Evan to the side to see just what I'd gotten myself into, and decide where to go from there. If this trail continued like this, none of us were going to make it to camp in one piece. I couldn't imagine my little brother on this thing and *not* hurting himself. What was I thinking, heading down a trail I'd never been on and knew nothing about when my little brother was following behind?

The guilt barely had time to settle in before my bike rolled onto level ground. I went just far enough so I was out of the way of the other campers flying down the trail before leaping off my bike and throwing it to the side. The trail was narrow, but I flew up it, managing to balance on the very edge while dodging the bikes speeding past. The excitement that had been on their faces two minutes ago was gone. Terror was more the look of things now.

I was counting off each bike that passed me. They were all managing to make it down the Descent of Doom on the seat of their bike, instead of somersaulting over it. Thank God. Helmets might have protected heads, but a person would need full-body armor to walk away from a fall on this part of the trail.

"Wait for me at the bottom of the hill," I shouted as they whizzed by.

Ten. Eleven. Twelve. Thirteen. I counted off, one at a time, and after thirteen whipped by me, there was a break in the procession. No one else was coming. There was a bend just behind me so I wasn't able to see up to the start of the descent, but I was just letting myself start to hope that Harry had punched his brakes before following his sister leaping off the proverbial cliff when I heard it.

The cry.

His cry.

My little brother's.

I choked on my own cry as I barreled up the rest of the trail. I lost my footing when I got to the bend in the trail and wiped out, but it didn't slow me down. I crawled until I was able to push myself up and had just lunged around the bend when I saw it.

Mayhem.

Destruction.

My worst nightmare.

Take your pick.

"Harry!" I powered up the rest of the trail like I wasn't climbing a solid 15 percent grade. "Harry!" I cried again, but if he'd heard me, he didn't answer.

I flew to the ground beside him. Evan had gotten to him

a moment before I had, along with the guy who'd been right behind Harry. Evan started throwing the bike off Harry, while the other guy looked like he wasn't sure what to do.

The front wheel of Harry's bike was bent. I tried not to even think about what kind of crash would have caused a bike wheel to bend.

"Hey, Danger Zone, how many toes am I holding up?" Evan crashed down onto his knees beside Harry once he'd tossed the bike aside.

Like the guy gaping down at Harry across from me, I stayed just as frozen.

When Harry didn't answer, Evan snapped his fingers in his face and held up three fingers again. "How many toes am I holding up, Harry?"

Harry cleared his throat. "Three," he whispered.

"This is serious." Evan managed a smile as he continued to hold his three fingers above Harry's face. "Because these are not toes."

Harry creased his forehead, confused. Then he smiled. "That was a good one," Harry said, his voice just as loopy.

Evan shrugged. "Anything hurting?" He was keeping his cool, but I could tell he was worried. When Harry answered with a shrug, Evan asked, "Can you move your toes?" He waited for Harry's feet to move. "Your hands?"

When Harry started to move his hands, he grimaced. "My wrist."

Evan nodded. "Do you mind if I check it real quick?"

Harry shook his head and moved his arm toward Evan.

Evan had barely put his fingers on Harry's wrist before Harry screeched in pain.

"Stop! You're hurting him," I cried.

He let go instantly. "The girl who just led a beginners'

group of mountain bikers down an advanced trail accusing me of hurting a camper?" Evan's brows went high as he continued, "Can you say *irony*?"

I was too upset to argue.

"Do you think you can sit up, big guy?" Evan asked Harry, totally calm. It reminded me so much of Callum he might as well have been the one kneeling across from me. No wonder Callum put so much trust in his counselors. Too bad it didn't apply to me.

"Yeah. I think so." Harry's voice was still a whisper, but it was getting stronger. The shock must have been wearing off. Or maybe it was just setting in.

When Harry started to rock himself up, Evan put his hand behind his back to help him the rest of the way.

"You've either sprained or broken your wrist. I'm not sure which, and I don't want to feel around anymore since it's sore." Evan lowered his head so it was right in line with Harry's. "We're going to need an X-ray to know for sure, so let's get you back to camp."

Harry nodded, looking at Evan the whole time.

"Are you okay with me carrying you to camp? There's a shortcut I know, and it's only about a mile." Evan waited for Harry's answer, but I could tell he was in a hurry to get him moving.

Harry took a breath. "I'm okay to walk." I was just about to object when he added, "Really. It's just my wrist, and that way we'll get there faster."

"Then how about we get going?" Evan stood up, holding his arms out when Harry did the same, just in case he went down. "There's this cute nurse who works the day shift at the ER in town. If we hurry, I'll introduce you."

"You've been to the ER before?" Harry asked, taking his

glasses from Evan after Evan cleaned them off on his shirt. I didn't know how they were still in one piece.

"So many times they all know my name by now." Evan winked and pointed at a scar on his forearm, before pulling up the sleeve of his shirt on the same arm and revealing an even longer, more jagged-looking scar. "That's just my left arm. It would take until midnight to show you the rest, and by then the cute nurse will be clocked out for the day."

Harry smiled. The real kind, not the rummy, loopy, I'm-in-shock kind. "What about my bike?"

"Leave it. I'll come back for it later." Evan kicked at the front wheel of Harry's bike. "Nice job, by the way, on taco-ing your tire. Seasoned pros only get the bragging rights of taco-ing a tire once or twice in their lifetimes. You've got skill, my man."

"I think it's more a lack of skill that's to blame for . . . taco-ing my tire, but thanks." Harry cradled his injured arm against his chest as he stared at his bent bike wheel.

"Hey, you okay here?" Evan moved up beside me and lowered his voice. "I don't think it's broken, but it's definitely sprained. I need to get him back, so that means you're responsible for the rest of the campers." Evan nudged me. "Preferably with no more injuries or busted bike wheels. Think you can manage that?"

He waited for me to answer, but I couldn't give him one. How could I get fourteen people to camp safely after what had happened?

"Listen, about a tenth of a mile past the bottom of this hill, there's a trail that Ys off to the right. Take it. Do not— and I repeat a million and one times—do not continue on this trail. It goes from this"—Evan flashed his arms down the steep descent—"to gnarly real fast. Take the right up ahead and you'll all be back in camp in a half hour."

I couldn't imagine a trail getting even more "gnarly" than what I'd already experienced. Bottom of the hill. Tenth of a mile. Y to the right. I repeated the instructions in my head until they were stuck.

"I'm not sure I can do it." My voice sounded small and pathetic—the way the rest of me felt, too.

"You don't have to be sure. You just have to do it." Evan unsnapped his helmet and balanced it on the end of his handlebar. He'd propped both Harry's and his bikes up against a couple of trees just off the trail and then followed after Harry. who was already cutting through the trees. "See you at camp."

Harry was gone. He hadn't said good-bye. He hadn't even been able to look at me. Not that I could blame him. He trusted me, and I'd let him down. I should have been more careful. I should have done this, I shouldn't have done that—but I knew I had to fix my mistake.

I had to pull myself up by my shoelaces and get this done.

I had to be strong. When I'd never felt weaker.

I found the guy who was still huddled on the side of the trail. "Do you think you can grab your bike and walk it down to the bottom of the trail?"

"Yeah, yeah. I think so." He didn't sound confident, and he certainly didn't look confident.

"Would you rather walk? I'll get your bike down." I climbed the trail until I'd reached the guy's bike spread across the edge of the trail. "After you," I said.

"I knew he was going to crash. I watched him. . . ." The guy shook his head, his eyes wide. "It's the worst feeling, watching a kid fall like that and not being able to help him."

I made myself look away from where Harry had crashed. "Let's go check on everyone else. They're probably wondering about us." I started walking down the hill with his bike, and he finally started moving. The trail was steep, so we took each step slowly.

"Are you okay?" he asked me.

I thought about Harry. I thought about my parents. I thought about my life. "No," I said, answering that question truthfully for the first time in months.

TWENTY

Fourteen campers rolled into camp fifty-two minutes later. Fifteen had left for the ride. Fourteen out of fifteen might not have been bad odds in some situations—like, say, a pop quiz or maybe a winning streak—but it was unacceptable when it came to people's lives and what should have been an easy, breezy bike ride.

The camp was pretty quiet when we returned, matching the mood of the whole bike ride. Everyone knew what had happened to Harry and was worried, and even though I tried playing it off like he was going to be just fine and in good hands, I'd been experiencing an internal freak-out. It was all I could do not to throw my bike to the ground the second we hit Camp Kismet and leap into the first moving vehicle I came across heading into Flagstaff.

As it turned out, I didn't have to wait long before an old truck rolled up next to the bike shed just as I was locking the last one up. It was the same truck we'd used to haul the rafts to the river, and for a moment, my heart stopped. I wasn't sure what I was going to say to Callum yet. I didn't know how I was going to explain myself, if I was even going to try.

That was when I noticed who the driver was.

"I was just heading to the hospital to check on Harry. Want to catch a lift with me?" Ben had already leaned across the seat and thrown open the passenger door.

I finished locking the shed and leaped into the truck, hoping Ben was a fast driver. "Thanks," I muttered.

"No problem. Your mom left with Harry, and I waited to leave until you got back, figuring you'd want to go check on him yourself." Ben glanced in his rearview and both side-view mirrors before going. Forward. So much for hoping he was a fast driver. I'd be lucky if Mr. Safety-Conscious maintained a steady five below the speed limit.

"My dad went with them, right?" I asked as the truck crawled through the camp.

"Your dad left earlier today, so he wasn't here. I guess he had to get back to California to take care of something." Ben shrugged.

"I didn't know anything about him going back home."

"It must have been urgent," Ben suggested.

My teeth ground together as I focused on taking slow breaths. I knew I shouldn't have been surprised Dad had up and bailed on us with the excuse of "something urgent" needing to be taken care of, and maybe I wasn't really all that surprised . . . but I was pissed. It had been his idea to come here; he'd been MIA pretty much the entire time and fled the scene without any warning on the very day his son could have used the presence and support of his dad.

Figured.

"Harry . . . ," I started, swallowing the ball that had formed when I'd said his name. "Did he seem . . . okay?"

"He seemed good. Harry's a tough little guy." Ben smiled at the road as we crept along. "I had Evan drive them to the ER since your mom was in something of a panicked state."

I rolled down the window and leaned my head against the door so I could breathe in the fresh air. "Are you going to fire me?" I shifted on the seat. "It's okay if you do. I understand. I didn't do my job of taking care of the campers."

"No. I'm not." Ben tapped the brakes when a chipmunk scampered across the road a hundred feet in front of us. "You're human, so you make mistakes every once in a while. Comes with the territory."

My eyebrows came together. I wasn't sure what the point of his speech was, but it sounded like I wasn't getting the ax. Yet.

"But . . . ," I started, wondering just how much of the story he'd gotten from Evan and Harry.

"Callum's made plenty of his own mistakes, too. Evan too. And you can add my name to that list." Ben waved his hand. "That's the way we become better. Whether that's becoming better as a camp counselor or a big sister or a person in general, making mistakes along the way is inevitable. It's the painful part of the growing process."

I wondered how many mistakes a person was allowed to make before the growing-pain excuse expired.

"Mind telling that to Callum? Because I'm pretty sure I'm going to get a serious lecture when he sees me." I bit the corner of my lip. "Not that I don't deserve it . . ."

"Callum already knows that, but I think he sees something special in you. That's why he holds the bar a bit higher."

My head turned toward Ben. "Something special?"

"The way you pick yourself up, dust yourself off, and keep going. How you take care of Harry. He expects more from you because you're capable of more."

I slumped lower in the seat. "I'm not convinced."

When Ben came to a stop sign, he checked both ways, three times, before turning onto the road leading into Flagstaff.

"That's usually the way it goes. We convince everyone else first, but we're usually the last to realize just what we're capable of. Human nature."

I didn't have anything to say after that, and since we were almost to Flagstaff, I was starting to get antsy. I couldn't wait to see Harry. . . . At the same time, I was terrified to see him.

"Hey, you know who else that mistake policy applies to?" Ben said when we were stopped at a red light.

I was bouncing in my seat, able to see the hospital up ahead. "Besides everyone?"

"Dads. And moms." He must have not noticed my eye roll, because he kept going. "They make just as many mistakes as you and me because they think they're doing the right thing."

I bit my tongue to keep from replying. Ben obviously thought one way, and I thought the other.

When he pulled up to the emergency room entrance, I mumbled a quick thanks before flying through the door.

"Meet you inside," he called after me, but I was already rushing in.

"Harry Ainsworth?" I said, sliding to a stop at the reception desk. The woman just pointed her finger, and I started sprinting in the direction she'd indicated.

I could hear the familiar sound from a few doors down. Harry was laughing—I could have cried with relief. If he was laughing, he wasn't in pain. He was going to be okay. Laughter meant okay, right?

And then I heard the other voice coming from the room. I recognized that one, too.

I didn't think before bursting into the room. Two surprised faces turned my way. One was smiling. One was not.

I froze in place.

"I'll give you and your sister some privacy, Harry." Callum

stood up from the chair he'd been in and lifted his hand above Harry's good arm.

Harry high-fived him so hard the slap echoed through the room.

Callum shook his hand like it was stinging. "Easy there, Hulk. One sprained wrist is enough for one day."

"See ya, Callum!" Harry called after him as he headed for the door. *Marched* might have been the more fitting word for it, though.

"No more acrobatics on a mountain bike, okay?" Callum wouldn't look at me as he passed. It was like I'd become invisible or something.

Harry laughed again, waving good-bye.

Callum waved back and left the room, closing the door behind him. He hadn't acknowledged me with even one look.

With Callum gone, the room grew quiet. I swallowed and looked up at Harry. He was sitting on the edge of an exam table, his wrist bandaged, and he was staring at the floor, swinging his legs, waiting.

I didn't have a clue what I'd say when I finally got to see him, so I went with what came naturally.

"I'm sorry," I said, rushing toward him. I was crying. "I'm so sorry, Harry. I never should have turned onto a trail I wasn't familiar with. I should have stuck with the plan and not been a stupid, stupid idiot." I crashed down onto the spot beside him and wrapped both arms around him, resting my head on his shoulder. I was still crying. I didn't think Harry had ever seen me cry before. "I'm sorry you crashed, and I'm sorry you got hurt, and I'm sorry you're in this emergency room, and I'm sorry I'm such an irresponsible disaster of a sister." I paused long enough to sniff and catch my breath. "And I'm sorry I'm getting tears and snot all over your favorite T-shirt."

Harry wound his arm around me. He patted it. Gently. Like he was trying to comfort me. "It's okay, Phoenix. I'm okay," he said. "You're not a disaster of a sister, either. You're, like, the best sister ever."

That made my soft cries turn into sobs. Harry's pats became harder the louder I cried. "Why are you crying? I'm okay. Better than okay because I got a cool bandage out of the deal." Harry raised his bandaged wrist in front of me, which, of course, made me cry even harder. "Major bragging rights."

"I'm supposed to take care of you, not send you crashing down a steep trail you shouldn't have been on in the first place."

"You didn't know that was going to happen." Harry's shoulders lifted.

"But you trusted me. And I totally crapped all over that." I wiped my face off with the back of my arm.

"No, you didn't."

"Yes, I did," I argued.

"No. You didn't."

I closed my eyes and held him tight. I knew we'd been lucky today. Things could have ended so much worse than one sprained wrist. The bike and ground had taken most of the damage, but next time Harry might not be so lucky.

"Yes. I did. You're never going to trust me again. And I don't blame you for it, either."

Harry stopped patting my back, but he left his arm where it was. "What do you mean? You're my sister. Of course I still trust you."

"Really?"

"Of course. You're my big sister. So that's, like, a get-out-of-jail-free card."

I heard the even heel strikes step through the door, but I didn't pull away from Harry. I wasn't ready to get a lecture from

Mom on responsibility yet. I was just waiting for her to go bad cop on me, but instead, she sighed. The mostly tired, relieved-sounding kind.

"Mind if I wiggle in there?" She wound her own arms around Harry and me and held us tight.

"I love you." Her whisper was kind of broken, but her arms tightened again.

After shaking off the surprise of hearing those three words come from Mom, I added, "I love you, too, Harry." I tried to wipe my eyes with the sleeve of my shirt so she wouldn't see I'd been crying.

"I was including you in that, you know, Phoenix." Mom's hand combed through my ponytail. She hadn't done that in years. "I love *you*, too."

Harry was grinning, like this was some kind of fun family reunion at an amusement park. He didn't notice or get that Mom and I were teary. "I love you," he chimed in, then paused. "Just in case either of you are wondering, I meant that for you both." His legs started swinging from the exam table. He was getting antsy, ready to get out of there.

"I love you," I whispered. When I glanced over at Mom, it was like I was seeing the real person that I'd been missing. Or maybe she'd been there the whole time—she'd just been in hiding. "Both," I added.

When she smiled, I did the very un-teenage-daughter thing to do. I smiled back.

TWENTY-ONE

I waited until Harry was asleep before sneaking out. I didn't notice the small table lamp burning on the kitchen table until my hand was on the front door.

"Where are you off to at this hour?" Mom twisted around in her chair and lowered her reading glasses down her nose. She quickly gathered the papers on the table and stuffed them into a folder before I could get close enough to see what she was working on.

"Studying." I turned around so she could see my backpack. It was full with books and everything . . . not that I was planning on getting much studying done tonight. I had something else more important to do tonight. Like confront Callum.

"And this requires you to leave the cabin at"—Mom turned her wrist so she could check her slim silver watch—"ten-thirty at night?"

"I'm studying with someone. You know, a study session." I hoped my face matched my voice—innocent.

"Who's this 'study session' with?"

I licked my lips, stalling.

"It's Callum, isn't it?" Mom added a second later.

I looked away and shrugged. "Yeah. So?"

Mom turned around in her chair until she was almost facing me. "So . . . I'm wondering if it might be a better idea if he came here to study."

My skin started to prickle. "I'm just meeting him over at the staff cabins. Outside at a picnic bench. Not in his cabin doing . . . whatever you think we might be doing."

"If I was worried about *that,* I'd be locking you in your room instead of having a constructive conversation and thinking about letting you go."

I half groaned, half exhaled. "Mom . . ."

"I've noticed the way you are around him, Phoenix." Her voice was still in control. "And I've noticed the way he is around you."

I stopped. "What do you mean? How he is around me?" I was fishing, but I wanted to know if I wasn't the only one who'd noticed that the way Callum was with me was different from the way he was with others.

Mom blinked at me like she couldn't believe I was asking for an explanation. "It's the way you two can be in opposite corners of the dining hall but seem to know exactly where the other is. Or it's the way I've seen him watching you when you're talking with another guy, the same way you watch him when another girl approaches him."

I was shocked by Mom's transformation. How could someone who last spring had been too distracted to notice I'd dyed my hair blue with Kool-Aid after our track team won regionals now pick up on the way Callum and I were around each other?

We hadn't been obvious; at least I didn't think we had. I couldn't believe the queen of oblivious had figured us out.

"Listen . . . Mom . . . ," I started, no clue what to say next.

"I'm not looking for an explanation or a confirmation or a

denial." She shook her head once. "I just want you to know that I've noticed something between you two, and that I'm hoping you'll think about what you're doing before getting any deeper. At the end of the summer, you're parting ways. Remember that when you feel those butterflies."

I wanted to mention about the furthest we'd gone were a few innocent nudges and hand brushes. I looked away and put my hand on the door. "Okay" was all I said, but I was thinking a lot more. I was thinking about just how right she was and that maybe before Callum and I took that next step, maybe I or he or both should hit the brakes and barricade ourselves in friend territory. We lived different lives. We lived in different parts of the state. We had different plans for the future. . . . Well, one of us had plans while the other had question marks.

"Do you mind if I take off? I really need all the time I can get to study." Right before she was about to answer, I added, "And I promise I'll give some thought to the deeper-waters thing, okay?"

Mom started to smile. "You're a smart girl—I know you will, but I wouldn't be doing my job if I at least didn't bring it up. Oh, and Phoenix? I'd like to talk with you about some other things."

Talk about some things. I knew to most kids, those words were like the kiss of death. Especially coming from a parent's mouth. For some reason, instead of feeling like a cornered cat, my whole body relaxed.

"Harry too?" I asked.

"I think just you for now."

"Harry's a part of the family. He deserves to know what's going on."

Mom thought about that for a few seconds and sighed. "Harry too."

"I'm working late tomorrow night, but how about the night after? My shift ends at five, I think. Maybe after dinner?" I felt weird talking to my mom like this, like we were comparing calendars and trying to pencil each other in.

"Works for me." She waved at me before sliding into her seat. "Don't stay out too late."

I hustled across camp with my backpack thumping against me. I figured the quicker I got there, the less time in between I had to change my mind. As expected, Callum was camped at the same picnic table, a stack of study guides spread out around him. Either he was really focused or he was keeping up the Phoenix-doesn't-exist act. My money was on the latter.

"Is this really your plan? To ignore me the rest of the summer?" I started, moving a few steps closer.

I waited for him to say something, but he didn't. He stayed frozen. His shoulders might have tensed up some, but that was it.

"How's the studying going?" I glanced down at what he was working on, but he slammed his book closed. "Was that a reaction? To something I just said?"

His response to that was stacking his books and packing them. He was going to get up and walk away. I didn't know what I'd been expecting, but not this. Not him bailing before I had a chance to apologize and attempt an explanation.

"Listen, Callum, I'm sorry," I said, throwing my backpack onto the table because it suddenly felt too heavy to handle. "I know I screwed up and I know I let you down and I know I probably deserve to be ignored, but I really just need you to know that I'm sorry, okay?"

I felt like I was talking to a wall for all the reaction I got. It had been easier when he'd been sitting; it was harder to face him at eye level.

"Just what exactly are you sorry for?" he asked coolly. "That you didn't do what you were supposed to or because your brother got hurt because of that?"

I swallowed. "Both."

"Yeah, well, sorry if I find that hard to believe. You've spent the summer trying to prove you know best." Callum shrugged out of his flannel shirt and tossed it down on the bench. He was getting fired up, but at least he was talking to me.

"I am sorry." I threw my arms in the air. "I don't have an excuse, and I don't have a good reason for doing what I did. I'm sorry."

He pinched the bridge of his nose like I was giving him a headache. "Why didn't you follow the route you were supposed to take?"

How many times had I asked myself that same question in the last six hours?

"I don't know. Because I didn't." I dropped onto the bench because standing was a chore. "I let stuff get to me I shouldn't have. I didn't think it would be that dangerous. I made a mistake. I'm human. It happens."

He huffed under his breath. "You make a lot of mistakes."

I lifted my shoulders. "I'm really good at the human thing."

"How can I ever trust you again after this? First the permission slip lie? Now this? These are big things, Phoenix. I need to know that someone else isn't going to get hurt because you decide to do your own thing. I need to be able to trust you out there. And you need to be able to trust that Ben and I know what we're doing when we put together these activities."

"The honest answer is that you can't," I half shouted. "It's not like I'm trying to screw up. It just happens. I made a mistake and I'm sorry. I'll try harder next time."

"When Evan told me what trail you took off on"—Callum shook his head—"I couldn't believe it."

"Why not?" I said, blinking.

"I fractured a couple of ribs going down that trail two summers ago. And I knew what I was doing. Thinking of you on it . . ." He cut himself short and turned away so his back was facing me.

I raised my hands up on the picnic table, reeling. "You were worried about *me*?"

"Of course I was worried about you. I worry about all the counselors. Just like I worry about all the campers." He shrugged like it was no big deal, but his face gave him away.

"Yeah, but you didn't mention anything about those campers or the other counselors just now. You said when you thought about *me*"—I stuck my thumb into my chest—"on the trail. You didn't bring up anybody else."

His shoulders tensed. "You're splitting hairs." He was trying hard not to make eye contact.

"Why can't you look at me?" I asked, stepping around the end of the picnic bench.

"I *can* look at you just fine. I'm just choosing not to."

I rolled my eyes. "Fine. Why are you *choosing* not to look at me?"

His neck cracked when he rolled it around. "Because you're driving me crazy, Phoenix." His voice was strained. "One minute you're teasing me about keeping up during morning runs, and the next you're leading a bunch of inexperienced riders down Suicide Trail. You're helping me with these damn study guides and then you're ignoring me in the hospital like I'm not even there."

"Wait." I lifted my hand "Nice try, but that was *you* who ignored *me* in the hospital."

"I was only following your lead. You were the one who walked into that room and pretended I didn't exist." That was when he slipped and finally looked at me. "I'm so angry at you right now—I'm so not in control of my emotions—I might kiss you. . . ." The skin between his brows was lined deeper than I'd ever seen it. "And that's the problem. Phoenix. I can't kiss you."

"Why not? I like you, Callum, and now I know you like me, too." Yeah, because that made everything so much easier. Or not.

"You shouldn't." He shook his head and ground his jaw. "We can't both like each other or else it's going to be impossible for me to keep this up."

My heart was beating so hard. "Keep what up?"

"Pretending I don't feel anything for you. I can't keep that up if I know you feel the same way." I moved fast, and before he could lunge out of bounds, my hand found his wrist and wound around it.

When I moved closer, sliding my hand down his wrist until our fingers were knotting together, he closed his eyes. "Don't."

I was close enough I could smell whatever he'd used to wash his hair, mixed with the outdoors that seemed to cling to him no matter what time of day. Fresh and musky. Clean and earthy. "Why not?" I asked, almost in a whisper. You know, in case any of the trees were eavesdropping.

"Because you're going so many places. Fast. And I'm going maybe a couple of places. Real slow." His eyes were squinted shut, but his fingers were tightening around mine. Why was the thought of us so hard for him to consider?

"I'm not worried about places right now." I pressed my other hand to his chest, testing to see if that was okay. He didn't flinch but instead seemed to melt into me a little.

"You should be."

I sucked in a breath. "If you're not going to kiss me . . ." I paused and bit my lower lip, studying his at the same time, wondering what it would feel like moving against mine. "I'm going to kiss you."

Under my hand, Callum's chest started moving faster. I hadn't seen him breathe this hard even after a strong sprint finish. "Don't."

I smiled, knowing that for once, I'd won an argument between us. I moved closer, until our bodies were almost touching. Close enough, I could feel the warmth coming off him. "Can't stop me."

That was when he finally opened his eyes. The conflict was gone from them. "I know." He tugged me a little closer with his hand. And now our bodies were totally up against each other.

My fingers curled into his chest, gripping a handful of his shirt. I had a seriously strong urge to tug it off, but I beat my hormones back. For now. Kissing first. Shirt maneuvering later.

He pressed into me a little harder, just enough I fell back a couple of steps until I felt the edge of the picnic table bump against me. This was it. We were going to kiss. Finally. After weeks of flirting and dodging, grinning and glaring, we were taking the leap.

When he stayed like that for another minute, watching me as if he was waiting for something, I tipped my head. "What?" I asked, because I thought I'd made it pretty damn glaringly obvious that he could kiss me.

When his gaze dropped to my mouth, his eyes went a little darker. "You made me a promise. I'm just waiting for you to pay up."

My stomach fluttered a few times and before I could second-guess myself, I pressed up on my tiptoes, pulled him closer with the grip I had on his shirt, and stared right into his eyes as my mouth moved toward his. He didn't blink.

His lips felt hard at first, almost unyielding, but they thawed a whole second after mine touched them. I watched his eyes close before mine followed, and then I kissed him.

I kissed Callum O'Connor. Soft and sweet, even a little unsure.

Finally.

And then he kissed me back. Hard and lingering, like he'd never been so sure of anything before.

His hand found my waist, and his arm slid around it as his body kept mine pinned against the picnic bench. He tasted like sunshine and a storm, and he kissed as though we had forever and had run out of time.

He kissed me like I'd wanted to be kissed my whole entire life—like I was everything.

TWENTY-TWO

I spent the rest of the night thinking about the kiss. What night was left after we finished the actual kissing. Which wasn't much.

Eventually, we got to studying. For a while. Before getting back to the kissing part. I wasn't sure how we were going to figure out how to study together now that we'd officially crossed (slash catapulted) over the line, but we'd have to figure it out because I might have liked kissing Callum, but I also needed to score well on my SATs.

Mom was in bed when I'd tiptoed in sometime before the sun rose, and I'd instantly fallen asleep when I crawled into bed.

My alarm was blaring an hour and forty-five minutes later. Not cool.

I was scheduled for a tempo run this morning, two miles of warm-up, four miles of tempo, and a mile or two of cooldown. A tempo was a beast to run after a good night of sleep, so I knew I was in for a session of suffering.

Snagging a banana from the counter, I had it down in four bites, and before I'd swallowed the last of it, I was out the door and jogging down the trail.

I tried to concentrate on my pace, my breathing, my form, but I couldn't. All I could think about was Callum.

The way he kissed. The way I kissed him. The way he felt. The way he touched me. How his hands were rough and callused to look at, but soft and gentle when they touched me. I thought about how I'd never felt half the things I had last night with him when I'd been with other guys. How I'd wanted to do so much more than just kiss. How I would have let him if he hadn't been so frustratingly restrained.

Unlike Keats before him, who'd seemed to view making out as a necessary evil or an appetizer leading to the main course, Callum seemed perfectly happy making out as long or as little as I let him. He hadn't been rushing to move on to something else, or let his hands wander into off-limits territory, or left me feeling guilty when the kissing led to nothing else. He hadn't muttered anything about me being a tease, or anything about a guy having different needs than a girl. Instead, he smiled the kind that was my favorite, kissed my forehead, and walked me to my cabin. He even waited until I was inside the door before leaving, just like he had the night before.

Not that I'd been watching him or anything, or noticed the way he seemed to move a little lighter now. And I definitely hadn't noticed when he'd thrown his head back and let out a little whoop when he was almost out of sight of the cabin. No, I hadn't fallen that hard that fast yet. Not even.

That was what I was still trying to convince myself of when I heard a familiar set of footsteps pounding up behind me.

"So you take advantage of me at night and bail on me in the morning." Once he caught up to me, he slowed his pace to match mine. "Wham, bam, thank you, sir. I totally didn't take you for that kind of use-and-abuse girl."

My watch beeped. I'd just hit two miles—warm-up time

was over. I went from an eight-and-a-half-minute mile pace to a six-and-a-half. Callum matched my pace, not missing a beat.

"I thought since you didn't get to bed until four in the morning, you might want to sleep in today instead of running eight miles," I said, trying not to smile because a person shouldn't feel like smiling if they were doing a tempo run. Crying was more the correct response.

"And I thought *you* would have wanted to sleep in after going to bed at four in the morning instead of running eight miles." He slid close enough to nudge me with his elbow. Just that one little touch made my spine feel like it was liquefying. "But then I remembered who you were and how you probably wouldn't let mono keep you from a training run." He nudged me again. "So here I am."

When the trail opened up a bit, I felt safe taking my eyes off it for a quick second. My eyes swelled the instant I looked over at him. "Why aren't you wearing a shirt?" My voice was two octaves too high, but for good reason. I'd never seen Callum run without a shirt. Given the way we'd been making out, I knew he'd totally planned it. He was trying to throw me off my game.

"You managed to tear my shirt last night, and I didn't want to chance the same thing happening this morning. I only brought a few with me, so I need to ration them." He kept going on about his precious shirts and how I was a destroyer of them or something like that, but I was too focused on what I was doing to pay close attention.

He'd paused just long enough to take a breath as I was tucking the neck of my shirt into the back of my running shorts. I knew the moment when he glanced over and saw that I'd followed the trend and taken off my shirt, too. I knew because that was when I heard a sharp intake of air, right before he wiped out, making sounds with his mouth and body that probably woke up the whole forest.

I braked to a stop and paused the time on my watch before rushing to him. He was sprawled out on the trail, leaves and little twigs sticking from his hair and dirt painting his face and the rest of him.

"Ow."

I bit my cheek to keep from laughing once I knew he was okay, save for some scraped palms and knees. Oh, and a potentially bruised ego.

"Did you just trip?" I crouched down beside him and plucked a twig from behind his ear.

"No, I just wiped out."

"On a trail that you know like the back of your hand?" I repeated a phrase I'd heard said about Callum a lot—that he knew every hill, valley, and trail within ten miles of Camp Kismet *better* than he knew the back of his hand.

"I was distracted." He shook his head a couple of times and looked up at me. Or he looked up at my chest area.

I snapped the shoulder strap of my sports bra. "Please. You've run track for how many years? Lived in California for how many? You've seen as many girls in sports bras as you've seen guys in baseball hats."

Callum leaned up on one elbow, giving a little wince. He'd taken a hard fall. If I'd known he'd go all stuntman on me, I might not have taken off my shirt. Or maybe I still would have. Especially seeing the way he was looking at me now. "Yeah, but none of those girls have been the same one I was making out with the night before."

I gave his chest a light shove, but my hand didn't move away. Instead, it stayed there. I'd touched his chest through his shirt last night, but not like this. Not with my skin warm against his.

My heart was already beating fast from the run, but it picked up even more when his hand covered mine, flattening it against his chest and holding it there.

"Hey, klutzy, I've got three and a half miles left of a tempo to finish. Think you can get on your feet and suck it up?"

He let me continue to pluck the leaves and twigs from his hair, looking like he was in no hurry to move. "That's a lot of *up*-ing. I just took a serious spill and who knows what kind of injuries I might have sustained. Or, God forbid, a concussion."

I sighed and dusted his forehead off. He looked like he'd been tumble-dried in a compost pile. "I'm not sure how I feel about being with a guy who isn't as tough as I am."

"And I'm not sure how I feel about the girl I'm with thinking she's tougher than I am." He rolled his head and held out his hand. "At least give me a lift. Then we'll get after those three and a half miles."

Popping up, I grabbed his hand, and just as I started to pull him up, he gave my hand a yank, and I went from upright to lying on top of him. My breath whooshed out from the surprise, the impact, and the fact that I was lying on top of Callum. While he was shirtless and I was in a sports bra.

I didn't realize I'd been sweaty until my skin was against his, but now it was almost all I could notice, the way it almost made my skin stick to his, like Velcro.

"How's that for sucking it up?" He smiled at me, where my face was hovering just a bit above. I could feel his breath on my neck, warm and even.

"We can't keep doing this," I breathed, trying to focus on something other than his hand drawing patterns along my spine. I succeeded. But instead of that hand, I focused on his other, which was busy slipping behind my neck while his fingers tangled into my hair. "Making out when we're supposed to be studying. Making out when we're supposed to be training. If we don't show some restraint, we're not going to wind up doing anything but making out."

His forehead creased. "And this would be a bad thing?"

I shoved his chest, but I didn't exactly move away. "Only if your definition is failing the SATs and getting kicked off the track team for huffing and puffing your way to the finish line with a five-minute eight hundred."

Without warning, he kissed me. His head lifted from the ground and his mouth found mine, and he kissed me. The same way he had last night—like I was everything. Like I was a beginning and an end.

When he was kissing me, it was easy to forget that summer would be over soon. We were almost halfway through, and eventually, my nights together with Callum would be over.

When I pulled away from him, he let me go. I knew enough about his strength to know he wouldn't have if he hadn't wanted to. That messed with my head, too. He wanted me to stay, but he was letting me go. He wanted one thing, and I wanted the other . . . and he respected it.

"What's the matter?" Callum curled his legs up and adjusted his shorts as he watched me pace a few feet in front of him.

"I don't know." I was biting my thumbnail. I hadn't bitten my nails in years.

"Something's the matter." His voice was calm.

"Nothing's the matter." I continued to gnaw on my nail, pacing fast enough for the dust to break around my shoes. "Or everything's the matter. I don't know. I can't tell."

"Okay, so let's cross nothing off the list because there's nothing to talk about if nothing's wrong. What's everything wrong?"

I spat out a chunk of nail. Gross. If Callum thought my nail hygiene habits were just as disgusting, he didn't show it. "Besides *everything*?"

"Top of the list." A minute passed. "Your dad leaving?" he suggested gently.

When I shot him a surprised look, he shrugged. "Harry told me yesterday in the hospital."

I huffed. "I don't care what my dad does."

He looked up at me like he could see into me. "Is that why you look like you want to cry?"

I swiped my arm across my eyes just in case. "It's just that this was his whole idea, coming here, you know, and he bails. Doesn't say good-bye; he just leaves."

Callum let that hang in the air for a moment. "Maybe he's got something important to do."

"Maybe he's got more computer screens to cuss at and walls to daze off at." I kicked a small rock in the middle of the trail. "He's the reason everything is falling down around me, and he isn't doing anything to fix it."

"You don't know that." He lifted one shoulder. "And you don't want to start giving other people power over your life. That's a tough habit to break."

I stared into the trees. "Personal experience?"

Callum shook his head. "My brother was a big fan of the victim mentality. Blamed everything on our dad. He felt powerless, but really, he'd just chosen to give his power away."

My teeth ground together—Callum wasn't giving me the typical lip service most people did when I unloaded my baggage. It wasn't the first time he'd challenged me when others would have just consoled me. "I'm not giving my power to anybody, but I can still blame my dad for screwing up our lives and leaving."

"If he left, like, left for good, he wouldn't be calling to check in, you know?"

"He hasn't called to check in," I said.

"Harry said he's talked to him."

My mouth opened, but nothing came out. How did Callum know that and I didn't? "Why hasn't he called me?"

"You wouldn't answer? You'd let it go to voice mail? You'd hang up? You wouldn't talk? You wouldn't let him get a word in?" He was listing things off on his fingers.

"Yeah, yeah. You made your point four points ago." I sighed, knowing he was right. I wouldn't have answered if Dad had called me. I didn't want to talk to him. But I had a million good reasons for not wanting to talk to him, too.

"So your dad's the matter." He clasped his hands together. "What else?"

"Everything else."

"Ice cream sandwiches? Monarch butterflies? Sunny days? Buttercups?" He was listing things off on his fingers again.

I looked over at him and crossed my arms. "You're a pain in the ass."

His smile stretched. "You're welcome."

I kept pacing. "I'm worried about Harry's wrist. I'm worried about my mom and if this new version of her is here to stay. I'm worried the campers and Ben and the other counselors won't trust me after what happened yesterday. I'm worried about testing really, really well on the SATs this fall, and I'm worried I won't be able to run anything faster than a sub-seven with all the stress and distractions I'm dealing with. I'm worried about saving up enough money for a car, and I'm worried that I won't get into college. I'm worried about being on my own next year, and Harry being basically on his own . . . and neither of us able to do it."

I could have gone on, but I didn't want to sound even more pathetic.

"That's a lot to be worried about," Callum said finally.

My eyebrow peaked. "You think?"

I heard him take a breath. "But it seems kinda pointless worrying about all those things that may or may not happen."

He was right, of course—but that didn't change the way I felt. Waste of time and energy or not, I was still freaking out about everything coming my way.

So I moved on to the topic I hadn't brought up yet. "I'm worried about us."

When I looked over at him, he didn't seem surprised. He almost looked like he'd been expecting this, just waiting for me to mention it. "What's got you worried?" he asked, patting the ground in front of him.

I moved closer until I was a few feet away, then plopped down on the trail so I was facing him. I drew my legs together like his and did my best to ignore the overwhelming pull I felt being this close. We were close, but I wanted to be closer. "What people will think," I started. "What will happen at the end of summer. How we'll be able to be together and still get important stuff done like training runs that last longer than twenty minutes and study sessions where we actually open the books." I tapped my watch, where the time still read twenty minutes. We would have been close to finishing our run if we hadn't gotten "sidetracked" at mile two.

"I don't care what people think, and I don't think you do, either." He paused, giving me a chance to disagree. He was right, though; I didn't really care what people thought. Too much. "If it makes you happy, during our runs and studying, we'll adopt a no-kissing policy. Maybe setting that aside for ten-minute breaks." His grin was definitely tilted higher on one side.

"*Five*-minute breaks."

"Oh yeah, sorry, I forgot you were the restrained one." He didn't roll his eyes, but his voice more than made up for it. "And as for the end of summer, add that to the list of pointless things to worry about. We can't call the future, so why waste time worrying about it?"

I linked my pinkie with his and nodded.

"Is there anything else?"

"It's just things are moving fast," I started, drilling my tongue into my cheek. "Yesterday afternoon you wouldn't look at me in the hospital, and this morning we're kissing practically topless."

"Topless?" Callum made a face. "You're wearing a sports bra."

I felt a smile coming. The worst had to be over. "Sure, *now* it's a sports bra." Callum smiled, too, looking as relieved as I was that we'd navigated through the heavy stuff. "I'm just saying I think we've felt something for each other for a while, and now that we've admitted that . . ." I felt myself almost blushing. Having this conversation with him was all kinds of awkward. "The physical part is trying to catch up. Like, *really* trying to catch up. I just don't know if I can trust—"

"I swear to you," he interrupted, looking me straight in the eyes. "I won't do anything without checking with you first. You just want to kiss? Fine. You just want to hold hands?" He made a bit of a face, like he was grimacing. "A hesitant and reluctant fine, but still, I'm down. I won't push you any further than you're ready to go."

My smile had gotten bigger. Not because I needed him to confirm all that, but because I could see he was almost as uncomfortable as I was talking about this stuff. It was kind of a relief to see a person like Callum squirm.

"I know that," I said, leaning toward him. "I trust you. It's me I'm not sure I trust."

His jaw dropped in mock surprise. "You trust me? This? Coming from Miss Trust Issues herself?"

"Of course. You haven't given me any reason not to."

Callum looked at me. Like, really looked at me. "Plus maybe I might have earned some trust, too?" He waited for my answer. I made him wait a little longer.

"Maybe." I might have been more convincing if I hadn't still been smiling at him.

"Okay, so you're not sure you can trust yourself when it comes to keeping your hands off me. I totally get that." I swung an arm around just so I could punch him, but he grabbed it and he kept my hand in his.

"You're no help," I said with an exaggerated sigh.

"Okay, clearing the filthy thoughts from my head now." He gave his head a violent shake and thumped it a few times with his palm. "Still trying." A few more whacks, and then his face cleared. "So how do you learn to trust yourself?"

My shoulders fell, along with everything else. "I have no idea."

TWENTY-THREE

It was Talk with Mom Night. I'd been dreading and looking forward to it ever since she brought it up the night of Harry's accident. Part of me was ready to know just what was coming, and part of me wanted to keep my head in the sand.

I'd been in such a rush to clean up after the crafts session I'd led that I'd spilled a bottle of glue, which had mysteriously lost its lid, and dumped half a container of shocking-green glitter in the process of wiping up the glue.

"Thanks for your help. I would have been there all night." I caught myself just before mussing Harry's hair. He'd confronted me a couple of days ago on how it made him feel like a baby when I did it. A month ago, he couldn't get enough, and now it made him a baby. He was growing up. That was a good thing, I reminded myself.

"You bet." Harry inspected the bandage covering his wrist. It was sparkling with shocking-green glitter.

"Don't worry. I'll change it when we get to the cabin," I said, guessing what he was thinking.

He shrugged. "Why were you and Callum looking at each other so weird before we left just now?"

I stopped in the middle of the trail heading toward our cabin. "What are you talking about?" I reminded myself to play it cool because Callum and I had been careful. No one had picked up on us yet. Least of all a ten-year-old boy.

"You know. You guys were being all weird."

I made myself keep walking. "How were we looking at each other?"

Harry made duck lips as he thought about it. "The way me and my friends look at each other when we're trying to say something, but someone else is around and we don't want them to hear. You know, when we have a secret we want to keep private."

So much for thinking we'd been secretive. "Callum and I do not look at each other that way."

Harry shoved his glasses up on his nose and huffed. "What's going on? Is he still mad at you about the accident?"

I practiced my most convincing voice in my head before replying, "No."

"Still giving you the silent treatment because you totally let him down?"

I sighed and elbowed him. "No, nothing like that."

"Then what *is* it like?" This time he was the one who stopped in the middle of the trail.

Moving a little closer, I scanned the area. Nothing but trees, trees, and trees. "You can't tell anyone."

"Not even Mom?"

"*Especially* not Mom."

I cocked an eyebrow so he knew I meant business. He threw his arms up. "Okay, fine. What?"

My eyes squinted as I reconsidered telling him. Harry was trustworthy, but he was ten. Most ten-year-olds could barely spell *trustworthy*, but I was tired of everyone keeping secrets from us. I couldn't control what my parents chose to keep from us, but I could control what I kept from Harry. As little as possible was my goal.

"Callum and I are kind of, you know, seeing each other." I put my hands on my hips. Then dropped them back at my sides.

Harry's face crinkled up. "Seeing each other?" he said slowly. "Haven't you guys been doing that since, like, you first met?"

It took me a second to understand what he was getting at. Yeah, I was so talking to a ten-year-old boy. I tried again. "You know, we've been getting kinda serious?"

Harry blinked. "Eh, shocker, Phoenix, but you have always been serious, and Callum . . . he doesn't seem like the nonserious type, either."

I shook my head and did one more scan of the area. And how 'bout them trees? "We're dating, okay? Seeing each other, getting serious . . . in a dating kind of way."

Harry's whole face flattened with shock. "Whoa," he said "Like a boyfriend-girlfriend kind of way?"

"I didn't say that."

Harry started to get animated then. Spinning in circles and giving off *woots*. "Holy smokes. Callum is your boyfriend?"

"I don't know I'd call it that."

That was when an arm rung around my waist before he pulled me to his side. I could have jumped out of my skin if it wasn't so plastered in Elmer's Glue. "Well, I don't know what you'd call it, but I'd call you my girlfriend." Callum grinned over at me and fired a wink, before holding his hand high up in the air for Harry.

Harry didn't even pause before leaping up and smacking a solid high five. "My sister is dating the coolest guy at camp. Mind blown."

"My life's purpose. To date the cool guy at camp," I dead-panned, totally straight-faced.

When Callum lifted his hand again for Harry to high-five, I intercepted it.

"Yeah, yeah, I get it. You guys are best pals and on each other's side. Fabulous. But we have to see Mom, and you"— I pointed at Callum—"have a practice test to complete before dinner."

He grumbled, but I knew he'd do it. He'd been going through a couple of mini practice tests every day since we started studying and with his persistence and my savvy when it came to researching just about any topic on the Internet— test-taking anxiety in this case—his scores were getting better maybe due to some creative scoring on my end. But I wasn't ready to tell him about my extra help yet.

"Yes, ma'am." Callum gave a little salute and smiled as he started backing away. "Hope 'the talk' goes okay. Meet me at the Swallow Lake beach later?"

Callum had introduced me to a private beach close by camp last night where we were supposed to spend a couple of hours studying. That hadn't worked out as well as we'd planned. "For studying?"

"Whatever you want," he answered with a big grin. Then he disappeared down the trail.

"You just told him to go take a test, and he listened, like, lickety-split." Harry snapped his fingers, blinking at the spot Callum had disappeared. "You're a drillmaster, Phoenix."

"Why, thank you." I gave a little bow before wrapping my arm around Harry's shoulders and pressing on. I wanted to get this over with.

The cabin was just up ahead when I noticed Harry's face line with concern. "Phoenix? Do you know what this is about?

I've had lots of talks with Mom before, but never one I've had to schedule with her."

My fist curled around his shoulder. "I've got an idea."

When Harry swallowed, his whole throat moved. "Are we going to be all right?"

"Of course we're going to be all right. I've got your back no matter what. I'll look after you no matter what." I paused at the bottom of the cabin's stairs. "You know that, right?"

Harry was staring up the stairs like they were insurmountable, but when he glanced up at me, his face cleared. "Yeah, I know that."

Before I could catch myself, I mussed his hair. If he was irritated, he didn't show it. Instead, he exhaled and climbed the steps with me.

"Mom?" I called through the screen door. The main door was open.

"In here!" she called as the scent of . . . *baking* fanned over me. Harry sniffed at the air as we exchanged a look like neither of us could believe it. Mom used to bake—pies, cookies, and breads—but not recently.

"Cookies," Harry sighed with another sniff before charging into the cabin.

"I'm just pulling the last batch from the oven." Mom was standing in front of the stove, skillfully sliding cookies from the baking tray to a cooling rack. Oatmeal chocolate chip. Harry's and my favorite. "Go ahead and have a seat at the table, you two. I'll be right over." Mom wiped her hands off on her jeans after licking a few gooey globs of chocolate from her fingers.

Harry sprinted to the table and crashed into a chair so quickly he almost sprained his other wrist, but I stood there watching her. It was like she'd transformed into the mom of my childhood, dancing around the kitchen to whatever song she had blaring on the radio, letting me whack metal pots with wooden spoons while she experimented with some new recipe. Flour in her hair, her sleeves rolled up to her elbows, the smile on her face . . . I had a sudden urge to run and wind my arms around her so she could soothe and kiss and pat all my problems away like she used to be able to.

That was when I reminded myself that the problems of a seven-year-old were entirely different from the problems a seventeen-year-old encountered. They were trivial in comparison.

"Phoenix?" Mom paused when she noticed me standing at the door.

I shifted and flushed the urge to let her comfort me away. "Do you need any help?"

"Yes." She waved at the table where Harry was already helping himself to a towering plate of cookies. There were three glasses of milk at the table, too. "I need help eating those cookies. Every last one of them."

Harry grinned over at her, his teeth all coated in chocolate. He lifted his second cookie in the air.

Mom motioned at the chair beside Harry and waited for me. When I took a seat, she looked between us, the happy calm seeming to drain from her face. When she took her own seat across from us, she shifted restlessly. I'd picked up a cookie, but so much for eating it. Not when I felt like my heart was lodged in my throat.

"I want you both to know that no matter what, your dad and I are going to take care of you. You're going to be okay, and we're going to get through this."

Mom glanced at the wall clock, like I did when I couldn't wait for class to be over. She hadn't even really started talking and was already counting down the seconds until we would be finished.

Not good.

"You both know that your dad lost his job two years ago and that things have been . . . difficult since."

Sure, if *difficult* was the code word for *disastrous,* then sure, things had been *difficult.*

"Your dad made good money at his job, money we depended on to pay for the house and school and lots of things." She slowly twisted the glass of milk in her hands, staring into it. "When he got laid off, he wasn't able to find another job that paid anything close to what he was making, so we knew he could either take a lower-paying job and we'd have to make some changes, or he could keep searching for a similar-paying job and we could hang on for a while . . . until things ran out."

"Things being money," I added, sounding impatient. I didn't need a recap of the past; I needed a general sketch of the future.

"Instead of uprooting you kids, we chose to hold on to the life we'd been living, hoping . . ."

I snorted over the *hoping* part, wondering when unicorns and magical lands were going to show up in this conversation.

"It didn't work out the way we'd hop—" Mom stopped when I snorted again. "The way we'd *planned.* Your dad wasn't able to find the same kind of job and things—*money*—has run out." She was looking at me the whole time, but it was that statement that shifted Harry's attention from the cookies to the conversation.

"We don't have any money?" He swallowed the bite he'd been chewing. "Are we, like, poor?"

Mom's eyes went glassy instantly. She was going to cry. I was watching, waiting for the first tear to fall, when she lifted her shoulders, sniffed, and forced a small smile aimed Harry's way. "We have money, sweetheart. We're not poor." She didn't blink as she talked to him. "But we can't keep holding on, watching that money shrink, keeping our fingers crossed. It's time to make some changes. That's what I want to talk about."

Harry bobbed his head, but he looked nervous. I might not have looked it, but I felt nervous.

"We have to move," she said. The glass of milk stopped twisting. "We've got to leave our house and move to another one."

Harry's face went white. "My Legos? My computer? They're goners, aren't they? I'm never going to see them again?"

Mom shook her head as hard as I did. "No, Harrison, your Legos and computer and everything else are just fine. That's why your dad left. He's home, packing up the house so we can bring everything with us to the new house."

"The new house will be in the same school district, right?" I scooted forward in my chair. I knew we were losing the house. I'd known for a while. I knew downsizing and budgeting and all those adult things would be involved, but I'd just assumed we'd stay in the same general area so Harry and I could stay at the same schools.

Mom's face answered my question on its own. My lungs collapsed, and I couldn't breathe. "That's what we really wanted, Phoenix. We did everything we could to find a place where you and Harrison could stay at the same schools, but our neighborhood is expensive." Mom exhaled and dropped her eyes. "Too expensive for our present situation."

I glanced over at Harry, expecting him to be freaking out. Instead, he looked a little concerned, but that was about it. I was the one who felt like the room was closing in on me.

"Where are we moving to?"

"We're moving a little inland—somewhere in Riverside County. You'll be attending Jefferson High, and Harrison . . ." Mom bit her lip and shook her head. She looked kind of defeated, like she'd been beaten down so many times she couldn't peel herself off the ground again. "We're still trying to figure that out."

"Riverside County? Jefferson High?" My hands curled into fists in my lap. This was worse than I'd thought. "I've never even heard of Jefferson High, and I'm supposed to spend my senior year there?"

"Phoenix," Mom warned, indicating toward Harry.

Harry was twisted in his seat, his head moving from me to our mom like we were playing a tennis game.

My nails were digging into my palms enough it hurt. I didn't stop, though. "Do they even have a cross-country team? Do they even have a track? What's an Ivy League school going to think when my application shows me transferring from one of the best schools in the state to Jefferson High?" My voice made it sound like Jefferson were Alcatraz. "Everything I've worked for . . . I'm one year away . . . and you guys are doing this to me?" I slammed the table in front of Harry. The cookies rattled on the plate. "To *us*?" I imagined Harry stuck in some new school. The kid would spend most of his classes probably stuffed in custodian closets and garbage cans.

"I know, Phoenix. I'm sorry." Mom's eyes were welling again, but her voice was controlled.

"No, you don't know!" I shot out of my chair so fast my knees banged the edge of the table. The milk from my glass spilled over the sides. Another mess to clean up. "And if you were sorry, you'd be doing something about this instead of baking cookies."

In his chair, Harry looked like he was about to cry as he

rubbed at his upper lip, but I couldn't stay to comfort him. I had to get out of here. I had to get away from her before I threw the plate of cookies at her face. The cookies . . . yeah, because that made up for ruining your kids' lives.

"Where are you going?" she called as I stormed toward the door.

"If I thought you cared, I might actually tell you." When I'd shoved through the screen door, I paused long enough to fire a glare at her. "But it's pretty clear you don't give a damn about my future."

TWENTY-FOUR

Life was back to normal.

I wasn't talking to my mom again. She wasn't talking to me much, either. Maybe it was because we'd said enough or didn't have anything else to add. We were moving out of the school district.

It was such a helpless feeling, having my whole life pulled out from beneath me. I'd spent most of the week just trying not to think about it.

It was easier to say than do most of the time . . . except those times I was with Callum. Or on my way to seeing him, like I was now.

I'd just finished yet another long day of decoupaging and friendship bracelet weaving, and only a hard ten-mile run had helped me to recover from my bout with creativity.

The rain had started a little while ago, but unlike everyone else, who'd grabbed one of the loaner umbrellas, I went without. It hadn't rained in weeks, and the change in the weather was refreshing, if not a relief. The gray skies and rain more matched my mood than the blue-sky, sunny ones.

The walk from the dining hall to the staff cabins was only

a few minutes, but I was pretty much soaked by the time I bounced up the stairs to Callum's cabin. He'd been leading an advanced group of mountain bikers earlier and should have gotten back a couple of hours ago. Usually, he stuck his head in the dining hall to wave and make sure I hadn't taken a butter knife to my wrists after a papier-mâché project gone bad.

Today, though, I hadn't seen him. Not since our morning run, at least, which we'd actually completed. Without any "breaks."

So far, he'd taken his promise seriously. When we were supposed to train, we trained. When we were supposed to study, we studied. When we were supposed to take five-minute breaks . . . we usually took ten. Sometimes fifteen. Callum's test scores were still improving, too. Mostly thanks to his efforts, but a little thanks to mine and my creative strategies. But it was working. Callum and I were getting it right.

It felt like the only thing in my life that was.

When I knocked on the cabin door, I didn't hear the usual rushed sound of footsteps approaching. I didn't hear anything. I leaned over the porch railing to peek in the window. It didn't look like anyone was inside. It was just late enough I guessed the other guys Callum bunked with were probably out doing their own thing.

I knocked again, and when there was still nothing, I turned the doorknob. It was unlocked, so I pushed the door open.

"Hello?" I called. "Anyone here?"

No answer.

"Callum?"

I was about to let myself in to dry off and get a jump on studying, when the bathroom door at the end of the cabin opened a little. "Come on in!" Callum called, his head appearing in the crack of the door. "I'm just getting out of the shower.

Make yourself comfortable. You know, if you can in a cabin shared by four guys."

He smiled the one that made my throat go dry, but it already was. Something about him mentioning the shower and me realizing he was very likely naked behind that door made my throat, knees, and heart malfunction.

He was just ducking behind the door again when he stopped. "Did you swim through a river to get here or something?" His eyes moved down my body. More slow than quick.

"Rain. Cotton." I pinched the cuff of my sleeve. I felt like I was wringing a sponge. "It happens."

"Why don't you grab a change of my clothes and throw them on? I just did laundry, so my dresser's fully stocked."

"With clothes that are size Ripped?"

"With clothes that are condition Dry." He pointed at his dresser beside his bunk. "Come on. Everyone else is gone for the night, so you don't have to worry about anyone seeing you not topping the fashion charts."

"Oh yeah, because that's my priority." I ran my hands down my outfit. Camp Kismet shirt, denim cutoffs, and Tevas. And a messy ponytail. *Vogue* had nothing on me.

Callum chuckled, giving me another one of those looks. Another one of those looks he'd been giving me a lot lately. The ones that made me think he was picturing me the same way I was picturing him at the very moment. As far as acting on it, he'd been a saint. His hands hadn't wandered out of bounds once, but his eyes sometimes told a different story. He could control his body, but not his thoughts.

Right now I wished it were the other way around.

"You look great no matter what you're wearing. Even if it's one of my ratty old flannels," he said, pointing at the dresser again. "Middle drawer is shirts. Bottom is pants. Help yourself."

"What's in the top?" I headed for his dresser, not because I was cold from my wet clothes, but because he seemed adamant. My wet clothes were the equivalent of a cold shower and as my totally inappropriate thoughts could confirm, I needed an extra-cold one.

"There's nothing in there you'd want to put on, I promise." He opened the door a little more when I kept moving toward the dresser. Maybe if I moved just a little more . . .

And nope. He wasn't opening the door any wider, but I caught a nice glimpse of his abs, and that was no small thing. Guy runners had great stomachs, but the sprinters ruled the ab world. Emerson had once whispered to me that the guy sprinters on my track team had abs that were grab-your-ankles good.

I'd thought she'd been exaggerating. And then came Callum's abs . . .

"No, but there's probably something in there I'd have fun taking off." I raised a suggestive eyebrow in his direction.

He wet his lips, moved like he was about to slide through the door . . . then slammed it shut behind him. A long sigh followed, echoing under the door.

We'd both been feeling the tension. Bad.

"How was today's adventure in crafting?" he called as I pulled open his middle drawer.

"Agonizing." I fingered through a few of his shirts until I found my favorite flannel of his, the black-and-red checked one that I teased made him look like a lumberjack. "How was your adventure in advanced mountain biking?"

"Dreadful," he answered instantly. "Total torture. Flying down mountains at forty miles per hour. Rolling over Prius-size boulders. Agonizing, every mile of it."

"If you're trying to make me feel better, it's working." I

checked the door to make sure it was still closed before shim-
mying out of my wet shirt. It landed on the wood floor with a
loud thwack. I slid into Callum's flannel like I was in a speed-
dressing contest. I don't know why, but standing half naked
in his room, right next to his bed while he was hot out of the
shower a whole ten feet away was a tad intimidating and tempt-
ing at the same time. "Ben doesn't trust me to lead the outdoor
activities anymore, does he?" I asked in an effort to distract
myself as I wrestled out of my shorts.

Callum was quiet on the other side of the door.

"Hello? Don't make me come in there and force the answer
from you." I lightly tapped on the wall like I was knocking on
the door as I buttoned up his flannel. It was so big it could
have been a dress on me, so instead of reaching for a pair of
pants, I grabbed a rolled-up pair of wool socks and slid them
on my feet. There. Dry. Except for two pieces of underwear I
was not going to replace with anything of Callum's.

"That's supposed to be a threat, right?"

"Except I don't make threats," I answered with just enough
insinuation I knew he'd picked up on it.

"Have you talked to Ben about it?" His voice was a note
high—yeah, he'd definitely picked up on my meaning.

"No, but his message is pretty obvious." As I rolled up the
cuffs of Callum's shirt, I inspected my hands. Where dirt had
been under my nails at the beginning of the summer, now rub-
ber cement and tempura paint was.

"Well, how do you feel about it? Do you feel ready to
get back out there and be responsible for that many people
when the danger is more than a runny glue gun or an open
safety pin?"

I took a moment to think about that. Long enough to lay
my shirt and shorts over the heater to dry.

"What do you think?" I asked, pulling a few books from my backpack before leaning it against the heater, too. "Would you free me from crafts hell if you could?"

He was quiet again. "If you felt ready, then yeah, I would."

"And if I didn't?"

"I think you just answered your own question." The bathroom door opened, and he came out. A plume of steam followed him. I swallowed and imagined a litter of kittens batting at a bunch of butterflies. Anything to distract me from where my mind wanted to go.

I never knew until recently that I had such a dirty mind.

"Do you trust me?" I was still kneeling by the heater, stacking books, but I had to know. Nothing seemed more important, not even what my unruly hormones were trying to convince me of.

Callum hadn't noticed me crouched over by the heater when he'd first stepped out. When he did, he stopped dead in his tracks. "You're not wearing any pants."

I hadn't felt self-conscious about it before. At least before he looked at me like I was standing in front of him in a scrap of sheer fabric, curling my finger at him.

"Stop trying to distract me from the topic." I tugged at the hem of the flannel as I stood up.

"You're the one wearing nothing from the waist down, and I'm the one who's distracting?" He closed the bathroom door and leaned into it. It looked more like he was gluing himself to it.

"I've lived in cutoffs that show way more leg than this thing." I swiped my hand across where the shirt fell just above my knees. "And I'm not wearing *nothing* from the waist down. I've got on underwear."

Callum scrubbed his face. "Not helping."

"Come on. It's a simple question: Do you trust me?" I leaned into the wall behind me and looked at him across the room. Obviously, neither of us trusted the other to get any closer with him fresh from the shower and me running around in his shirt.

"Right now, that is not a simple question. My head's so dizzy you could ask me my name and it wouldn't be a simple question." When he shook his head, smacking at it with his palm, I laughed.

"Fine. I'll throw a blanket on and cover myself." I padded over to his bed in his thick wool socks that already had my feet all toasty warm and threw the covers open before crawling in. I dropped my stack of books on the nightstand. "Better?" I asked as I layered the sheets and blankets over myself.

"Oh yeah. You're crawling into my bed half naked." He shoved off the door and rolled his eyes. "*So* much better."

"Do you trust me?"

He moved to the heater and turned it up a few degrees. "As the guy who cares for you, absolutely."

"And as the other guy? Whoever that is?" I watched him move to the table pushed against a wall at the front of the cabin. That was where we usually studied, but tonight I was kinda digging his bed. It smelled like him, which made me picture him sleeping in it, which made me imagine what it would be like to be in it with him.

"Exactly. There isn't one." Callum opened the book we'd left off on last night and slid into one of the chairs. "The only one I want to be, and the only one I am when I'm with you, is the guy who cares for you."

I folded my hands over my book. "So you trust me?"

He smiled. "So I do." He held up a book and stuck his finger in it. "Picking up where we left off last night?"

I lifted my own book. "Math problems. They make my world go round."

"And here I'd been under the impression that was my job."

"Strong in this one, disillusionment is," I said in my best Yoda voice. When he laughed, it was definitely more the kind of laughing that was at me instead of with me.

I was barely through my first problem when Callum leaned away from his book. "How are things with your mom?"

My shoulders went tense. The topic of parental units had been a sensitive one this week after I found out Harry and I would be in a school district that wasn't exactly known for its above-average test scores or state championship sports teams. Jefferson School District was well known for a few things, though: its dropout and pregnancy rates.

"About the same as they were yesterday when you asked," I answered.

"And how's Harry dealing with things?"

I was thumping my pencil against my workbook. Spending so much time together, we'd clearly picked up on a few of each other's habits. "He's dealing better than I am."

"That must make you feel at least a little bit better about the move." Callum was keeping his voice level, not because he was an impartial party when it came to The Move, but because he was almost as opinionated as I was. He was upset because I was upset, and we were both upset, because at my old school, I was a whole hour closer to where he and his mom lived. At Dropout Pregnancy High, a two-hour drive across some seriously congested interstates separated us.

"It makes me feel a ton better that he's okay with it, but that doesn't mean it's okay."

He nodded and slid the wet strands of hair behind his ears. "You know why they didn't tell you, though, right?"

"They're selfish jack-holes?"

"They didn't want you to worry," he said after popping off a quick laugh.

"It didn't work."

"But they didn't know that. They were hoping they could fix things before you or Harry had to find out. Before things had to change." His voice was the equivalent of a warm hug, and usually I would have let myself be comforted by it, but not right now. Not with this.

"They lied because that was the easy thing to do. The path of least resistance." I drew my legs up to my chest so he couldn't see my face. I didn't want him to see me cry, and I felt close to crying the angry kind of tears.

"Lying to someone you care about isn't easy, Phoenix. Whatever a person's reason or justification for it, keeping the truth from a person you love is never easy."

He didn't say anything after that, and when I heard his pencil scratching across his book, I lowered my knees enough to get a glimpse of him.

Callum was focused on his workbook, moving through each problem almost methodically. As it turned out, there was so much information and advice on how to overcome test anxiety we'd been on information overload for a few days. After that, though, we were able to sort through what worked for him and what didn't, and each day he got better. Each practice test he took, he improved.

He'd slipped into a light gray thermal shirt that clung to him in all the right places, and he was wearing my favorite pair of jeans. My stomach started the process of tying itself into knots, so I distracted myself with something other than my study guide. Mathematical proofs were just not going to do it for me tonight.

I glanced over at his nightstand. A couple of study guides were stacked on it, his headlamp, and two photos. I knew the one was of his mom because he carried a photo of her in his wallet, too. Callum had the same brownish hair she had, and the same smile. She was really pretty but had this tough look about her. Maybe *tough* wasn't the right word; maybe it was more strength I saw when I looked at her picture.

I could only imagine the strength it took to raise two boys alone in California, a state not exactly known for its stellar cost of living.

It was the second photo that caught my attention. "Is this your dad?"

Callum didn't look up from his book. "Yeah."

"I thought you never knew him." Their dad was holding an about-two-year-old Callum in one arm and his brother in his other arm. Both of the boys were smiling. Their dad was, too.

"I didn't. Not really. Every once in a while, when he needed a place to crash or ran out of cash, he'd come home for a 'visit.' Which I figured out later meant he came home to raid Mom's coffee can of money and throw down a few home-cooked meals before skipping out on us again. You know, usually right when my brother and I were just getting used to him being back." Callum's pencil starting whacking at his book. "He's a real piece of work, my old man."

"But you keep a picture of him on your nightstand," I said gently. "You must have some good memories, too."

"I keep the picture close by to remind me of the kind of person I don't want to become, not to remind me of the person pretending to play dad in that photo."

I turned from the picture to look at him. His forehead was creased and his back was tense. He might have looked like his dad, but he wasn't like him. "You're a good person, Callum. You've got nothing to worry about."

He managed a smile and then returned to studying. Or at least pretending to study. I knew he was because I was pretending, too. Crawling into his bed had been a bad call because now it was the only thing I could focus on. His bed. Me in it. Scheming ways to lure him into it.

I needed to move to the desk where he was if I actually wanted to learn anything tonight. But I was wearing his shirt, and even though it covered more skin than my everyday outfits here at camp, the way he looked at me in it was like I was prancing around in lingerie. So I stayed put.

My pencil went from my hand to my mouth to behind my ear, and back to my hand again. My feet wouldn't stop bouncing as I tried to focus on the problem in the study guide instead of the question playing on repeat in my head. I'd wanted to ask the question for a while, but I'd chickened out each time I'd come close.

"Have you ever had sex?" The words spilled out all at once, sounding more like *haveyoueverhadsex*.

Callum's face flattened from the concentrated one he'd had as he slowly turned away from his workbook. "And how 'bout them isosceles triangles?"

My cheeks were hot and probably fire red, but I didn't care. He looked almost as uncomfortable with the question as I did.

Callum set down his pencil and closed his book. "Is that you asking because you want to know the truth? Or what you hope is the truth?"

I bookmarked my spot with my pencil and closed my book. "You really have to ask me that?"

He glanced at the door for a moment before he turned in his chair toward me. "I just know from personal experience that when a girl asks a guy if and who he's been with, she usually wants to hear he's never looked, touched, or been with anyone else. That he's never even *thought* about wanting to look, touch, or do."

I lifted my shoulders. "Not this girl. This one will take the cold, hard truth all the time, every time."

Callum rolled his neck. I heard it crack. His eyes stayed on mine the whole time, though, giving me a chance to change the subject or change my mind on the "cold, hard truth" thing.

I didn't blink as I stared back.

He clasped his hands together. "Yeah, I've been with a few girls before." He was still looking at me, so I tried not to show anything that might have cut him short. "But that was a long time ago."

My heart was thudding in my ears, and my stomach was twisting. It wasn't the good way I was used to them feeling when Callum's mouth was on mine or when his thumbs scrolled along my lower back. It was the other way.

"You're eighteen," I said. "How long ago could it have been?" My voice didn't sound right, so I cleared my throat.

His hands unclasped, then clasped together again. "I got an early start."

I wasn't going to ask just how early. My imagination could fill in that dot, dot, dot just fine.

"And since?" My voice sounded normal, but now it was too quiet.

"My brother got a girl pregnant when he was sixteen." He rolled his neck again; it cracked twice that time. "That scared the shit out of me and made me realize I didn't want to have sex again until I could imagine raising a kid together, you know? 'Cause that's forever. I'm not cutting and running like my dad did."

My eyes narrowed as I tried to wrap my head around it. "So you're saying you don't want to have sex with someone unless you can see marrying her and living happily ever after?" I'd heard a lot of reasons for either waiting or not waiting to have sex, but this was a foreign concept coming from the mouth of a guy.

"No, I just don't want, in the crazy event I did get someone pregnant, the mom to be someone who can barely take care of herself, let alone a kid."

I didn't know what to say. Were we really having this conversation?

"You've given it a lot of thought." I wiggled my toes under the blankets, burning off some nervous energy. Callum and I were talking about sex—there was no shortage of nervous energy bouncing around.

"I kinda did it backward, though. Had sex, then thought about it, but"—he shrugged—"it is what it is."

After that, awkward silence. The kind that made me reach for my book and wish I could be working proofs instead of rolling in awkward silence.

I'd just opened my book when he shifted in his chair. "Have you ever been with anyone?"

I had gone from bouncing my toes to tapping my feet against the mattress. He'd just admitted he'd been with other girls before. I was about to tell him I had the experience of a nun. "Is that you asking for the truth? Or what you hope is true?" I asked, delaying the inevitable for a few more seconds. I wasn't embarrassed or anything by my lack of experience in the intimacy department, but admitting it to Callum felt really personal—like I was sharing a deep, dark secret instead of how many, few, or no guys I'd slept with.

"Do you really have to ask?" he repeated, his smile as thin and stretched as a crescent moon.

I sucked a slow breath in through my mouth. "No," I said. "Close, but no, not all the way."

Callum leaned forward in his chair. "And this is the real truth version?"

I turned my hand up. "That's the cold, hard truth version." The skin between his brows creased. *Really?*

I slid my ponytail over my shoulder. It was still wet and had formed a damp ring on the back of Callum's shirt. "Why are you acting all surprised?"

"Because it's not that common." His hands had been resting on the arms of the chair, but now they were gripping them. I watched his knuckles fade to white. "So if we . . . you know"—he shrugged, filling in the unsaid—"I'd be your first?"

My legs squeezed together. Did that mean he was suggesting he be my first? Volunteering for the position? "And I'd be your fourth or fifth," I counted out on my fingers. "Special."

"Hey, that didn't mean anything." He scooted his chair closer so it was just at the end of the desk.

"Says every guy in history, but it had to mean something." I slid up on his bed. I hadn't realized how far I'd let myself recline. "Or else you wouldn't have done it. Again. And again."

Callum exhaled as a frustrated look settled on his face. He was quiet for a minute, staring out the window at the rain still pummeling down. His face cleared suddenly. "Have you ever eaten a porterhouse steak?"

I wasn't sure I'd heard him right. We'd just been talking about sex, and now he was bringing up steak? "Not following."

He stared at the window a little longer before looking at me. "A porterhouse steak is like the best damn thing in the whole world. There is nothing better in this galaxy or the next one over. Nothing."

I wasn't a big red-meat eater, so I shrugged. "Okay, I believe you."

"Have you ever eaten packing popcorn?"

My nose curled. "Now, that I definitely have not eaten."

"Yeah, well, I have." He must have seen the question on my face. "Don't ask. Big brothers and dares—that's all I'm going to say. Anyway, it tastes like chemical air and goes down like sandpaper. The worst stuff ever."

"In this galaxy and the next one over?"

He smiled at me. "Exactly."

"I feel like you're trying to make a point, but the packing popcorn is throwing me." My eyes narrowed as I tried to figure out what had gotten us from sex to comparing substances of a questionably edible quality.

Callum looked at me, like the answer should have been obvious. Then he pointed at me. "*You* are the porterhouse. The best. All those other girls, any other girl, they're packing popcorn." He shook his head, never breaking eye contact. "They hold no appeal, and yeah, sure, I might have tried a bite, but I sure as hell am not doing it again."

My chest hurt right then. I experienced that tightness I'd heard described before but never actually felt. I thought I knew the name for the feeling, but I wasn't sure I was ready to say it out loud yet.

"So I'm a big slab of meat?"

He chuckled. "I think my point more had to do with them being packing popcorn, but yeah"—one shoulder lifted and stayed there—"you're the best damn porterhouse steak in this galaxy and beyond."

"You really love your analogies, dove boy."

He grumbled and shook his head, giving me a look that told me he knew I was giving him a hard time. "Fine. Still not convinced?" He suddenly shot from his chair, lunged across the room, and sprang up onto the top bunk above me, and in one smooth motion, he leaped from the bunk to the rafters.

With one hand clamped around one of the beams, his other arm and the rest of his body stretched out beneath, he smiled down at me, still swinging from his insane leap. "There," he said, pointing at the floor below him. "That's where those other girls are, and here"—he smacked the beam with one hand, now swinging from just one arm—"is where you are, way up here." Instead of grabbing onto the rafter again, he let his arm fall at his side. Show-off. "But we're talking each inch from there to here is like a mile. Or a thousand. The point is, they're down there and you're up here." His gaze dipped from the floor to the roof before landing on me. "Now, can we just stop talking about it? Before I run out of analogies and superhuman feats, and quite possibly break my neck?"

I couldn't stop smiling up at him, swinging above me like a monkey to make a point. When I'd asked Keats to tell me how he felt about me, he'd lowered my hand to his crotch to "show" me what I did to him. Yeah, I'd take Callum's version any day.

"You've made your point," I shouted up at him. "Come down before you hurt the cabin."

He waggled his brows, and instead of swinging to the top bunk the way he'd come, he dropped to the floor. It wasn't exactly a kiddie-size drop, either. When his feet hit the floor, a sharp grunt followed.

"Are you okay?" I scrambled up, tossing the books from my lap. "What did you break, sprain, or damage?"

With a grimace of pain on his face, he half stumbled, half fell closer, until he'd fallen right over me. I shrieked, worried he really had hurt himself, then one arm found my waist, pulling me close; the other moved to the headboard, shoving on it until he'd lowered us into a more horizontal than upright position.

My thighs squeezed together feeling him on top of me. All of him on top of me.

"That worked better than I'd planned." His arm lowered from the headboard to my ponytail. He wound it around his fingers, burying his hand in the base of it.

"Are you okay?" I managed. His hips shifted above mine, and instead of moving to the side like they typically did, he fitted them over mine. The blankets were still between us and everything, but it wasn't like they provided that much of a buffer. I could still feel him.

"I'm very okay." His hand tightened in my hair, and just when I thought he was going to kiss me, he stopped. His eyes cleared a little. "Listen, if there's anything I do, anywhere I touch, that doesn't feel right, let me know, okay? I'll stop." His lips brushed mine gently. "You set the pace."

I bobbed my head and wiggled my arms free from beneath him. He was touching me in all the right places, and I wanted a turn. "Okay." Wow. I did not have that sultry bedroom voice I'd imagined or hoped I would.

"You can trust me. You know that, right?"

I bit my lip when he shifted again. He was just trying to find a comfortable position, but every time his hips moved against mine, "comfort" wasn't on my mind.

"I wouldn't be here if I didn't trust you." I moved my hand behind his head. "It's okay," I whispered before his lips dropped to mine.

I froze for a second, like I always did when he kissed me, but he knew how to unthaw me. His tongue traced the seam of my lips, parting my mouth before touching mine.

I kissed him back, moving my other hand down his side. I'd passed the frozen stage and moved on to the unable-to-breathe one. It didn't matter what we did or how long we did it—I never moved past this stage. A rumble vibrated in his throat when my kissing moved past the slow-and-sweet category. His hand stayed buried in my hair, the other one snug around my waist, but I wasn't as content to keep my hands glued in place.

The one sliding down his side stopped at the waist of his jeans. Slipping my pinkie just inside, I skimmed it across his stomach, slowing when it got to the middle. His chest started falling against mine harder, faster. When I traced the line a bit lower on the return trip, he trembled.

Just one little pinkie. Barely skimming his skin. If that could make him tremble, I wondered what doing other things would do to him. It made me want to find out.

I didn't stop kissing him as I flattened my palm against his stomach, and this time I slid it up the canyon of his abs, stopping on his chest. My fingers curled into him, trying to pull him closer.

His kisses deepened, like he was trying to pull me closer, too.

I didn't remember reaching for the bottom of his shirt, but I did remember pulling it over his head and arms. I didn't remember where I threw it, but I did remember the way he looked hovering above me without a shirt, his mouth parted from breathing hard, his chest moving like something was trying to escape from it.

He sat up, straddling me, as he started unbuttoning the flannel I was wearing. He hesitated after the first button, looking at me like he was checking to see if this was okay. I'd barely nodded, and the next button was free. The rest followed in what felt like no time at all. At first he kind of froze, looking down at me with that conflicted look I'd seen on him before. I didn't want him to stop. I didn't want to go all the way yet, but that didn't mean I wanted him to stop.

Shoving up from the mattress, I let the flannel slide off my shoulders and pulled the sleeves free from each arm.

We were at eye level, and I could tell he was trying to keep his eyes on mine, but it was so hard I could almost make out the beads of sweat forming at his hairline. Harry would have said he had the self-control of a Jedi Master . . . but it felt wrong thinking about my little brother when I was deep into make-out territory.

Just as I started to move toward him, his eyes captured mine. I couldn't remember a time I'd ever seen them so alive, not even that time on the river. "God, Phoenix. I can't breathe when I'm with you."

When his hand reached for mine, I reached for his. "When I'm in your bed and just removed my shirt?"

His fingers slid through mine and he smiled. "*Anytime* I'm with you."

He was just pulling me closer—or was that me pulling him closer?—when the cabin door fired open and someone strutted inside. Callum moved quickly, throwing the covers over me.

"Holy . . . !" Ethan braked to a stop, his mouth dropping as far as his jaw would allow from the looks of it.

"Turn around!" Callum hollered.

Ethan kept doing everything *but* turning around while I started wiggling into Callum's flannel again.

"That meant now, asshole!" Callum popped off when he noticed Ethan still staring.

Callum's jaw set as he reached for something on his nightstand. He fired a pair of balled-up socks at Ethan and managed to whack him across the face.

"Dude, you guys just made my summer." I couldn't see him thanks to the tensed chest barricade blocking me, but Ethan's voice was the equivalent of high-fiving a packed room.

Callum's shoulder tensed so much his neck almost disappeared. "Shut the hell up, Ethan."

Fastening the last button, I slid from behind the human wall.

Callum grabbed my hand and tugged on it, but when I stayed my ground, he let me go.

Ethan's grin stretched from ear to ear as I grabbed something off Evan's nightstand. I didn't figure he'd mind me borrowing it, especially when he found out what I'd used it for.

"Someone told you to shut the hell up, right?" I plastered on a smile as I approached Ethan.

"Maybe," he said around a shrug. "Selective hearing."

I kept the smile in place as I rolled to a stop in front of him. It wasn't until I'd started pulling on the item of Evan's that Ethan's face started to change. I heard Callum's footsteps moving up behind me, but he didn't force his way between us. He was letting me take care of this.

When I figured I'd pulled enough free from the roll, I tore it off with my teeth. This stuff was tough.

Ethan gave an overdone shiver. "Duct tape?" His smile pitched high on one side. "I didn't take you for the kinky type, New Girl, but here you go. Do your worst." Clasping his hands together, Ethan held his wrists up for me to bind.

That wasn't the body part I had in mind, though.

Stepping a little to the side, I lifted the piece of tape higher, past his neck, and before he knew what was happening, I had it stretched tightly across his mouth.

I gave it a few rubs, just to make sure it was good and stuck, and then I smiled up at him like I was the most innocent thing on this side of the planet. "There. How's that for kinky?"

Behind me, Callum barked out a laugh and followed me toward the door, but as he was passing Ethan, Callum clapped his hand over Ethan's shoulder. "Warned you."

TWENTY-FIVE

"You've got it wrong."

That was all I'd heard today, and this last one was the tipping point.

"That's never going to hold."

Across the table, Harry scooted down the bench a little, like he was worried that when I blew, he was in the worst possible location.

"And how do you know that, Gretchen?" I twisted in my seat and looked at her. I was the counselor leading Lincoln Log Mania scheduled this afternoon in the dining hall, but she'd taken the reins from me on this like she had just about every other craft, project, and game I'd been in charge of the past few weeks.

She was pretty much the queen of indoor recess.

"The base you built." She moved up behind me and waved her hand at the Lincoln Log house I'd spent the last three hours of my life building. "The foundation is all wrong. Everything you build on top of it is not going to hold if you don't get the base right." Gretchen gave my Lincoln Log shack another sad wave before shaking her head and moving down the line, barking suggestions and comments as if she was running the activity.

Like I cared if she was.

I was so sick of being trapped inside the dining hall day in and day out, cleaning dried glue from the tables and picking tiny beads up from the floor I was about to go Mount St. Helens all over this place.

If it hadn't been for my morning runs and evening "study" sessions with Callum, I would have been committed days ago. There was only so much crafting one person could take, and I'd hit my limit after the first day. Crafts just weren't my thing. Creative expression was something I equated with medieval torture practices.

I hadn't been scheduled to lead anything even remotely outdoorsy. Although when I'd complained about that to Callum earlier in the week, he'd brought up that I'd gotten to forage for leaves and flowers with the "crafts bunch" before locking ourselves up in the dining hall to layer them into presses. That was *not* my idea of enjoying the great outdoors, but I knew he'd just been trying to cheer me up, so I let him . . . and then I *really* let him.

Callum had been my saving grace lately, Harry had been my welcome distraction, Dad was still MIA, and Mom I'd just done everything I could to steer clear of. I wasn't ready to talk yet after everything she'd told us. I wasn't sure I ever would be, because what was there to talk about? It wasn't like I could talk myself out of this. What was coming was coming.

"You can build that as high as you want, but it's just going to fall apart at the slightest wobble." Gretchen had made her way around the table and was across from me now, shaking her head between my "house" and me. "You might as well start over and get it right this time."

My teeth ground together. Harry scooted farther down the bench, shoving his friends with him.

"It's fine. Thank you—so much—for your concern, but I built it just fine. How's yours coming along?"

Hint, hint.

"Finished." Gretchen waved down at the end of the table, where what looked like a Lincoln Log estate had been constructed. I checked the clock on the wall to see if I'd accidentally let seventy-two hours pass when I thought it had just been three. No can do. We hadn't even reached the two-hour mark, and I was about to take a couple of the longer, narrower Lincoln Log pieces and jab my eyes out with them. "Kind of like how your house is going to be if the table does this." Grabbing on the edge of the table, Gretchen gave it a shake. It wasn't that much of one really, but it was enough.

My house fell over.

"See what I mean? If you don't get the foundation right, you might as well just start from scratch." She shrugged and managed to both give me a look of sympathy and pity, before moving down the line.

Grabbing the base of what had been my house, I dropped it onto the floor after shoving off the bench. Heads whipped around as Lincoln Log building came to a standstill. "I'll be right back," I announced to the group, but no one made eye contact.

I marched through the dining hall, stormed into the kitchen, and didn't stop to give it a second thought before pounding on Ben's office door. I couldn't take it anymore. If this was how I was going to spend the last two weeks at camp, he could just fire me because I'd had it.

Crafts paraphernalia would haunt my nightmares for the rest of my life after this summer.

"Come in," Ben hollered.

I was already shoving open the door.

"Phoenix?" It was like he was surprised to see me. "Aren't you leading Lincoln Log Mania right now?"

"That's why I'm here." I started pacing in front of his desk. "I can't take it anymore."

Ben leaned back in his office chair and wrapped his arms behind his head like he was relaxing. At least one of us was. "You can't take *what* anymore?"

"Being the crafts activity bitch. Day in. Day out."

If Ben was surprised by my word choice, he didn't show it. Instead, he did a slow spin in his chair. "I thought you were enjoying it."

My eyes widened into saucers. "Who did you hear that from? *Masochist Illustrated*?"

Instead of answering, Ben did a couple more spins in his chair. "And am I to take it that the reason you're sharing this with me is because you'd like me to do something about it?"

I wiped my hands off on my shirt. I was so worked up I was actually hand sweating. Gross. "Yes, but if you can't, then I'd like to know so I can give you my notice."

Ben smiled at his desk. "Your *two-week* notice?"

I sighed. There were only two weeks left of summer. "So are you saying I'm wearing the crafts bitch crown the rest of summer? Because if you fire me, I don't need to worry about the notice thing."

"Have you done something that would give me a reason to fire you?" Ben steepled his hands in front of him. "Because I guess these days an employer has to have a really good reason for firing someone. Lawyers and their red tape."

I thought about that. I didn't have to think long. I'd probably done half a dozen things that were worthy of a firing. Leaving my Lincoln Log hell being the most recent offense.

"Take your pick. If there's a right way to do it, chances are I've done it wrong."

Ben made a face. "That's how we learn. We can't do it right the first time all the time."

"So does that mean you'll take me off crafts duty?" I stopped in front of his desk. I couldn't read his face. He could have been experiencing nirvana as easily as he could have been getting a cavity filled. With Ben, sometimes it was hard to tell. "Or does that mean you're firing me?"

Ben smiled at his messy desk again. "Have you expressed your dissatisfaction to Callum?"

Most of the camp knew Callum and I were an item. Not because we were all open and PDA about it, but because Ethan couldn't keep his mouth shut and duct tape only worked for so long. Ben knew about us because Callum had told him. He said he didn't want it to feel like we were going behind his back.

"Yeah, only about every single day," I answered. Callum had taken the brunt of my whining and complaining.

That was when Ben's smile faded and his forehead creased.

"What?" I moved closer. "What is it?"

"I appreciate you bringing this up to me because I want to know when one of my employees is unhappy, but I'm afraid you're talking to the wrong person if you're hoping to get your schedule changed." Ben looked up at me, reading the question on my face. "I don't make the counselors' schedules." My breath stopped before he said it, because I already knew. "Callum does."

That feeling of getting the wind knocked out of you? I'd only had it happen once, but there was no way to forget how it'd felt. It was the exact way I was feeling now, but I hadn't fallen from the tree I'd been trying to climb this time. This time, I'd just fallen from the fairy-tale branch.

"Callum makes the schedules?" I said to myself, dazed.

"I thought you knew." Ben sat up in his chair. "I thought that the reason you'd spent the last few weeks in the dining hall was because you'd requested it. I didn't know he was the one who was . . ."

What Ben left unsaid, I filled in the blank. "Lying to me?"

Ben shook his head. "Not what I was going to say." He shook his head again. "I know how Callum feels about you, and believe me when I say—"

"Where is he?"

Ben turned around and stared out his office window. "He had the afternoon off. Was going to spend a few hours rock climbing."

"Which spot?" I didn't know how I could sound so calm when it felt like a fireworks display was going off inside me.

"Patterson Ridge."

"Thank you." I started moving for the door. "Can you check in on Lincoln Log Mania, maybe? Gretchen's doing a great job leading it, but just in case the campers decide they've had enough . . ."

"I've got it covered." Ben spun around as I was closing the door behind me. "Phoenix? He cares about you. No matter what he did or why he did it, he did it first because he cares about you. Keep that in mind."

I paused in the doorway. "I think you're confusing care for control."

Ben shook his head. "Maybe *you* are."

I wasn't in the mood to get into an argument with Ben when I had one with Callum's name written all over it. Closing the door behind me, I jogged through the kitchen, through the dining hall, and had found my stride by the time I'd hit the central lawn. I wasn't wearing my sneakers, but I could run pretty fast in my Tevas.

Patterson Ridge was about a mile from camp and was one of the more technical faces to climb. Which meant it was Callum's favorite. He never took the campers here when it was rock-climbing day, but he spent plenty of his afternoons off here. I'd joined him last week and been amazed by how easy he made climbing a vertical, seemingly smooth rock wall look. He climbed "free," which meant he didn't use a harness and carabiners or anything. To me, it seemed suicidal, but he brought an inflatable mattress with him and positioned it below where he'd be climbing. You know, so if he did slip, hopefully it would break his fall. Before he broke his neck.

Or, in today's case, I broke his neck instead.

It didn't take me long to get there, but instead of giving me a chance to cool down, it did the opposite. So when I rounded the last bend of trail that put me in front of the forty-foot rock wall, I was feeling nuclear.

Callum was about halfway up the wall, managing to keep his movements in line with the air mattress he had stationed below him. He was in an old pair of cargo pants and his climbing shoes, and had ditched his shirt on a tree branch. His hands were white with chalk, and even from back here, I could see how much he was sweating. It was the dead of the afternoon on a ninety-degree day, and he was climbing a hot rock wall—he was lucky he hadn't turned into a puddle.

I was about to shout up at him but swallowed his name when I saw him bracing for a tough move. There was a spot on the wall where a lip stuck out a couple of inches, but it was a few feet up and over. The only way to get to it was to jump.

He checked the mattress below him, stuck his free hand in his chalk bag, and sucked in a breath I knew he'd hold until he'd made the jump. Every muscle spanning his back broke through his skin right before he leaped. His foot pressed off the foothold and his arm reached up.

My heart stopped, just like it had when I'd watched him do this last week. His fingers weren't connecting—they weren't going to make it. He hadn't given himself enough of a lift.

Just when I was about to rush forward to make sure the mattress was in the right spot to catch him, his fingers caught the lip. The veins in the arm holding his entire weight bulged through his skin, and then his foot found a tiny crevice to wedge into.

I didn't know I'd been holding my breath until it all came out in a big rush.

He didn't pause a beat to celebrate the victory. He just kept climbing, making his way up on handholds and footholds that were impossible to see from the ground.

Now that the worst part of the climb was over, I remembered why I was here—and it wasn't to gawk at him gliding up the side of a rock.

The first step I took, my foot cracked a twig in the middle of the trail. Like he didn't have anything else to concentrate on besides the sound of a twig snapping, Callum stopped climbing.

He was already smiling when he looked down. "And my day just keeps getting better."

I felt that familiar pull. The one that made me feel like when I was with him, everything was okay. I was going to miss that. "You might want to climb down for this."

His shoulder lifted. "All right." He worked his fist from the crack he'd wedged it in, and let go. I rushed forward a step, but he'd crashed into the air mattress before I could take another.

He didn't grunt or take a moment to shake it off. He just rolled off the mattress and leaped up. His smile hadn't moved.

"And look." His arms thrust down at the air mattress. "I brought a mattress."

I didn't look at it. If I did, I might remember what we'd done on that mattress last week, and then I'd crumble. I couldn't crumble. I had to stay strong.

"You lied to me."

Callum's smile held. "So I shouldn't have brought a mattress?" He thought I was messing with him.

My arms crossed. "I'm being serious, Callum."

He motioned between the mattress and me. "I am, too."

"You lied about Ben being the one who'd been making my schedule." That was when his smile started to fade. "Because it's *you* who makes the schedule, and *you* who are responsible for my stint in crafts hell."

He exhaled and hung his hands on his hips. "I didn't lie to you, Phoenix. I might have omitted a few things, but I never lied to you."

I could actually feel my blood warm—that was how quickly the anger inside formed. "You had me believe it was Ben who made the schedules."

"No, you made yourself believe that. I just didn't do anything to make you think differently."

"Why didn't you tell me?"

"Because I was afraid of this." When he lifted his hand to wave between us, his hand had left a chalky handprint hovering just above his hip. "I was worried you wouldn't get it and would be pissed first and understanding second. And forgiving last," he added, cracking his neck like I'd seen him do a hundred times before.

"Yeah, well, you were right," I fired back.

He was still sweating and breathing hard. Probably because he was dehydrated from sweating a gallon of water climbing that thing. I shouldn't have, but I moved toward his metal water canteen and tossed it over at him.

Callum studied the bottle in his hand, the skin between his brows creased. "I'm confused." His gaze went from the bottle to me, where I was almost shaking from being so upset.

"Yeah, just imagine how I feel finding out the guy who said—no, the one who *promised* he trusted me—is the same one who doesn't trust me enough to lead a few people on a two-mile hike that has a whole elevation gain of twenty feet." When he stayed quiet and still, refusing to take a drink of water, I stomped. "You said you trusted me!"

"I know what I said." His voice was quiet.

"But clearly you don't."

His eyes flashed. "Don't tell me what I do and don't think." Then he threw the water bottle onto the mattress like he was staging some kind of thirst strike.

Fine. Like I cared.

"Fine. I'll ask again since I'm a little sketchy on the topic." I had to work my jaw loose to get the next part out. "Do you trust me?" His mouth opened to answer instantly. "And don't even think about lying to me again."

His mouth snapped closed, and the muscles of his neck went rigid. "I've never lied to you once, and that's not going to change."

I waited. Good luck talking his way out of this.

His eyes closed for a second. "As your boyfriend, I trust you," he started, each word coming slow. "As the lead counselor responsible for every camper here, I needed you to earn back some of the trust you'd lost."

My shoulders fell. "So you don't trust me."

His eyes flew open. "I'd trust you with my life."

"Just not the lives of the other people here at camp." I waved my hand dismissively, which set him off.

"There's a hell of a lot more room between trusting some-one and not trusting someone. Or haven't you learned that yet?"

"I don't know. I think I learned a whole lot about trust this afternoon."

"It's black-and-white to you. So this or that. There's no room for error and no room for mistakes. How's a person sup-posed to live up to that kind of a standard?"

"Listen, it is really cut and dried, Callum. I either trust you or I don't. You either trust me or you don't. You can't kinda, sorta, maybe trust me. Sorry, it just doesn't work like that."

He was glaring into the trees, the same way I was glaring at him. "You know, this is as good a time as any, I guess." Mov-ing toward his pack he'd propped up against a tree, he lowered down and unzipped it.

I stood there watching him, confused. I felt so close to crying or exploding or melting I couldn't even guess what he was doing.

"Look who can't trust who." Callum stuck his arm up from where he was crouched on the ground. In his hand was a wad of papers.

"Am I supposed to know what you're talking about?" I took a step closer, but that was when it clicked. He didn't need to bolt up and move closer like he was, sticking his finger at the papers like he was trying to light them on fire. "Callum, let me explain . . . ," I said, scrambling. I'd come here ready to battle him because of what he'd done, not defend myself for what *I'd* done.

"Oh, I think you explained yourself pretty good when you inflated the scores of every single practice test I've taken the past month." His fingers opened, and the whole stack of papers flew to the ground.

I moved toward the scattered papers, wanting to pick them up and explain. "How did you find out?"

"When I took a practice test on my own this morning and instead of the twelve hundreds I'd been killing it with lately, I barely managed an eight hundred." When he moved, he walked across the tests, grinding them into the dirt. "I wondered if I was having an off day or something, so I pulled all of these old ones out and realized pretty quick that I've been having a whole month of off days. Kind of like the rest of my life."

"It was only to boost your confidence, you know? To make you think you were really making a lot of progress so you wouldn't give up." That was when I felt the tears. "You've gotten better and better with every test. You *have* made improvement this summer."

"Just not exactly the kind of improvement you were hoping for, right? Not the kind that says *college-bound*." Callum moved to the rock wall and leaned into it. He wouldn't look at me.

"I was only trying to help. If I'd known you'd find out, I never would have done it." I couldn't stop staring at the scattered tests. I'd had the best of intentions when I'd overlooked a few wrong answers on each one, not that any of that mattered now.

"The funny thing is I wasn't even going to bring it up." Callum shrugged, looking all cold and removed. "My plan was to spend the afternoon clearing my head and climbing some rocks, and then burn every last one of these later tonight. I figured you hadn't meant much by them and probably were just trying to stroke my confidence a little." He tilted his head against the rock so he was looking up into the trees. "But then you reminded me just how trust works in your world, and either you do trust me or you don't." He paused and sniffed, sounding as removed as I'd ever heard him. "And, by the same token, that I either can or can't trust you."

I wanted to run to him right then. To put my arms around

him and say I was sorry and do my best to explain and make him understand where I'd been coming from and why I was such a damn wreck on the trust subject.

I was too late.

Callum pushed off the rock and was throwing his pack on a moment later. "Well, consider this me making my mark in the can't-trust-you box." He wouldn't look at me as he walked by. "I already know where you made yours."

"Callum," I whispered.

He didn't stop.

"Don't," I said louder, turning and watching him leave.

"Don't *what*?" He spun around. "I've had enough people in my life think I couldn't make it anywhere on my own without a handout. I sure as hell don't need my girlfriend to think the same. Just leave me alone, Phoenix."

I could hear my breath echoing in my ears.

"Callum, please . . ."

He kept moving down the trail. I'd screwed up. Seriously. "We always knew the summer would come to an end, Phoenix. It just came two weeks earlier than we'd planned."

TWENTY-SIX

I ran alone now. I studied alone, too. It felt like I did everything alone.

I supposed that came with the territory when the only person who trusted me was my kid brother.

Twelve days had gone by since Patterson Ridge, and I'd felt every second of them. Everyone said time eased pain, but from my experience, I could confidently say that was a load of bull. Time didn't ease any of my pain—it intensified it. Made it sharper. More noticeable. More overwhelming. More everything of a painful nature.

I couldn't just "get over" Callum like I had with Keats. Because Callum wasn't just any other guy. He was *that* guy.

So yeah, I'd gone from a mess to a wreck in under two weeks. I wondered where I'd be in another two weeks. Outlook wasn't exactly sunshine and roses.

That morning like the past eleven, I beat my alarm clock out of bed. Mostly because I couldn't sleep—another delightful side effect of feeling as if my heart had been ripped from my chest and diced into ribbons.

I tiptoed out of the room, careful not to wake Harry because he'd been on high alert with me lately. Most of the time when I caught him looking at me, it was as if he was on prisoner suicide watch, or whatever the big-sister version of that was. His wrist was still bandaged up, but getting better. By the start of school, the brace would be gone. Even Mom was fretting over me lately—she wasn't exactly sure what I needed, but it didn't keep her from trying.

Instead of stopping for my usual banana or breakfast bar, I continued through the kitchen and opened the squeaky cabin door as quietly as it was capable of.

The air was chilly this early, cooler than yesterday morning, and that one cooler than the one before. Summer was coming to a close, and as much as I wanted to pretend it never would, I knew I had two mornings left here before it was back to . . . wherever. Somewhere, California.

I wasn't ready to admit this was the end, though. No white flag waving yet. I still had a couple of days. Two days to figure out my whole entire life.

Yeah, 'cause that wasn't daunting or anything.

My shoulders slumped as I dropped down onto one of the stairs to pull on my running shoes. I wasn't actually expecting him to be waiting for me, leaning up against that beaten-up, old pine tree in front of the cabin steps, but I still checked for him every morning. I think part of me was hoping he'd show up one morning, running shoes and smile in place, like nothing had happened between us. I knew I'd be able to forget the past if he could. It didn't even seem that important anymore—what each of us had done that hurt the other. Best intentions gone way off the rails, right?

I knew that now—why couldn't I have realized that twelve days ago when it could have made a difference?

It took two tries to get my laces tied, and I was just thinking about forcing myself off that stair when the door wailed open behind me. The sound was so shrill it made me wince.

I figured it would be Harry, coming to give me the "look-over," but when I glanced back, I almost fell off the step I was perched on.

"Perfect morning for my first run in two years, don't you think?"

I whipped my head around and felt every muscle in my body tighten. "When did you get here?" The chilly air had clearly gotten to my voice, too.

"Late last night. Or early this morning, depending on how you look at it. I didn't want to wake you and Harry."

I glared into the trees. "We're leaving in two days. You missed the whole summer. Why come back now?"

"And miss a morning run like this? That was worth the six-hour red-eye drive."

I could barely talk to Dad. I was so angry at him and the circumstances and . . . I was just so, so angry.

Shoving up from the step, I started to leave. "Have a nice run."

"Phoenix." His voice was different, less faked and more real. I rolled to a stop but didn't look back.

I heard the stairs creak as he walked down them. "I'm sorry," he said, his voice catching on the last syllable. I felt something clump up in my throat. "I'm so, so sorry, sweetheart. I know I've let you and Harry and your mom down, but I'm going to do everything to make it right. I'm going to fix this, all of it. . . ." He paused to clear his throat. It sounded like he had something stuck in his throat, too. "If you'll give me a second chance. I don't deserve one and I haven't earned one, but I'm asking for one."

I'd been holding my breath. I only knew this because when

I finally took a breath, I sucked in a gasp of air. My shoulders were quivering, and as much as I wanted to run away, I couldn't move. My feet were stuck in place.

Wasn't it too late? What had been done had been done—our house wasn't ours anymore, Harry and I were leaving our schools, friends, everything familiar. What was there left for him to fix?

I didn't know he'd been moving closer until I felt his hand rest on my shoulder. It was hesitant at first, like he was expecting me to step to the side or swipe his hand away. I didn't move, though. It was the first time my dad had touched me with something resembling affection in a long time. I'd forgotten how strong his hands felt, and how strong they made me feel—like there was nothing that could hurt me when he was close.

I hadn't known I'd missed him until right then. I'd been so focused on being angry and disappointed and betrayed I'd blocked out what was at the core of all that—missing him. The real dad, not the shadow one.

When I exhaled, I felt everything inside relax. Or maybe I felt everything coming back together. I wasn't sure.

"I'm sorry." When his voice broke again as his hand squeezed my shoulder, I turned around.

"I'm sorry," he rasped, his throat bobbing. Lifting his arms, he slowly wound them around me and pulled me to him. It was gentle and restrained—he was giving me the chance to break away if I wanted.

But instead I found my own arms wrapping around him. I hugged my dad. He hugged me back.

I cried. He cried, too.

I wasn't sure I'd forgiven him or moved on or felt any less scared of the future, but I had my dad back, and for now, that felt like enough. I could work on the rest later.

"Harry . . ." I sniffed and moved my head from his chest to look up at him. The rims of his eyes were wet. "He can't go to a public school, Dad. You know that, right? He's spent all his life in private schools, and he's got the brain of a high schooler in a ten-year-old body. We can't do that to him. You know that, right?"

Dad's face crinkled when he smiled at me. He'd shaved and looked like he'd gotten a little sun, but he still looked old—like time had held him down and beaten him good and aged. He wiped the tear winding down my face. "I know that, Phoenix. And that is something I've managed to fix already."

I straightened. "You enrolled Harry in private school?"

"There's a good one a half hour away from the new house. He's enrolled, and it's all been paid for. At least for the next three years, but that will be long enough for me to get back on my feet."

I didn't know exactly how much Harry's last school had cost, but it wasn't cheap. Given that our family's financial status was dire, I couldn't figure out how Dad had managed to prepay three years of tuition just like that.

"How?" I asked.

"I sold my Mustang. Some guy paid asking price and everything."

"You sold your Mustang?" I sounded dumbfounded because I was. My dad loved that car so much I'd actually caught him sleeping in it a few times. Some people would save the photo albums or the family pet in the event of a fire—Dad would have saved his classic Mustang. I never thought he'd sell it. Actually, I thought he'd probably want to be buried in it.

"Ink's still wet on the title transfer." He said it was no big deal, but I knew better. It was a giant deal. He'd sold his most prized possession so his son could go to a nicer school for the next few years.

"Thank you," I said, sighing. Harry would be okay. Sure, it would be a different school, but the same kind of school. After this summer playing social butterfly, he'd probably make friends at this one.

"You're welcome." Dad looked at me for a minute like he was waiting for something. There were so many somethings he could have been waiting for; it could have been anything.

"What?" I asked.

"Isn't there anything else you might be worried about?" he asked. "Any*one* else you might be concerned about?"

My eyes drifted to the cabin. Mom and I hadn't exactly made up, but we were at least talking again. It took me some time, but I realized I couldn't be pissed at her because she'd gone and told me the truth when that was what I'd been wanting her to do the whole time. She couldn't help it if that truth sucked.

"I think Mom will be okay, you know? I mean, yeah, the move's going to be hard on her like all of us, but she's strong. She'll be okay."

Dad's face lined, almost in amusement. "I agree, but that anyone else I was referring to was you."

I shifted. "Oh."

"There you go," he said.

"Well, yeah, I guess I'm a little worried about what's going to happen." I cleared my throat and kept staring at the cabin. "It's my senior year and everything's changing. It's a lot to take in."

"It is your senior year, and I know how hard you've worked." Dad rubbed his chin, like he was still sporting a semi-beard. "It's not fair to you to change schools and teams when you're one year from making another big change into college."

I bit the inside of my cheek instead of nodding my

agreement. It wasn't fair. But I'd come to realize I couldn't depend on fair when I was planning my life.

"That's why, if you want to, Emerson's family has agreed to let you live with them this next year so you can finish your senior year at North Shore." Dad threw his arms in the air like he'd just announced I'd won the lottery, but I could tell his excitement was kind of forced. He wasn't eager for me to move out a year earlier than any of us had planned.

For a minute, I let that settle in. I could spend the year at the same school, with my same friends, with my same teammates. I could graduate from one of the top schools in the state like I'd planned on. I could have exactly what I thought I couldn't have again . . . but I couldn't have it with my family.

Sure, they'd still be close by, but what would it be like not to share an after-school snack with Harry every day? What would it be like to not wake up to the smell of Mom's favorite coffee or fall asleep to the sound of the late-night news streaming from my parents' bedroom? Would I miss these things? Were they worth giving up so I could stay at the same school?

At the beginning of summer, I wouldn't have thought twice about my answer. It would have been yes. Harry would have been the hardest to say good-bye to, but I wouldn't have cared about anything else.

One summer had changed that. Or maybe one summer had changed *me*.

"You talked with Emerson's family about letting me stay with them?" Another tear slipped down my cheek. So much was coming at me, and the sun hadn't even risen all the way yet.

"Actually, I can't take the credit for that." Dad tipped his head at the cabin. "That was your mom's idea."

"Mom's?"

"It's a pretty good one, right?"

The ball in my throat doubled in size. I nodded because I couldn't get a word out.

"Is that a yes?" Dad circled his hand, waiting.

One second I wanted to say yes. The next I wanted to say no. It was such a huge decision to make, and one I hadn't even known was an option until five seconds ago. "Can I think about it?"

Dad sighed, kind of like he was relieved. "Of course you can. Take as long as you need, just maybe try to have an answer before the first day of school."

I smiled, sniffing. "I can do that."

He pulled me into a side hug. It felt so natural, so like we'd never stopped, I wound my arm behind him and hugged him. "So what about this run? Daylight's burning." He checked the horizon where the sun was just thinking about waking up.

"Lucky for you it's an easy day." I wound an arm over my head, stretching, then repeated with the other.

"Like I need you to take it easy on me." He pointed down at his sneakers, which had been trendy a decade ago. "I'll have you know I was my high school track team's fastest runner. My record in the mile still holds to this day."

I rolled my eyes. "That's because you graduated with a class of fifteen kids, and you were the *only* student on your track team that year."

He laughed, the kind I remembered from Christmas mornings and birthday parties. "Details."

I swallowed the new lump in my throat. It didn't move. "Ready?" I pointed in the direction of the trail in front of us.

Dad started jogging in place. "I was born ready."

Even though I was still sad about Callum, I laughed. Dad was back to dropping cheesy lines and acting like his family existed.

When I started jogging, Dad fell in right beside me. We hadn't made it far before he was already breathing like he'd just gone from sea level to ten thousand feet. We were barely clipping along at a nine-minute mile.

"We're only doing a mile or two, right?" He panted. "It's an easy day."

I tried not to smile. "Try eleven or twelve. Easy has more to do with the pace than the actual distance."

Dad groaned so loudly a squirrel started chattering down at us from a tree lining the trail. "Is that all?" He shrugged like it was nothing, but he was already sweating.

This time I didn't hide my smile. I wasn't running alone anymore.

"Hey, Dad?" I paused for a second. "Thanks for, you know, everything."

He looked over at me and smiled. He didn't stop smiling the whole jog. "Thanks for the second chance."

TWENTY-SEVEN

It was my last day as a Camp Kismet counselor. I'd come here hating it on principle alone, and now I was about to leave it, knowing I'd carry a piece of this place with me wherever I went in life. I'd left a piece of myself here, too.

I'd gotten in my last run earlier, and Dad had joined me, against my warnings that if he couldn't walk without limping, he really shouldn't run, but he'd insisted. Something about working through the pain, which, to me, sounded like a recipe for tearing a muscle, but I was thankful for the company. I'd missed my dad, the one who made me feel like I could do anything and that, even if I failed, I was still okay in his book.

It was almost eight when I headed to the craft closet to pull out the day's supplies. Now, this I wouldn't miss. Crafting. Being crafty. Making crafts. Living crafts. Breathing crafts. Dreaming crafts.

If I never saw another bottle of acrylic paint, it would be too soon.

Today was a simple-enough project—not even one I could mess up. We were decorating sticks that would be a part of the stick ceremony later at night. It was a long, time-honored Camp

Kismet tradition that on the very last night campers and staff would group around a campfire, and each one would stand up and talk about what they'd learned that summer before tossing their stick into the fire.

Sounded kind of hippie-dippie to me, but everyone talked about it like it was something as holy as getting to kiss the pope's ring or something. I wasn't planning on making a stick or getting up and talking, but I should be able to help a handful of campers make theirs.

I grabbed a few bottles of the dreaded glue, sequins, and paint, and—against my better judgment—a few bottles of glitter. I stacked the ribbon box on the top and slowly made my way into the dining hall, which was almost empty from the breakfast service.

Callum hadn't been there, in his usual seat, at his usual table, alone. Maybe he'd been out leading an early morning ride or maybe he'd just decided to sleep in an extra thirty minutes. I wondered if I'd see him again. I mean, I had to, right? We couldn't just leave for the summer without saying good-bye, could we? After everything? The thought of it made me ill.

He'd been avoiding me, ignoring me, and dodging me for the past two weeks, and I'd let him. The first week I'd done the same with him. But I didn't care how far he went out of his way to stay out of mine—tonight I was confronting him. At least to say good-bye, because, really, what was there left to say?

"You're like Martha Stewart's naughty niece." Someone slid into the bench at the table I was cleaning for the day's project. "Crafting never looked so good."

I grumbled under my breath. "Haven't you gone extinct yet?"

"The world's still spinning, isn't it?" Ethan cracked his smile, which might have worked on all the girls except me.

"What do you want, Ethan? I'm kind of busy here."

"Who says I want anything? Why can't I just have a normal conversation with you that doesn't revolve around me wanting something?"

"Well, like you said, the world's still spinning. . . ."

Ethan chuckled, watching me scrub the table with an anti-bacterial wipe. I yanked another wipe and tossed it his way. "Make yourself useful."

He circled his finger around his face a few times, that smile of his pasted into place. "I already am."

I groaned and started taking out my irritation on the table I was wiping. This sucker had never been so clean. "Is there a reason you're here? Other than to annoy the crap out of me?"

Ethan scrubbed at the table with me. "I need another reason than that?"

"When are you leaving? Soon, hopefully?" I slid onto the bench across from him and stopped cleaning. It was going to be a mess in ten minutes anyway.

"As soon as Evan pulls the truck around."

"You're not staying for the stick ceremony?"

"Why? Any chance of getting to second base with you after? Because I could be persuaded." Ethan stuck his hands on his chest and tried to hold a serious expression. It didn't last.

"Bon voyage." I waved at him.

He chuckled and checked the window. He was excited to head out. I guess I'd be eager to leave, too, but something was keeping me here. I didn't want to go, but I knew I had to.

"So you and Big Kahuna are splitsville, eh?" Ethan bounced his brows a few times. "Probably for the best. For you, at least."

Callum and I hadn't announced our breakup, blowup, whatever-you-want-to-call-it, just like we hadn't announced our getting together, but I guess everyone had figured it out.

"Why was it so crazy I'd want to be with him?" I asked,

trying to convince myself I was having a conversation about the pros and cons of fabric softener, not one about the guy who'd ruined me for all other guys.

"I don't know. You just seem ambitious, you know?" Ethan made a box with his fingers and looked at me through it. "So destined for the greatness thing."

"And Callum doesn't?"

He raised his hands, like I'd just accused him of something. "Hey, I like the shit out of Callum. He's the first guy I'd pick to be on my team in a zombie apocalypse—he'd be my Rick Grimes—but you know . . . this is the real world."

I switched to defensive mode. "You're saying he's not the guy you'd want on your side in the real world?"

Ethan didn't look away, even though I wasn't giving him a particularly kind look. "I'm saying he wouldn't be my first-round pick."

I wadded up the dirty wipes and threw them in the direction of the garbage can. They actually went in—my aim was improving. "Second?"

"More like last to second-to-last."

"That's harsh."

He shrugged, looking maybe ashamed for saying it, but not because he didn't mean it. "I dated a girl who goes to school with Callum." When I muttered a "Big surprise," Ethan gave a lazy wink. "Anyway, she knew all about Callum O'Connor."

"And she said he was a disaster?" Why did I suddenly want to find this girl so I could tear a chunk of her hair out?

"No, she said he's a reformed troublemaker. One of those guys at school everyone likes. Kinda keeps to himself like he does here, but a stand-up guy." Ethan looked out the window again. This time Evan and his truck were outside waiting. He spun around the bench and stood up. "Nice guy. Good guy.

Makes the outdoors his bitch, but in a classroom, behind a desk . . . not his thing."

"Not his thing?" I repeated as my hands curled into fists.

"Let's just say that you know how they call the student with the highest GPA valedictorian? You wanna know what they call the person with the lowest one?"

"Not really." I started to shake my head when it looked like he was going to tell me anyway.

"Callum O'Connor." He wasn't smiling, he wasn't trying to make a joke, he was telling it straight.

To distract myself from driving my fist into his eye socket, I started opening the craft bins and spreading the contents down the table.

Ethan rested his hand over mine to stop it for a second. Then he turned my hand over in his, and he shook it. All summer he'd been trying to con me into just about everything else, and here he was, shaking my hand like that was all he'd ever planned on.

Why did the boys of the world seem intent on seriously screwing with my head?

"Nice knowing you, New Girl. Good luck out there." He made a clucking sound with his mouth and slid his hand free.

"You've spent a whole summer with me, asked me out every time I accidentally made eye contact . . . ," I called after him as he started for the door. "And I'm still New Girl?"

"I don't know, it just stuck. Kind of fitting, right? You're trying to figure it all out. Got that born-yesterday look to you. 'New Girl' works."

"I knew enough to stay away from you!"

He laughed as he punched open the door. "You make a point." Ethan tilted his chin at me. "Catch ya in another life, Phoenix."

I leaned into the table. "You know my name."

Evan blared the horn when Ethan didn't budge from the door. Ethan waved his middle finger his brother's direction. Another, longer horn sounded. "I knew it before I said one word to you." With a wave, Ethan gave me what was possibly the most real smile I'd seen from him.

Through the window I watched Evan's truck leave. I was still looking through the window a few minutes after it had peeled away when someone showed up across from me. I figured it was the first camper who'd signed up for stick decorating, but it wasn't.

"Not that I don't encourage initiative with my counselors, but what are you doing here getting everything set for the crafts today?" Ben swept his hand down the table and last at me, like he was confused.

"Just getting things ready before the campers show up," I said, hiding my confusion about as much as he was his. "Just like I have every day for the past month."

"You think you're scheduled for the crafts today," Ben said like he was talking to himself.

"Yeah?"

"You didn't check the schedule."

My eyebrows came together. "No?"

Ben sighed, then shuffled through a few pages on his clipboard before holding it up in front of me. I glanced at the crafts column. "Naomi's scheduled to lead crafts today?"

"So I've got the last day off or something?" I asked.

Ben sighed again, then stuck his finger at a different column on the schedule. My name was there. Beside the hiking box. Inside which was written, *The last hike of the season.* The Matterhorn was the route listed.

I swallowed. I'd been serving a sentence in the prison

known as the craft room, and I was getting let out on the last day. I got to lead the last hike of the summer. From low woman on the totem pole to top one. How had that happened?

"Thank you, Ben." That damn ball was making its reappearance in my throat. I'd felt a lot of it lately. "Thank you so, so much. You don't know how much this means to me that you trust me enough to lead this, you know . . . after my string of screwups." I set down the container holding the beads. No more crafts for me.

"I'm glad it means so much to you, but don't you remember?" Ben tapped the schedule with his knuckles. "I don't make the counselors' schedules."

My breath caught. How could I have forgotten? At least for a second. "You mean, *he* . . . scheduled me for the hike?"

"*He* did."

I had to turn around so I could sink onto the bench. My knees were temporarily out of order. "Where is he?"

Ben was quiet.

"Ben?" I twisted enough so I could see him. "Where's Callum?"

He was quiet for another second, and then he shifted. "Gone. He left late last night after drawing up today's schedule."

"Gone?" The word wasn't computing.

"I'm sorry, Phoenix."

I dropped my head into my hands. Callum had avoided me for two weeks. He'd scheduled me for the big last hike of the season. And he'd just left without saying a word? Without explaining why?

"He's gone," I said to myself, hoping that the sooner I accepted it, the sooner I could move on.

"Why?" My fingers curled into my scalp.

"Why did he leave?" Ben moved closer, but I could tell he

didn't know what to do: Pat my shoulder in sympathy or suggest I pull myself up.

I shook my head. "Why did he schedule me to lead the Matterhorn hike?"

From the corner of my eye, I noticed Ben shrug. "Because you earned his trust back."

After that, I didn't know what to say. I didn't know what to think. I didn't know what to do.

"Are you going to be okay? Campers will be lining up outside for the hike in a few minutes."

I blinked a few times and stood up. My smile was still in place when I turned toward Ben. "I'll be great."

His face cleared before he held his arm out in the direction of the front lawn. "Then, lead on."

I practically sprinted from the dining hall, and when I burst through the door, I sucked in the fresh air like I'd been locked up in some dank, stinky basement for years.

Thanks to the cool morning, I'd put on my hiking boots instead of my Tevas, so other than grabbing a pack from the shed and filling a couple of water bottles, I was ready to go.

A few campers were already waiting on the lawn when I returned with the pack. I went through it twice, to make sure it had everything I'd need in the event of an emergency . . . and then I checked it once more just to be safe.

By then, all fourteen campers who'd signed for the hike had shown up. As I went through the checklist of having campers check their water bottles, their boots, and their pack straps, I moved around them, giving a hand or a high five as I passed. I hadn't just learned how to get a group of people through a hike from Callum; I'd learned how to make sure they enjoyed it.

I crouched down to double-check my own laces right before

we left. Three miles up, three miles down. I should have been nervous. This was the first outdoor activity I'd led in weeks. It was the big final hike of the summer. Disaster had struck the last time I'd been responsible for a group of campers.

It wasn't nerves that I felt, though. It was something else. Something different and new and something I couldn't put a name to. Confidence? Courage? Those weren't quite right. Close, but not close enough.

I knew the route. I knew I'd stick to the route. I knew everything would be okay. I knew I could handle it if it wasn't. I knew we'd all make it to the end.

"Okay, everyone. Ready?" I stood in front of the campers and waited for their attention. "We're going to stick together, stay together, and work together. Any questions?"

One of the older guys in the group raised his hand. He was smiling. "About that together part . . ."

A chuckle spread among the campers.

"Together. That's our marching beat today, people."

Doing one last head count, I turned in the direction of the trailhead. I checked my pace. I checked the line behind me every minute. I checked the trail for loose rocks and tree roots. And then I started over. I knew what I was doing. I'd been trained by the best.

Callum. I couldn't not think about him, especially on a day like this, leading the last hike of the season, the same one I'd done with him on my first day. Instead of feeling like losing him had made me weaker, I focused on how having him in my life—in whatever way I had and for however short a time it had been—had made me stronger.

I wasn't weaker because of Callum O'Connor—I was stronger.

That was what I focused on as I set out on that hike, climbing higher with every step.

TWENTY-EIGHT

I'd done it. Fourteen campers had made it to the top safely. Fourteen had made it down safely. One counselor had done the same.

The last hike of the summer was over, suitcases were packed, and storage sheds had been swept and locked. The summer was over. At least almost over.

I would have been happy to skip on the stick ceremony, but the other three members of the Ainsworth family were going and adamant that the fourth would be as well. I would have rather spent the night lying on the beach by the lake and staring up at the stars, but they had it in their heads that the stick ceremony was not to be missed. Apparently, I was the only one who hadn't drunk the Kool-Aid when it came to the ritual of spilling one's guts in front of a bunch of people before dropping a stick in a communal fire.

"Come on. This will be great." Dad nudged me as we found our spot in the ring of campers already circling the campfire. It didn't look any different from the other campfires we'd had every night for the past few months.

"Great is a matter of perspective, and coming from mine, this is the definition of child abuse." I nudged him back.

Mom was shaking open a blanket for us all to sit on. She'd even packed a snack bag filled with popcorn and licorice. This might not have been the movies, but I appreciated the effort she was making to keep us all together. Harry crashed onto the blanket with a grumble. He was down with the stick ceremony, but he'd been grumbling the past couple of weeks about something else. With this being the last night here, his grumbling had hit record highs.

"My wrist is fine. The doctors are just trying to ruin my life."

"Next summer." I crouched down beside Harry and took my turn. Dad and Mom had exhausted just about every comforting avenue. "You'll be big enough to do the ropes course, and your wrist will be perfect. The year will fly by."

"No, it won't. It will crawl by." Harry was picking at the grass with his good hand and glaring at his bandaged wrist like it was to blame for everything.

"Harry, it will. I promise." I put my hand on his shoulder, but he shrugged it off.

"Whatever."

I sighed, not having anything else to say. I knew the ropes course was important to him, but he was acting like it meant the difference between life and death. I'd never seen him so disappointed over anything—finding out we'd lost our house and were changing schools included. I guess this was the ten-year-old-boy dream, and it was just out of reach. What he wanted most and couldn't have.

I knew the feeling.

As I was thinking what I could possibly say to make him feel better, Ben weaved his way to the campfire. It was cold tonight so everyone was bundled up pretty good, except for him. He was still rocking his tie-dyed camp shirt and khaki shorts. It gave me chills just looking at him, so I tucked my jacket around me tighter, although it wasn't really a jacket.

It was a flannel shirt. The same one I'd worn the night during the rainstorm. The same one I'd buttoned on, the same one he'd unbuttoned, the same one I'd left his cabin in later that night. He'd never asked for it back, and I'd never exactly been eager to return it, and now he was gone.

I wondered how much I'd think about him after I left here. I wondered how long I would. Would he eventually go away, like a bruise fades with time? Or would he always be there, like a wound that might get better but leaves a scar behind?

"Welcome to the stick ceremony." Ben clasped his hands together and looked into the crowd. "We all come together at the end of the year to share an experience that touched us. Some people talk about something they learned, some talk about something they need to confess, some talk about a problem they're dealing with." Ben turned to face the fire. "It doesn't matter what you say, so long as you say it." Ben walked around the campfire a few times, not saying anything. Everyone was quiet, looking as afraid to move as their neighbors next to them. Finally, Ben clapped his hands. "Let the ceremony begin." He waved his arms like he was inviting everyone to speak at the same time.

No one went, though. Not for the first minute. Not even the second. People who'd been holding their sticks in front of them tucked them beneath blankets or sat on them. I watched campers who didn't seem to have an off switch when it came to talking seal their lips shut.

From the corner of my eye, I noticed Ben looking around the group. If he was surprised no one was leaping up to expose their soul, he didn't show it. He might have been the least uncomfortable person here, though.

Everyone else was keeping their eyes forward, afraid to make eye contact. A few people actually had beads of sweat dotting their foreheads. A couple on the outskirts slipped away like no one could see them, though I knew everyone did.

At the five-minute mark, still no one had spoken. I hadn't made a stick or anything, but it was a stick ceremony, right? Any stick should do. Scanning the ground for something that could work, I found a "stick." If that was what you could call it, because it was more twig than stick.

My fingers curled around it, and I paused another second, giving someone else a chance to suck it up and go first. No one.

So I stood, taking my stick-twig with me. Every eye around that circle zipped my way. The collective sigh was almost deafening.

"Hey, everyone." I waved as I stepped around and through people on the way to the campfire. It had gotten so small it was mostly just embers now. Nothing but ashes. "I'm Phoenix, in case you didn't already know that." I paused, feeling like the newest member of the Idiot Club. I was a camp counselor. I knew everyone by first name and most by last, too—of course they knew my name. So far, this stick ceremony was really life changing.

What had Ben said? People talked about a problem? Something they'd overcome? Something they'd learned?

I looked into the crowd as if somewhere out there I'd find my lightbulb. Instead, I found Ben looking at me, his face turned up in an expectant expression. Then he circled his hand like he was prompting me. *Just say what you need to say.*

There it was. I got it.

The breath I'd been holding came out in a whoosh. "I

learned a lot of things this summer, but the most important thing I learned was something about myself."

Ben smiled at me across the crowd of campers, flashing me a thumbs-up.

I almost wanted to run, but I stayed. I'd started, so I'd finish.

"I have trust issues. Or I had them. Someone helped me work through them this summer." I noticed campers scanning the crowd, looking for him because they knew—they'd probably learned something from him, too. "Callum taught me it wasn't everyone else I needed to learn how to trust; it was myself . . . because I'm not sure you can really trust another human being until you can trust yourself first." I stared into the fire, at the ashes scattered around the perimeter of the fire pit. Ashes—the perfect place to rise from.

"I needed to figure out I'd be okay no matter what came at me. I had to trust that I was strong enough to make it through anything. I know that now. That's what he was trying to get me to understand, I think. That I'd be okay." I found myself staring at my family again. We were a mess—foreclosure, bankruptcy, dysfunction, school change—and we'd be okay. All of us. "Sometimes you just have to go with the flow when things are at their worst. Save your strength for when it will really count."

I stopped at the edge of the campfire and thought about the girl I'd come here as and the one I was leaving as. Stronger . . . and more vulnerable at the same time. I couldn't have gotten here without Camp Kismet and Callum. "I learned a lot from Callum this summer, but I figured this out on my own. Trust is a lot like love. Actually, I don't think you can have one without the other." I studied the campfire pit. It was nothing more than ashes now, no real visible embers to see. When I dropped my stick into it, a mound of ashes exploded into a cloud. A moment later, the twig caught fire. It didn't seem possible that something so bright and alive could rise from something so dead-looking. But it did. All the ashes needed was something to bring it back to life. "And I love Callum O'Connor."

TWENTY-NINE

I left right after.

Declaring my love in front of a group of people wasn't the route I would have preferred to go, but since the person I wanted to admit it to was gone, that was all I had.

Saying it out loud was important. It made it more real. Callum might never know, but that was okay, because I did. I'd fallen for him. In a hundred different ways. This summer was supposed to suck. It was supposed to go down in the annals as worst ever.

It couldn't have been better.

I couldn't stop thinking about how tonight was my last night at Camp Kismet. How it might be my last night *ever* here. I wasn't sure Ben would want me back. Who knows? A lot could happen in a single day, let alone one whole year.

There were a lot of places at camp I loved, but there was one place in particular. Close to the public beach on Swallow Lake—but not so near that the random camper would find it— there was a small patch of beach surrounded by trees. It was so dark out there it felt like I could see every star in the sky. Callum said it was a good substitute when he couldn't make it to the observatory.

To me, the observatory was a substitute for the beach, where I was heading after creeping away from the ceremony. The summer had been filled with work and runs and studying; I'd only made it here a couple of times, but I was taking the night off from studying.

When I could just make out the silver lines rippled across the lake from the moon through the trees, I clicked off my headlamp and finished the last little bit on my own. I wanted to give my eyes a chance to adjust to the dark so the stars would really stand out when I stepped onto the beach.

Along with the light reflecting off the lake, there was something else glowing just up ahead. I hadn't seen it at first because I'd been too far back, but it was bright and orangish in color. Then I smelled it.

A campfire. Small from what I could see, but there was definitely a campfire burning on the beach. On the two visits Callum and I had made, we'd never seen anyone else. In fact, Callum had said he'd never seen anyone here in all the summers he'd been coming to camp. He might have been the only person besides me who knew this patch of beach. So I shouldn't have been surprised he was . . .

Here.

I was able to just make him out standing in front of the fire, facing the woods. Most people who made a campfire on a beach faced the water. He was turned to the trees. Looking into them. Like he was expecting someone to show up.

I wanted to run the rest of the way to him. I couldn't believe he was here.

I wanted to freeze in place just as much for the same reasons. Why was he here? Was he waiting for me? Did he even want to see me when he'd proven the opposite the last two weeks?

My heart overruled my head, and I jogged the last few

yards down the trail. When I shot onto the beach, he didn't look half as surprised to see me as I was to see him. In fact, he barely flinched when I burst from the trees.

I took a whole half second to catch my breath. "You."

He rubbed at the scar at his temple. "You."

I swallowed, hoping my heart would drop back into place. "What are you doing here?"

"Waiting for you." He motioned between me and the small campfire.

"And you just knew to be waiting at this exact place at this exact time?"

"I spent the entire summer with you. If I couldn't figure out where you'd want to be on your last night at camp, I wouldn't have really gotten to know you, right?" His forehead creased when I stayed back on the trail instead of moving closer.

"But I thought you left. Ben said you were gone."

"I did leave. I made it halfway home before turning back."

Feeling finally returned to my legs. I took a few steps closer to the fire . . . and him. "Why'd you come back?"

He shifted and looked into the fire. I could see the small flames reflecting in his eyes. "Because I finally got it." He crouched down next to his backpack and pulled something out.

"Finally got what?"

"Why you changed my test scores." He held something up for me to see. It was a practice test—I'd taken enough to know what they looked like from a mile away. "It wasn't to hurt me. It was to help me."

"But I told you that at Patterson Ridge the day we got into that huge . . . you know." I paused. "Yeah, I upped your scores to help you, but that doesn't change that I went behind your back and lied about it." I moved toward the campfire because it was cold and because I wanted to be as close to him as he'd let me. Up until two minutes ago, I'd been convinced

277

I'd never see him again, and here he was, ten feet away and talking to me.

"But this is why you did it. Here's the proof." Callum tapped his finger at the top of the test, where I could just barely read the score circled at the top.

"A twelve hundred," I read.

"And that's the real score. Not the 'enhanced' version." He turned the test around and stared at the score, shaking his head like he couldn't believe it.

"You did it." I smiled, crouching down by the fire across from him. "I knew you could."

"Yeah, well, you were the only one who believed it." He tipped his head back and looked up at the sky. There were so many stars out here the sky looked more light than dark. A slow smile formed. "I took this test at a rest stop on my way home. I needed to clear my head from thinking about this summer . . . us . . ." His eyes dropped to mine for a second. *"You.* I pulled this test out of my pack, camped out on a bench, and didn't look up until I was done. When I graded it, I couldn't believe the score. I double-checked. Then I triple-checked." He pulled something else from his bag. Another test. "And then I took another test just in case the last one had been a fluke and I'd gotten lucky."

I leaned in to read the score on that one. Eleven-eighty. "No fluke."

He shook his head, his eyes flashing. "You weren't just another someone treating me like I was going nowhere fast. You were one of the only people who looked at me and believed I could go anywhere I wanted." He stood up and looked across the fire at me. "So you lied about my test scores." His shoulder lifted. "You did it because you cared about me. Would you do the same thing again if you got a redo?"

I thought about that for a second. I didn't have to think long. "No. I've learned my lesson."

"See? That's all that really matters."

I felt my eyebrows come together; was he saying what I thought he was? Had he forgiven me? Gotten over me lying to him? "It is?"

"That's all that really matters to *me*." He paused, his throat bobbing when he swallowed. "And I'm hoping that will help you understand why I did what I did."

"Why you didn't tell me you were the one who'd taken me off the outdoor activities?"

Callum leaned over to grab a big stick and started prodding the fire. He nodded. "I should have told you about being in charge of the counselors' schedules. I should have told you I was the one who'd scheduled you for craft duty and why I'd done it." His eyes closed as he rubbed his forehead. "I told myself I could separate being the lead counselor from the boyfriend, and I thought I could, but it didn't work."

I watched the glowing embers float into the sky from the fire. I watched them until they burned out. "I get why you did it, though, you know? I probably would have done the exact same thing if I'd been in your position." I held my hands toward the fire. It was just a small one, but it was keeping me warm. "You were responsible for the campers' safety. I hadn't exactly proven myself trustworthy in that department, so you did what you had to do. I might have been pissed when I found out, and maybe still am a little because you didn't feel you could tell me, but I get why you did it."

Callum looked into the fire, the skin between his brows drawn. He looked like he was trying to read something he couldn't make out. "I am responsible for the campers' safety. That's true. But I'm responsible for the counselors' safety, too, and I'd be lying if I didn't admit I was extra concerned for yours. I did what I did because I needed you to earn some trust back, sure"—he exhaled as if he was confessing a crime—"but also because I let my overprotectiveness get in the way."

He'd said a lot—he'd *explained* a lot—but it was what he said last that I latched on to. "You did what you did because you cared about me," I said.

It wasn't a question, but he answered it anyway. "Yeah."

"Would you do it all over again if you got a redo?"

His head shook. "Hell no."

I moved closer to the fire, but it was only because I wanted to be closer to him. We could have held our arms out and reached each other if it weren't for the fire standing between us. "Then that's all that really matters."

"It is?"

"That's all that really matters to me." A smile twitched at the corners of my mouth.

"This coming from the girl who didn't believe in second chances when it came to trust?" He stuffed his hands into the pockets of his jeans.

"From the very one."

"You've come a long way."

I eyed his pack. "So have you."

For a minute, we were quiet. There was still probably a lot left to be said, but for now this felt like enough.

"I'm sorry, Phoenix." He shifted his weight onto one foot, staring at the fire. "I'm sorry I walked away from you that day and avoided you the past two weeks and left without saying good-bye. I'm sorry it took me getting to the California state line to figure it out." He started moving around the fire, coming toward me. A smile looked like it was pulling at his mouth. "In case you didn't notice, I'm a slow learner."

"And I'm sorry I accused you of lying to me before hearing your side of the story first."

He didn't stop moving closer until he was standing right in front of me. He didn't stop there. His hand found mine. Heat fired up my arm from his touch, spreading to my fingertips. His thumb skimmed my knuckles. "And I shouldn't have sucker punched you about trust issues."

I still felt like I was trying to swallow my heart, but now a few other vital organs were misbehaving after his confession. Like my lungs. And brain.

Our fingers tangled together tighter. I'd missed the roughness of his palms, the softness between his fingers, the strength I could feel in him every time his hand was holding mine.

"You know what?" I started. "Maybe that's what makes us kinda great—not being afraid to call each other out on our shit."

The corners of his eyes lined like he was considering that. "You are definitely not afraid to call me out on my shit."

"And you are definitely not afraid to call me out on mine." When we laughed, it echoed across the lake.

Then his expression changed. He tugged me closer. "We're great in other ways, too, you know?"

"Like?" I was breathing so hard my chest was bumping into his with every breath I took.

His eyes dropped to my mouth. "I'd tell you, but I'd rather show you." His hand slipped inside the flannel shirt, winding around my waist until it pressed into my lower back. When he slid a bit closer, so our bodies were touching from our chest to our feet, my mouth parted.

I wasn't sure if I had kissed him or he had kissed me, but it didn't matter how we'd gotten here—what mattered was that we'd made it.

We kissed like we had two weeks to make up for. We kissed like we might have a lifetime to make up for. My hand stayed locked with his; the other skimmed up his chest before capping over his shoulder. This kind of kissing required a solid grip, because, damn, I felt like my knees were about to fail.

When he pulled back, he was breathing hard. Harder than I was, even. I tried pulling him back to me, but he braced in place and raised his hand. He kept it raised as he moved around the side of the campfire. I followed him. He stopped and reached down to grab a stick. Holding it up, he lifted a brow at me and cleared his throat.

His eyes locked on mine as he dropped the stick into the fire. It caught instantly. "I trust you, too."

I watched the rest of the stick catch fire. Just like I'd watched mine. "You were there."

"To witness you profess your trust in me in front of everyone?" He looked up at me and smiled. "I wouldn't have missed it."

He'd been there. I should have known. I should have felt something. Maybe I'd been a little distracted by all the eyes gaping up at me, though.

"I believe the word I used was *love*."

Callum sat down on the beach and patted the space in front of him. I didn't have to wait for him to pat twice. "Yeah, but they're the same thing, trust and love, right?" He bent his knees and fitted me in between his legs before winding his arms around me. His chin tucked over my shoulder as we stared at the lake.

"Where did you ever hear that?" I didn't try to hide my smile—would have been pointless.

I felt his shoulders rise behind me. "From this crazy girl I went and fell in love with."

My heart stalled hearing that. When his lips pressed into my temple and didn't move, my eyes closed. Everything about this felt so right. Everything about *us* felt so right. Why hadn't we figured it out sooner?

"You're going home tomorrow, Callum. I'm going . . ." I wasn't ready to call it home—maybe I never would be. "Wherever I'm going. What's going to happen?"

He didn't answer right away, but just kept his arms around me until our chests were rising and falling together. I started the summer thinking I wanted the world. I was finishing it wanting him. I wasn't sure I could have either.

"I don't know." It was so quiet his voice echoed across the lake. "But I do know I love you and that we've got tonight. Let's worry about tomorrow tomorrow."

I twisted around until I was facing him. I slipped my legs over his and wrapped them around his back. "And worry about tonight tonight?"

His hand curved into my back and pressed me closer. "Do I look worried?"

EPILOGUE

What I was certain would be the worst summer of my life had turned out to be the greatest. We'd left camp weeks ago, but I knew it was a place I'd never really leave behind. It would stay with me.

Today I was doing a different kind of camping—the kind that involved parking it on the front porch, tapping my feet, waiting for a certain someone who was going to be late if he didn't show up in the next sixty seconds.

My smile started to form when I heard the familiar sputter of his motorcycle come around the corner. Callum was never late picking me up. Despite the commute and the traffic, he was always on time.

Before I could stand, the drawing on the toe of my sneaker caught my attention. Callum had sketched it with a big black Sharpie on our last date two weeks ago.

He'd written our names and drawn a bird beneath each name. Mine was supposed to be a phoenix—and his like a dove, but in the end, they looked the same. You couldn't tell the difference.

He was a bird. I was a bird. I guess it didn't really matter what kind we were. What mattered was that we could both fly. What mattered was that we both already had.

He'd barely rolled to a stop before I started charging down the walkway toward him. We only got to see each other every two weeks, so each second counted.

"You," he said, his arm winding around my waist.

"You," I echoed, letting him pull me close.

"What do you want to do?" Callum's arm tightened just enough as my legs pressed up against his.

I didn't stop there. Pivoting, I swung my leg over the motorcycle and sat down so I was facing him and my back was to the handlebars. I was more on his lap than the actual seat, though. Nice planning on my part.

Callum's eyes widened before he looked in the direction of the garage and front porch. My parents might have liked Callum, but he was still their teenage daughter's boyfriend, and that automatically made him suspect. The last time my dad had caught us making out, he'd cleared his throat and scooted his way in between us on the couch. Mortifying.

"Dad's at work. Mom's gardening. Harry's at Spencer's. We're good."

Callum's hand dropped around my back, and he inched me closer. Now I was pretty much just all on his lap. "Convenient."

"So convenient," I said, my stomach fluttering.

"Really, what are we doing today?" He cleared his throat when my hands capped over his shoulders and I wiggled just a teeny bit closer.

I lifted an eyebrow.

He swallowed and looked away, but his fingers curled into my back. "Besides *that*?"

"Besides that, I don't care. I'd be fine with only that."

Callum chuckled, shaking his head. "Didn't you have a

cross-country meet last night? Didn't you log seventy miles this week? Where do you get your stamina?"

"I guess you really just bring it out in me."

He gritted his teeth and hung his head back, like I was torturing him. "Congratulations, by the way. Another first-place ribbon to add to the collection."

"Thank you, thank you." I did a mini bow. "Who knew a school called Jefferson High would have a decent cross-country team?"

"Who knew?" He was teasing me. I let him because, as much as I'd worried, everything was working out. The new school wasn't too bad, and I'd made a few friends from the cross-country team, plus I still kept in touch with some of my old friends. The new house was small but clean and kind of charming, and Harry was loving his new school. Not only was it keeping up with him in the brains department, but he'd also made some friends, which he hadn't managed at the last school. Dad had found a job, and even though I knew it didn't come with any of the same reputation and pay as his last one, he seemed happy with it. Content for now.

Mom had even found a job as a receptionist at a dermatologist's office. I think she liked getting out of the house and contributing in that way. Plus she said the free skin-care samples were an added bonus.

Everything was good. Against the odds, we'd come out all right. Maybe we always had been. Maybe we always would be. Maybe it was more a matter of perspective than the actual reality of a situation.

"By the way, she'll kill me if I forget. My mom says hello," Callum said.

"Tell her I say hello back. And that she's welcome."

He shook his head. "Never going to let me live it down."

"Go figure. Your mom, you know, the person who gave birth to you and wants the very best for you, actually is supportive of you going to college. Who in the world would have thought it?"

"Done yet?"

I tapped my temple a few times. "Just want to relive that moment of her actually crying when she found that stack of college applications on your desk. Such a good memory."

"Unbelievable. You really won't ever let this go, will you?" He waved his hand in front of my face while I continued to replay the memory. "She wants to know when she'll see you next."

Callum's mom was awesome. For the overprotective mom of the guy I was dating, anyway. I'd only been to her house a couple of times, but she always made sure I knew I was welcome anytime.

"Since I kind of have a serious thing for her son, probably a lot."

Callum smiled. "That would be a lot of highway time."

"Yeah, but now that I have my own set of wheels, you don't have to be the only one who drives to me on our weekends." I nodded at the driveway, where a two-decade-old, mostly gray Honda was sitting. She had so many miles on her she shouldn't have still been running, and the interior was as beat up as the outside, but she was mine. I'd earned her, and she got me from point A to point B every time. I wouldn't have traded her for the flashiest, most expensive car in the world.

"That's one hell of a nice vehicle, but she's lacking something mine has."

I glanced from my car to his motorcycle. Not even. "What?"

Callum's hands pressed me closer. His lap shifted below mine, which did nothing to help relax the muscles balled up in my stomach. "The space and freedom to do this." He shifted below me again, his smile going crooked when a little breath slipped past my lips.

"Fair warning." My voice sounded off—I didn't have to wonder why. "You do that again, and I will not be able to control myself from what happens next."

"Sounds like our day's all planned out." He clucked his tongue and reached down into his backpack again. "But first, a present . . ." He pulled something shiny and big from his bag and held it in between us.

"A helmet?" My head tipped.

"Not just any helmet. Your very own helmet, you know, so you don't have to slip on my old, crusty one. You can crustify it all by yourself." He tapped the matte-black helmet he had on before lifting the new one out for me.

Okay, so some guys might have brought their girlfriends flowers or truffles, but flowers died and truffles got eaten. This was the kind of gift that lasted.

"I know you can take care of yourself and everything, but I've got to at least do my part." He turned it around in his hands, and that was when I noticed that something had been painted onto the shiny black surface.

"What's that?" I leaned in closer to get a better look. It was small and kind of abstract-looking, painted in brushstrokes of red, orange, and yellow.

"What do you think it is?" Callum's finger tapped above the painting.

"A phoenix," I said, brushing my thumb across it.

"Not just a phoenix. A phoenix rising." He lifted the helmet and slid it over my head.

"Are you getting all symbolic on me again?" I smiled at him as he fitted the chin strap on me.

"I don't know what you're talking about." His eyes flickered to mine and he winked.

"Look at us, all in love and stuff." I looked down at him fastening my chin strap and waved between the two of us.

He laughed. "And stuff."

"In love or not, you know what they say—long-distance relationships never work." I tried to hold a straight face.

He made his own version of a straight face. "I know."

"And you know what else they say?" I sighed like the sun had stopped shining. "High school romances never last."

He sighed with me. "I know. We're totally doomed." His second sigh was a bit overdone. "Now get over here and kiss me, already." Callum's fingers stayed on my chin, tilting it closer.

Just when I could feel the warmth of his breath on my lips, our helmets clanked together, which made us laugh. When we tried moving in again, same result. Kissing in helmets was challenging.

"How about this?" I suggested. "You come in from the left. I'll come in from the right."

"See what a brilliant brain I'm protecting?" Callum flicked the side of my helmet as he came in from the left. At the same time, I moved in from the right.

Finally, our lips made it to each other. His hands stayed on my face, and he didn't stop kissing me until I felt dizzy. It only took a few seconds for that effect to set in, though.

"Damn, look at how tragic we are," he whispered against my lips before pressing one more featherlight kiss into them.

"Let's get out of here." My eyes closed, trying to hang on to this moment.

He turned the key in the ignition. The motorcycle sputtered to life. "Ready when you are. But you might want to crawl behind me."

"Sounds nice, but I don't think so." I turned the key back over, and the engine died. Then I pulled my own set of keys from my pocket. "My turn to drive."

Half his face pulled up in a grimace. "You've been driving for how long now?"

"One month."

Full-on grimace now. "And that thing actually passed inspection?"

I kissed him on the cheek and slid off his lap. He followed right behind me. "Come on," I said, linking my pinkie with his. "Trust me."

ACKNOWLEDGMENTS

Bringing a book to life is a team effort, and I'm exceedingly grateful for the people who made this one possible.

First, to my editor, Phoebe Yeh, who is the kind of mentor a writer can only dream of working with. Your belief in me means more than I can convey. I'm lucky to have you, and have learned so much. Thank you for your guidance and patience.

To my agent, Jane Dystel, who took a chance on a writer just thinking about spreading her wings so many years ago. I've always known you're on my side, and your dedication and loyalty have been unwavering.

To all of my readers. If you've read just one or each and every one, I love you all. Your emails, messages, reviews, and comments mean more than this writer could ever put into words. You breathe life into my stories, making me better with each book because I never want to let you down. Thank you for your loyalty and kindness.

To my dad and mom, who were the first to read and believe in my stories. A child couldn't hope for better parents. Thank you for all the ways you've helped make this dream a viable career. I love you both.

To my daughter, who makes me a better person because I want to be the kind of mother she deserves. Your laughter fills my world with joy. You are my light and life.

And last, to my husband. You remind me every day why the best decision I ever made was saying *I do* on June 12, 2003. In our next life, I'll be waiting.

Anything was possible.
At least that's what it felt like.

NEW YORK TIMES BESTSELLING AUTHOR
NICOLE WILLIAMS

Falling for him was easy.
Staying together?

ALMOST I̶M̶POSSIBLE

READ A SNEAK PEEK OF
ALMOST IMPOSSIBLE **NOW!**

Chapter One

Anything was possible. At least that's what it felt like.

Summer seventeen was going to be one for the record books. I already knew it. I could *feel* it—from the nervous-excited swirl in my stomach to the buzz in the air around me. This was going to be the summer—*my* summer.

"Last chance to cry uncle or forever hold your peace," Mom sang beside me in the backseat of the cab we'd caught at the airport. Her hand managed to tighten around mine even more, cutting off the last bit of my circulation. If there was any left.

I tried to look the precise amount of unsure before answering. "So long, last chance," I said, waving out the window.

Mom sighed, squeezing my hand harder still. It was starting to go numb now. Summer seventeen might find me one hand short if Mom didn't ease up on the death grip.

She and her band, the Shrinking Violets, were going to be touring internationally after finally hitting it big, but she was moping because this was the first summer we wouldn't be together. Actually, it would be the first time we'd been apart ever.

I'd sold her on the idea of me staying in the States with her sister and family by going on about how badly I wanted to experience one summer as a normal, everyday American teenager before graduating from high school. One chance to see what it was like to stay in the same place, with the same people, before I left for college. One last chance to see what life as an American teen was really like.

She bought it . . . *eventually*.

She'd have her bandmates and tens of thousands of adoring fans to keep her company—she could do without me for a couple of months. I hoped.

It had always been just Mom and me from day one. She had me when she was young—like *young* young—and even though her boyfriend pretty much bailed before the line turned pink, she'd done just fine on her own.

We'd both kind of grown up together, and I knew she'd missed out on a lot by raising me. I wanted this to be a summer for the record books for her, too. One she could really live up, not having to worry about taking care of her teenage daughter. Plus, I wanted to give her a chance to experience what life without me would be like. Soon I'd be off to college somewhere, and I figured easing her into the empty-nester phase was a better approach than going cold turkey.

"You packed sunscreen, right?" Mom's bracelets jingled as she leaned to look out her window, staring at the bright blue sky like it was suspect.

"SPF seventy for hot days, fifty for warm days, and thirty for overcast ones." I toed the trusty duffel resting at my feet.

It had traveled the globe with me for the past decade and had the wear to prove it.

"That's my fair-skinned girl." When Mom looked over at me, the crease between her eyebrows carved deeper with worry.

"You might want to check into SPF yourself. You're not going to be in your midthirties forever, you know?"

Mom groaned. "Don't remind me. But I'm already beyond SPF's help at this point. Unless it can help fix a saggy butt and crow's-feet." She pinched invisible wrinkles and wiggled her butt against the seat.

It was my turn to groan. It was annoying enough that people mistook us for sisters all the time, but it was worse that she could (and did) wear the same jeans as me. There should be some rule that moms aren't allowed to takes clothes from the closets of their teenage daughters.

When the cab turned down Providence Avenue, I felt a sudden streak of panic. Not for myself, but for my mom.

Could she survive a summer when I wasn't at her side, reminding her when the cell phone bill was due or updating her calendar so she knew where to be and when to be there? Would she be okay without me reminding her that fruits and vegetables were part of the food pyramid for a reason and making sure everything was all set backstage?

"Hey." Mom gave me a look, her eyes suggesting she could read my thoughts. "I'll be okay. I'm a strong, empowered thirty-four-year-old woman."

"Cell phone charger." I yanked the one dangling from her oversized, metal-studded purse, which I'd wrapped in hot pink tape so it stood out. "I've packed you two extras to get you through the summer. When you get down to your last one, make sure to pick up two more so you're covered—"

"Jade, please," she interrupted. "I've only lost a few. It's not like I've misplaced . . ."

"Thirty-two phone chargers in the past five years?" When she opened her mouth to protest, I added, "I've got the receipts to prove it, too."

Her mouth clamped closed as the cab rolled up to my aunt's house.

"What am I going to do without you?" Mom swallowed, dropping her big black retro sunglasses over her eyes to hide the tears starting to form, to my surprise.

I was better at keeping my emotions hidden, so I didn't dig around in my purse for sunglasses. "Um, I don't know? Maybe rock a sold-out international tour? Six continents in three months? Fifty concerts in ninety days? That kind of thing?"

Mom started to smile. She loved music—writing it, listening to it, playing it—and was a true musician. She hadn't gotten into it to become famous or make the Top 40 or anything like that; she'd done it because it was who she was. She was the same person playing to a dozen people in a crowded café as she was now, the lead singer of one of the biggest bands in the world playing to an arena of thousands.

"Sounds pretty killer. All of those countries. All of that adventure." Mom's hand was on the door handle, but it looked more like she was trying to keep the taxi door closed than to open it. "Sure you don't want to be a part of it?"

I smiled thinly back at my mom, her wild brown hair spilling over giant glasses. She had this boundless sense of adventure—always had and always would—so it was hard for her to comprehend how her own offspring could feel any different.

"Promise to call me every day and send me pictures?" I said, feeling the driver lingering outside my door with luggage in hand. This was it.

Mom exhaled, lifting her pinkie toward me. "Promise."

I curled my pinkie around hers and forced a smile. "Love you, Mom."

Her finger wound around mine as tightly as she had clenched my other hand on the ride here. "Love you no matter what." Then she shoved her door open and crawled out, but not before I noticed one tiny tear escape her sunglasses.

By the time I'd stepped out of the cab, all signs of that tear or any others were gone. Mom did tears as often as she wrote moving love songs. In other words, never.

As she dug around in her purse for her wallet to pay the driver, I took a minute to inspect the house in front of me. The last time we'd been here was for Thanksgiving three years ago. Or was it four? I couldn't remember, but it was long enough to have forgotten how bright white my aunt and uncle's house was, how the windows glowed from being so clean and the landscaping looked almost fake it was so well kept.

It was pretty much the total opposite of the tour buses and extended-stay hotels I'd spent most of my life in. My mother, Meg Abbott, did not do tidy.

"Back zipper pocket," I said as she struggled to find the money in her wallet.

"Aha," she announced, freeing a few bills to hand to the

driver, whose patience was wilting. After taking her luggage, she shouldered up beside me.

"So the neat-freak thing gets worse with time." Mom gaped at the walkway leading up to the cobalt-blue front door, where a Davenport nameplate sparkled in the sunlight. It wasn't an exaggeration to say most of the surfaces I'd eaten off of weren't as clean as the stretch of concrete in front of me.

"Mom . . . ," I warned, when she shuddered after she roamed to inspect the window boxes bursting with scarlet geraniums.

"I'm not being mean," she replied as we started down the walkway. "I'm appreciating my sister's and my differences. That's all."

Right then, the front door whisked open and my aunt seemed to float from it, a measured smile in place, not a single hair out of place.

"Appreciating our differences," Mom muttered under her breath as we moved closer.

I bit my lip to keep from laughing as the two sisters embraced.

Mom had long dark hair and fell just under the average-height bar like me. Aunt Julie, conversely, had light hair she kept swishing above her shoulders, and she was tall and thin. Her eyes were almost as light blue as mine, compared to Mom's, which were almost as dark as her hair.

It wasn't only their physical differences that set them apart; it was everything. From the way they dressed—Mom in some shade of dark, whereas the darkest color I'd ever seen Aunt Julie wear was periwinkle—to their taste in food, Mom was on the spicy end of the spectrum and Aunt Julie was on the mild.

Mom stared at Aunt Julie.

Aunt Julie stared back at Mom.

This went on for twenty-one seconds. I counted. The last stare-down four years ago had gone forty-nine. So this was progress.

Finally, Aunt Julie folded her hands together, her rounded nails shining from a fresh manicure. "Hello, Jade. Hello, Megan."

Mom's back went ramrod straight when Aunt Julie referred to her by her given name. Aunt Julie was eight years older but acted more like her mother than her sister.

"How's it hangin', Jules?"

Aunt Julie's lips pursed hearing her little sister's nickname for her. Then she stepped back and motioned inside. "Well?"

That was my cue to pick up my luggage and follow after Mom, who was tromping up the front steps. "Are we done already? Really?" she asked, nudging Aunt Julie as she passed.

"I'm taking the higher road," Aunt Julie replied.

"What you call taking the higher road I call getting soft in your old age." Mom hustled through the door after that, like she was afraid Aunt Julie would kick her butt or something. The image of Aunt Julie kicking anything made me giggle to myself.

"Jade." Aunt Julie's smile was of the real variety this time as she took my duffel from me. "You were a girl the last time we saw you, and look at you now. All grown up."

"Hey, Aunt Julie. Thanks again for letting me spend the summer with you guys," I said, pausing beside her, not sure whether to hug her or keep moving. A moment of awkwardness passed before she made the decision for me by reaching out and patting my back. I continued on after that.

Aunt Julie wasn't cold or removed; she just showed her affection differently. But I knew she cared about me and my mom. If she didn't, she wouldn't pick up the phone on the first ring whenever we did call every few months. She also wouldn't have immediately said yes when Mom asked her a few months ago if I could spend the summer here.

"Let me show you to your room." She pulled the door shut behind her and led us through the living room. "Paul and I had the guest room redone to make it more fitting for a teenage girl."

"Instead of an eighty-year-old nun who had a thing for quilts and angel figurines?" Mom said, biting at her chipped black nail polish.

"I wouldn't expect someone whose idea of a feng shui living space is kicking the dirty clothes under their bed to appreciate my sense of style," Aunt Julie fired back, like she'd been anticipating Mom's dig.

I cut in before they could get into it. "You didn't have to do that, Aunt Julie. The guest room exactly the way it was would have been great."

"Speaking of the saint also known as my brother-in-law, where is Paul?" Mom spun around, moving down the hall backward.

"At work." Aunt Julie stopped outside of a room. "He wanted to be here, but his job's been crazy lately."

Aunt Julie snatched the porcelain angel Mom had picked

up from the hall table. She carefully returned it to the exact same spot, adjusting it a hair after a moment's consideration.

"Where are the twins?" I asked, scanning the hallway for Hannah and Hailey. The last time I'd seen them, they were in preschool but acted like they were in grad school or something. They were nice kids, just kind of freakishly well behaved and brainy.

"At Chinese camp," Aunt Julie answered.

"Getting to eat dim sum and make paper dragons?" Mom asked, sounding almost surprised.

Aunt Julie sighed. "Learning the Chinese *language*." Aunt Julie opened a door and motioned me inside. I'd barely set one foot into the room before my eyes almost crossed from what I found.

Holy pink.

Hot pink, light pink, glittery pink, Pepto-Bismol pink—every shade, texture, and variety of pink seemed to be represented inside this square of space.

"What do you think?" Aunt Julie gushed, moving up beside me with a giant smile.

"I love it," I said, working up a smile. "It's great. So great. And so . . . pink."

"I know, right?" Aunt Julie practically squealed. I didn't know she was capable of anything close to that high-pitched. "We hired a designer and everything. I told her you were a girly seventeen-year-old and let her do the rest."

Glancing over at the full-length mirror framed in, you bet, fuchsia rhinestones, I wondered what about me led my aunt to classify me as "girly." I shopped at vintage thrift stores, lived in faded denim and colors found in nature, not ones manufactured in the land of Oz. I was wearing sneakers, cut-offs, and a flowy olive-colored blouse, pretty much the other end of the spectrum. The last girly thing I'd done was wear makeup on Halloween. I was a zombie.

Beside me, Mom was gaping at the room like she'd walked in on a crime scene. A gruesome crime scene.

"What the . . . *pink*?" she edited after I dug an elbow into her.

"You shouldn't have." I smiled at Aunt Julie when she turned toward me, still beaming.

"Yeah, Jules. You *really* shouldn't have." Mom shook her head, flinching when she noticed the furry pink stool tucked beneath the vanity that was resting beneath a huge cotton-candy-pink chandelier.

"It's the first real bedroom this girl's ever had. Of course I should have. I couldn't not." Aunt Julie moved toward the bed, fixing the smallest fold in the comforter.

"Jade's had plenty of bedrooms." Mom nudged me, glancing at the window. She was giving me an out. She had no idea how much more it would take than a horrendously pink room for me to want to take it.

"Oh, please. Harry Potter had a more suitable bedroom in that closet under the stairs than Jade's ever had. You can't consider something that either rolls down a highway or is bolted to a hotel floor an appropriate room for a young woman." Aunt Julie wasn't in dig mode; she was in honest mode.

That put Mom in unleash-the-beast mode.

Her face flashed red, but before she could spew whatever comeback she had stewing inside, I cut in front of her. "Aunt

Julie, would you mind if Mom and I had a few minutes alone? You know, to say good-bye and everything?"

As infrequently as we visited the house on Providence Avenue, I fell into my role of referee like it was second nature.

"Of course not. We'll have lots of time to catch up." Aunt Julie gave me another pat on the shoulder as she headed for the door. "We'll have all summer." She'd just disappeared when her head popped back in the doorway. "Meg, can I get you anything to drink before you have to dash?"

"Whiskey," Mom answered intently.

Aunt Julie chuckled like she'd made a joke, continuing down the hall.

I dropped my duffel on the pink zebra-striped throw rug. "Mom—"

"You grew up seeing the world. Experiencing things most people will never get to in their whole lives." Her voice was getting louder with every word. "You've got a million times the perspective of kids your age. A billion times more compassion and an understanding that the world doesn't revolve around you. Who is she to make me out to be some inadequate parent when all she cares about is raising obedient, genius robots? She doesn't know what it was like for me. How hard it was."

"Mom," I repeated, dropping my hands onto her shoulders as I looked her in the eye. "You did great."

It took a minute for the red to fade from her face, then another for her posture to relax. "*You're* great. I just tried not to get in the way too much and screw all that greatness up."

"And if you must know, I'd take any of the hundreds of rooms we've shared over this pinktastrophe." So it was kind of a lie, the littlest of ones. Sure, pink was on my offensive list, but the room was clean and had a door, and I would get to stay in the same place at least for the next few months. After living out of suitcases and overnight bags for most of my life, I was looking forward to discovering what drawer-and-closet living was like.

Mom threw her arms around me, pulling me in for one of those final-feeling hugs. Except this time, it kind of *was* a final one. Realizing that made me feel like someone had stuffed a tennis ball down my throat.

"I love you no matter what," she whispered into my ear again, the same words she'd sang, said, or on occasion shouted at me. Mom never just said *I love you.* She had something against those three words on their own. They were too open, too loosely defined, too easy to take back when something went wrong.

I love you no matter what had always been her way of telling me she loved me forever and for always. Unconditionally. She said that, before me, she'd never felt that type of love for anyone. What I'd picked up along the way on my own was that I was the only one she felt loved her back in the same way.

Squeezing my arms around my mom a little harder, I returned her final kind of hug. "I love you no matter what, too."

Chapter Two

I was still staring through the bedroom window at the spot where Mom's taxi had disappeared. I wondered if she was looking out of her window, too.

My lip took the brunt of my nervous energy as my mind ran through a million worst-case scenarios when I thought about Mom on her own.

I tried reassuring myself that she'd be okay. She had those fancy agents and support staff that came with hitting it big. And she had her bandmates . . . which didn't give me much confidence, since I was the most adult of all of them. Probably put together. But they took care of one another.

She'd be okay. Everything would be fine.

I wasn't sure how long I'd been at that window when a soft knock sounded at the bedroom door.

"Come on in!" I forced myself from my perch and pasted on an unaffected face.

"I wanted to see if you'd like any help unpacking," Aunt Julie started as she stepped into the room. Her eyes landed on my suitcase and duffel, in the same spot they'd been dumped, still zippered closed. "Or some help getting *started* unpacking."

I was so used to living out of suitcases, I hadn't gotten around to thinking about putting away my stuff yet. There were so many other things that needed to be experienced before settling in, but Aunt Julie was on a mission. She was rolling up the sleeves of her crisp white oxford and tucking her hair behind her ears.

"Sounds like a plan," I said, grabbing my duffel, since Aunt Julie had already had dibs on the suitcase.

"We're so happy you're here, Jade. I know we haven't seen each other a lot and we only talk every once in a while, but you're family and you're welcome here anytime. I hope you know that."

Tossing my duffel onto the bed, I tugged open the zipper. "I know that."

"Truthfully, I'm surprised you never asked to stay before when we offered." Aunt Julie's forehead creased after she threw the suitcase top open. "A summer on the California coast is most teenagers' dream."

Shrugging, I dislodged my array of sunscreens and lined them up on the dresser in descending SPF order. "I love being on the road with Mom. Seeing new things. Meeting new people. Each day different from the last."

Aunt Julie unfolded my favorite pair of jeans in front of her, her eyes widening when she saw the holes in the knees and how "loved" they were. I'd found them at some vintage store up in Portland a few months ago and wore them all the time. Whoever owned them before me had worn them all the time, too, so they'd seen a lot of mileage.

"What made you decide to take us up on our offer this summer, then? This is the first time your mom's band is headlining, so it seems like you really wouldn't want to miss it." She folded the jeans back up neatly and tucked them into the bottom drawer of the dresser. As far back as they could be shoved.

"It's also my last summer before I'll graduate and be heading off to college." I grabbed my shower bag next, realizing I'd actually have a reason to unpack it and spread things on a counter. "I wanted to see what this suburban, normal-ish lifestyle is all about."

Aunt Julie laughed. "I bet you'll find you enjoy having a routine, a schedule, a stable environment. What your mother was thinking hauling a young girl around the world chasing some silly dream is beyond me."

She said it in a nice enough tone, but her words hit me wrong. Almost like she was questioning my mom's parenting.

"I had a routine. It *was* a stable environment."

"Jade, honey, the longest you ever stayed anywhere was two weeks."

My shoulders lifted as I rummaged around in my duffel. "The scenery might have changed, but not much else did. Mom was always there for me, the other band members, too. I had school, hung out with friends, had my hobbies. Our location on the map might have been different, but nothing else was."

Aunt Julie continued to unfold every item in my suitcase, trying to disguise the surprised look in her eyes when she unearthed yet another thrift store gem. "Friends? How did you manage to make any when your mom uprooted you every other hour?"

"I learned to be really friendly." I shot a big cheesy grin at her that made her smile, too.

"And homeschooling? Your mom didn't even graduate high school. How can she expect to teach her daughter things she never learned herself?" When Aunt Julie came to her third pair of cutoffs, in the same condition as the other two, she gave up unpacking with a sigh. There wasn't anything pink and pristine in there, if that was what she was hoping to find.

"Mom got her GED." I could tell she wanted to say something to that, but she didn't. "And she spends hours studying my lesson plans to make sure she's got it before it comes my way."

Aunt Julie's eyebrows disappeared into her hairline. "Meg flunked geometry. And biology, if I remember correctly."

And chemistry and home economics, too. "Some of the harder stuff we go over together. We've got a system. It works."

Aunt Julie sighed again as I searched for topics to steer the conversation away from my mom. Aunt Julie might have loved her sister, but she couldn't talk about her without sounding like my mom had betrayed her in a hundred different ways, a thousand separate times.

"You obviously want to go to college. It's irresponsible of your mother to not have done a better job to set you up for success." She paused, biting something back. "I'll find you a tutor for the summer. Someone good. Excellent. Someone who can try to catch you up with your peers."

"Actually, Aunt Julie," I cut in. "I've been ahead of my peers since kindergarten. No need to go in search of that good-excellent tutor. But thanks."

"Just because your mom says you're gifted doesn't mean

a top university will, sweetie. Sorry if that sounds harsh, but it's the truth."

My gaze wandered to the window again. I seriously needed a fresh-air break before I said something I'd regret. "No, but those tests I take at the end of every school year do. Oh, and those SAT score things, too." I shot her a pleasant smile, watching her reaction. From doubt to surprise, and a couple more repeats, all in less than ten seconds.

Before she could say anything else, I grabbed my cloth purse from the bed and threw it over my shoulder. "Do you mind if I go out and explore for a while? You know, get my bearings in this new land of suburbia?" I felt kind of weird asking for permission. Usually with Mom, I simply told her where I was heading and when I'd be back, but I guessed Aunt Julie wouldn't be so chill.

From the look on her face you would have thought I'd asked to streak down the block a few laps. "Where do you have in mind? We could head to the mall together and buy you some new clothes?"

The m-word. I shuddered at the idea. I hadn't set foot in one since I was four and Mom tried dragging me kicking and screaming to visit some lame Santa in Sarasota. We hadn't made it past the double doors at the entrance before she turned around and let go of her plan to torture me with spilling my guts to some stinky mall Santa.

"Actually, I was thinking I'd wander around on my own two feet. See what there is to see."

"You don't have anywhere particular in mind?"

Uh-oh. The tone. The one that was created to make teenagers feel like they didn't have a clue. Time to improvise before I got to experience the summer in a proverbial cell, or worse.

"I was thinking about finding a summer job. That's what a lot of teenagers do, right?"

Aunt Julie started to relax. A little. "Well, yeah, sure. I suppose so. Where did you have in mind?"

Anywhere besides the mall?

While I thought of a way to voice this without sounding like I was insulting her apparent love affair with my personal nightmare in brick-and-mortar form, she snapped her fingers. "You know, when I drove by the public pool earlier, I saw a sign saying they were still hiring for the summer. Is that something that might interest you?"

I think I visibly sagged with relief. "Yes!" I practically shouted. "That sounds perfect."

As Aunt Julie gave me directions, I tried not to look overly eager because I guessed that would alert her. I knew living together would come with plenty of growing pains. I might have been one of the more responsible teenagers around, but I'd lived on more parental trust than most of my peers.

Since I suspected Aunt Julie and Uncle Paul wouldn't be so laid-back about letting me come and go, I wanted to ease them into the idea. They had to see I could be trusted, so that when I asked to head out for a few hours, their minds didn't automatically picture me as the main attraction at some drunken orgy.

"Do you want me to drive you?" Aunt Julie asked, already reaching for her purse as we made it down the hall.

"It was a long flight and it's such a nice day, I'd like to walk. If you don't mind," I tacked on for good measure. If

I'd said that to my mom, she would have stared at me like I'd grown a second head.

"It's a bit of a walk. Little more than a mile. You should probably take Uncle Paul's bike, just in case."

I decided not to bring up that I frequently walked several miles to find a gas station that served Icees. At this point, I'd unicycle my way there if it meant getting a little alone time.

"The bike sounds great."